La carta de Clementina

La carta de Clementina

Sara Pennypacker

Ilustraciones de Marla Frazee
Traducción de María Natalia Paillié

GRUPO
EDITORIAL
norma
www.librerianorma.com

Bogotá, Barcelona, Buenos Aires,
Caracas, Guatemala, Lima, México, Panamá,
Quito, San José, San Juan, San Salvador,
Santiago de Chile, Santo Domingo.

Pennypacker, Sara
    La carta de Clementina / Sara Pennypacker ; traductora María
Natalia Paillé ; ilustradora Marla Frazee. -- Bogotá : Grupo Edito-
rial
Norma, 2010.
    160 p. ; 20 cm. - (Colección torre de papel. Torre roja)
    Título original : Clementine's Letter.
    ISBN 978-958-45-2455-3
    1. Novela infantil estadounidense 2. Vida familiar - Novela
Infantil 3. Escolares - Novela infantil I. Paillé, María Natalia, tr.
II. Frazee, Marla, il. III. Tít. IV. Serie.
I813.6 cd 21 ed.
A1245000

    CEP-Banco de la República-Biblioteca Luis Ángel Arango

Febrero de 2010

Impreso por Editorial Buena Semilla
Impreso en Colombia - Printed in Colombia

Edición: Carolina Venegas
Traducción: María Natalia Paillié
Diseño de cubierta: María Clara Salazar
Ilustraciones: Marla Frazee
Armada: Andrea Rincón

C.C. 26000620
ISBN 978-958-45-2455-3

Para mis hijos, Hilly y
Caleb, quienes abrieron
sus corazones para que
Clementina pudiera latir.
    —S.P.

Con este libro, ya son
tres Clementinas para mi
hermano, Mark Frazee,
el gurú del producto.
    —M.F.

Capítulo 1

—Juro lealtad a la bandera de los Estados Unidos de… ¡Auch!

En tercer grado, todo el mundo se empuja. Era Fabián-Froilán-Sebastián.

—Damián —susurró él.

El verdadero nombre de Fabián-Froilán-Sebastián es realmente Fabián. *Ahora* lo sé. Pero al comenzar el año solía llamarlo con los tres nombres porque no podía recordar cuál era el verdadero. A él le gustaba. Y ahora, siempre quiere que le agregue uno más. La semana pasada, me sugirió Alacrán, pero le dije: "No. Tiene que ser un nombre real".

—Bueno —dije después del juramento a la bandera—. Fabián-Froilán-Sebastián-Damián.

Mi profesor se dio cuenta y se jaló la oreja. Este es nuestro código secreto para la "Hora de poner atención". Entonces, me enderecé y puse atención, aunque solo estaba diciendo que cuando llamara a lista levantáramos la mano si estábamos presentes.

Pero inmediatamente después, se puso interesante.

—Clementina, ¿podrías por favor ir a buscar a la directora Gamba a su oficina?

Siempre que mi profesor necesita que alguien vaya a la oficina de la directora me envía a mí, porque soy muy responsable. Bueno, también es porque me envían tanto a ese lugar que podría encontrarlo con los ojos cerrados.

Eso lo intenté una vez. Es impresionante la cantidad de moretones que te pueden salir de tropezarte con una fuente de agua.

Cuando llegué a la oficina de la directora Gamba, ella alargó la mano esperando una nota de mi profesor que explicara cuál era el problema.

—Nop, ¡hoy no vengo para un tirón de orejas! —le dije—. Solo estoy aquí para llevarla a nuestro salón.

—Oh, está bien —dijo ella—. Ya es hora.

Mientras caminábamos por el corredor, le recordé que el viernes tam-

poco me habían enviado a su oficina para un tirón de orejas.

–¿Me extrañó? Mi profesor dijo que me había portado muy bien. Que ya estaba entendiendo cómo se trabaja en el tercer grado.

–Sí me di cuenta de que no viniste, Clementina –dijo la señora Gamba–. De hecho, me dijeron que habías tenido una muy buena semana. Felicitaciones. Tu profesor dijo que él y tú estaban en verdadera sintonía últimamente.

–¿En sinfonía?

–En sintonía. Significa que están trabajando bien juntos, que se entienden.

De vuelta en el salón, mi profesor se sentó en su escritorio y dejó que la señora Gamba tomara el control, porque ella es su jefe. Pero estaba sonriendo. La señora Gamba también estaba sonriendo, cuando dijo:

–Niños, tenemos algo que contarles.

Esto me hizo pensar que eran buenas noticias.

—Estoy segura —continuó—, de que todos saben que su profesor tiene un interés especial en el antiguo Egipto.

Sí, claro que lo sabíamos. Había momias y esfinges y pirámides desparramadas por todo el salón y, durante el último mes no habíamos hecho otra cosa que hablar de Egipto.

Y eso me gustaba. Mi maestra del año pasado solo hablaba de "Los días de antaño en la pradera". Eso habría estado bien, excepto que a ella solo le gustaba hacer gorritos y pan de maíz.

Yo quería hacer cosas de "Los días de antaño en la pradera" *afuera*, como enlazar búfalos y excavar en busca de oro y atrapar criminales mientras estos tomaban cerveza en las tabernas. Pero mi profesora del año pasado dijo, "Nop", y todo tenía que ser gorritos y pan de maíz y quedarnos sentados en la silla todo el día. "Además", decía ella, "todas esas cosas son de 'Los días de antaño del Lejano Oeste'". Casi me quedo dormida con solo recordar lo aburrido que fue el año pasado.

Pero no me quedé dormida, porque quería saber cuáles eran las buenas noticias.

—Cuando supe que el programa "Aventuras para maestros" de este año era una excavación arqueológica en Egipto —continuó la directora—, nominé a su profesor.

La señora Gamba parecía muy contenta y orgullosa, pero yo todavía no entendía por qué.

—Y estoy encantada de decirles que durante el fin de semana, ¡nos enteramos de que el señor Morcillo es uno de los finalistas!

Cuando la directora Gamba pronunció el nombre de nuestro profesor, todos contuvimos la respiración al mismo tiempo. Porque si no estás poniendo atención puedes equivocarte, y en vez de decir señor Morcillo, puedes decir "morcilla", como si te estuvieras burlando del profesor.

El primer día de escuela, me esforcé tanto por no equivocarme, que me equivoqué tres veces.

En el recreo, me disculpé y le expliqué que la única razón por la que dije mal su nombre fue porque estaba muy preocupada por decirlo mal. El señor Morcillo dijo que entendía y que además eso seguramente iba a pasar algún día.

Desde ese día, todos lo llamamos "profesor". No vamos a correr ningún riesgo.

Supongo que a la señora Gamba no le importaba cometer un error.

Probablemente pensaba: "¿Y qué si me envían a la oficina de la directora? ¡Yo vivo ahí!".

—El señor Morcillo se irá hoy después del almuerzo, porque pasará la semana con el comité de "Aventuras para maestros". Pero lo veremos de nuevo el viernes en el capitolio. Ahí, habrá una ceremonia para nombrar al profesor ganador, y estamos invitados. Luego, si lo escogen, el señor Morcillo viajará a Egipto para la gran aventura.

Todos contuvimos la respiración otra vez cuando ella dijo su nombre, y por eso casi me pierdo lo que dijo después. Pero no me lo perdí:

—Eso significa que se irá por lo que resta del año.

La señora Gamba siguió hablando, pero yo solo oía "se irá por lo que resta del año", y no pude oír nada más.

Miré a mi profesor. Esperé a que saltara y dijera: "Nop, lo siento, señora Gamba. No me puedo ir por lo que resta del año porque prometí estar aquí. A mis alumnos les dije: 'Seré su profesor este año'. Como todavía estamos en este año, tengo que quedarme y ser su profesor. No voy a romper esa promesa".

Pero no lo hizo. ¡Se quedó sentado en su escritorio sonriéndole a la señora Gamba!

—Esta es una oportunidad estupenda —estaba diciendo la señora Gamba en su voz de letras mayúsculas—. Debemos estar muy orgullosos del señor Morcillo.

Todos los niños aplaudieron e hicieron caras como si estuvieran felices por la "oportunidad estupenda" y orgullosos de nuestro profesor. Yo no. No creo que romper una promesa sea una razón para estar orgulloso de alguien.

Capítulo 2

Cuando hicimos la fila para ir a almorzar, mi profesor dijo:

–¡Adiós, nos vemos el viernes!

Todos los niños dijeron:

–Adiós, nos vemos el viernes.

Excepto yo. Mi boca hizo las palabras, pero mi voz no funcionó.

Creo que mis pies tampoco estaban funcionando. Todo el mundo se fue, y yo me quedé atrapada y de pie en la puerta.

–¿Sí, Clementina? –preguntó mi profesor–. ¿Está todo bien?

—Claro que sí —dije. Solo que mi voz todavía no funcionaba bien porque sonó como: "¡No!".

—¿No? —preguntó mi profesor—. ¿Quieres decirme qué pasa?

—¿Cómo es que no nos dijo? ¿Cómo es que el viernes dijo: "Nos vemos la otra semana"?

—En ese momento no lo sabía. La directora Gamba me nominó en secreto. Esas eran las reglas —dijo él.

—Bueno, ¿y qué pasará con todas las cosas que dijo que íbamos a hacer este año? ¿Qué va a pasar con el proyecto de aprender a sumar quebrados? ¿Qué va a pasar con el proyecto del clima alrededor del mundo? ¿Qué va a pasar con el amigo de la semana?

—Le dejaré el programa de enseñanza a la suplente. Todo eso lo harán con ella.

—Pero usted dijo que *nosotros* lo haríamos.

—No me necesitas para aprender esas cosas.

—¿Pero qué pasa con mi esfuerzo por entender cómo trabajamos en el tercer grado? ¿Qué pasa con que usted y yo estemos trabajando en la sinfonía últimamente?

El señor Morcillo se inclinó en su silla.

–Oh –dijo él–. Ya entiendo. Clementina, creo que ya vas comprendiendo cómo trabajamos en el tercer grado. Sin mi ayuda. Creo que tendrás éxito con cualquier profesor.

Lo miré con una mirada que decía que ya había oído ese chiste antes y que N-O, *no* era chistoso.

–En serio –dijo él–. Parte de mi trabajo es saber cuándo los alumnos están listos para algo. ¿Recuerdas la historia de la mamá y los pajaritos?

La recordaba, porque era su historia favorita. Cada vez que él comenzaba a contarla, todos hacíamos cara de "ahí va de nuevo" y nos mirábamos. Como los otros chicos no estaban ahí, yo hice la cara para mí misma cuando el señor Morcillo comenzó a contarla.

–La mamá pone los huevos y los cuida muy bien. Se sienta sobre ellos hasta que los pajaritos salen del cascarón y luego los mantiene calientes y los alimenta en el nido –dijo él.

Todos conocemos esa parte, la parte bonita. Es el final el que es horrible.

–Luego, un día, después de que los bebés han estado sentados en la rama afuera del nido por un rato, ¿sabes qué hace la mamá?

–Sí, lo sé –dije–. ¡*Enloquece!* De repente, los empuja de la rama. Creo que debería existir una cárcel de pájaros para mamás como ella.

–Pero tiene que hacerlo. Si ella no los empuja de la rama la primera vez, nunca sabrán que pueden volar. Las mamás saben cuándo están listos.

–Bueno, sigo creyendo que no debería hacer eso. Creo que debería decir: "Oigan, chicos, algún día, cuando se sientan seguros, batan sus alas, así", y luego, ellos podrán decir, si quieren: "Hoy no, gracias".

–¿Y tú le estás diciendo "Hoy no, gracias" a que yo me vaya?

Miré por la ventana y puse la boca recta, en forma de regla, para que no

dijera: "No, estoy diciendo: '*Este año no, gracias*'".

El señor Morcillo suspiró y señalando mi caja del almuerzo, dijo:

—Por qué no vas a la cafetería antes de que termine el almuerzo. Cuando regreses, la señora Ángel estará aquí. Creo que te sentirás mejor al conocerla.

Efectivamente, cuando regresamos, una señora con un vestido verde estaba sentada en la silla de mi profesor. Y sacaba cosas de una bolsa grande.

Fui a su escritorio para mirar.

Puso una taza con un letrero grande de "YO ♥ EL AULA" donde mi profesor ponía la suya de "TÉ PARA EL PROFESOR".

Luego, salió un paquete de autoadhesivos de "¡ERES UNA ESTRELLA!".

Una caja de pañuelos con botones y caracoles marinos pegados.

Una fotografía enmarcada de una rata rosada envuelta en una manta azul.

Un momento. Tomé la fotografía para mirarla más de cerca. Tenía la cola y las patas escondidas bajo la manta y era difícil verle los bigotes, pero eso era ciertamente lo que era: una rata rosada envuelta en una manta azul. Puede que la suplente no sea tan mala, después de todo.

La suplente me quitó la fotografía y me preguntó cómo me llamaba. Le dije, y luego me dijo:

—Bueno, Clementina, ¿no deberías estar en tu puesto?

—Todavía no —contesté—. Nuestro profesor nos deja charlar hasta las doce y media.

–Pues ahora la profesora soy yo, entonces, ¿por qué no te vas a sentar?

Así que, tuve que volver a mi puesto mientras todos me miraban. Odio eso.

La suplente se puso de pie y palmoteó.

–¡Buenas tardes, chicos! Me llamo señora Ángel.

Luego se dirigió al tablero y escribió su nombre en letras grandes al lado del de nuestro verdadero profesor. ¡Como si tuviera derecho a estar ahí!

Sr. Morcillo
♡Sra. Ángel♡

Se dio la vuelta y volvió a palmotear.

–Lo primero que vamos a hacer hoy –dijo–, es hacer una tarjeta para desearle buena suerte al señor Morcillo.

Entonces, tomó una pila de hojas de papel dobladas y nos dio una a cada uno. Luego dijo:

–Todavía no escriban ni dibujen nada.

Taché el dibujo de bandidos tomando cerveza en una taberna que ya había hecho. A veces, mi profesor me llama "La pluma del Oeste". Él

siempre da la orden de "No dibujen nada" *antes* de pasar el papel. Esta suplente iba a ser difícil.

La señora Ángel nos dijo que escribiéramos "¡Buena suerte!" en la parte interior de las tarjetas, y cuando todos terminamos, nos dijo que podíamos dibujar algo en la parte de afuera.

—¡Algo que lo haga sentir que tendrá suerte!

A mi lado, Lulú comenzó a dibujar lo mismo de siempre: tulipanes debajo del arco iris. Al lado de ella, su hermano gemelo, Tutú, comenzó a dibujar lo de siempre: un tiburón

zombi con dientes largos y puntiagudos.

Yo solía tenerles miedo a las cosas
puntiagudas, pero ya no.

Bueno, está bien, todavía les tengo
miedo.

Lulú se inclinó para hurgarle el
cuello.

—Tutú, él probablemente está teme-
roso de no ganar —le recordó ella—.
Deberías dibujar algo que lo haga
sentir que va a tener *suerte*.

Tutú se encogió de hombros.

—Los tiburones zombis me hacen
sentir con suerte —dijo él, y le añadió
unos dientes más.

Yo soy tan buena artista que siempre hago algo distinto. Puedo dibujar lo que sea. Entonces, saqué mis
marcadores e intenté pensar en algo
que le trajera suerte a mi profesor. Y,
por primera vez en mi vida, no pude
pensar en... NADA.

Me quedé sentada ahí, mirando el
dibujo tachado de los bandidos y sin
ninguna idea a la mano, hasta que
sentí que me empujaban.

–Brontosaurio –susurró Fabián-Froilán-Sebastián.

Casi digo: "No, porque tiene que ser un nombre real". Pero luego, pensé: bueno, yo tengo un nombre que es una fruta, ¿por qué no puede él tener el nombre de un dinosaurio?

–Está bien –le susurré de vuelta–. Fabián-Floirán-Sebastián-Brontosaurio. Pero eso es todo. Solo un nombre de dinosaurio. Ni estegosaurio ni braquiosaurio.

–¿Clementina? –la señora Ángel me había visto–. ¿Tú y Fabián están hablando sobre dinosaurios? Porque deberían estar trabajando en las tarjetas para el señor Morcillo.

Sentí que las orejas se me ponían tan calientes y llenas de vergüenza que pensé que el pelo se me iba a incendiar.

En el recreo, Fabián se disculpó por haberme metido en problemas.

–¿Estás molesta conmigo?

–No –le dije–. Estoy molesta con *ella*. Y con nuestro profesor. No debió irse.

—Probablemente no pudo evitarlo —dijo Fabián—. Probablemente la directora Gamba lo obligó a ir.

—¡Tienes razón! ¡Ella es su jefe y probablemente él tuvo que decirle que sí! Ya sabes que él todo el tiempo hablaba de lo mucho que le gusta estar con nosotros. ¡Probablemente nos esté extrañando en este momento!

—Síp —dijo Fabián—. Probablemente.

De repente, me sentí mucho mejor.

—Oye —dije—. ¿Qué opinas de Marián?

Fabián-Floirán-Sebastián pensó por un momento y luego suspiró.

—No lo sé —dijo—. No creo que un nombre de mujer sea buena idea. Ya es difícil tener que llamarse Fabián.

Capítulo 3

Cuando regresamos del recreo de la tarde, encontré una buena sorpresa: un plato de cartón con una tajada de manzana encima de cada pupitre. La señora Ángel probablemente estaba tratando de disculparse por haber sido tan mala. No pensé que una tajada de manzana fuera suficiente, pero estaba bien para comenzar.

Pero luego, también encontré una mala sorpresa: Silbido y Chichón estaban en la jaula, sin moverse. Nunca los había visto así. Después, recordé algo: los lunes por la mañana, lo primero que hace el señor Morcillo es escoger a alguien que ayude a cuidar los hámsteres durante la semana, un "ayudante de los hámsteres". El trabajo del ayudante es darles de comer y de beber a Silbido y a Chichón, de inmediato, puesto que los viernes solo les dejamos lo suficiente para el fin de semana.

El señor Morcillo no había escogido un "ayudante de los hámsteres". También había olvidado la promesa que les había hecho a ellos. Y ahora era lunes *por la tarde*.

Corrí hacia la jaula de Silbido y Chichón y les llené el plato de la co-

mida y la taza del agua. Les di unas palmaditas mientras comían y les dije lo mal que me sentía de haberlos olvidado. Como todavía se veían un poco flacos, tomé mi tajada de manzana y se las puse en la jaula.

—Clementina, tienes que sentarte —gritó la señora Ángel. Bueno, supongo que no gritó. Pero hizo que mis oídos me dolieran como si lo hubiera hecho—. ¿Y dónde está tu experimento de ciencia?

—¿Mi experimento de ciencia?

—Dejé una tajada de manzana en cada pupitre. Vamos a hacer un experimento de ciencia con eso. La tuya no está.

—Pensé que era un regalo —le expliqué—. Se la di a Silbido y a Chichón. Estaban casi muertos porque no los habíamos alimentado hoy.

Probablemente la señora Ángel se molestó porque le di una razón tan buena, porque dijo:

—Lo siento. No hay más manzanas. Tendrás que compartir con alguien la manzana para observar el experimento.

—Puede quedarse con la mía —dijo Lulú.

—Puede quedarse con la mía —dijo Tutú, casi al mismo tiempo.

—Puede quedarse con la mía —dijo Fabián-Floirán-Sebastián.

Supongo que todos estaban cansados de que la señora Ángel fuera desagradable conmigo porque me ofrecieron sus tajadas de manzana.

Pero la señora Ángel decidió que "No".

—Está bien. Clementina podrá observarnos a todos.

Eso hice, y no me perdí de nada.

Si se deja una tajada de manzana al aire, se tornará marrón debido a la oxidación. Pues qué bien…

La directora Gamba regresó, justo antes de que se terminara la última clase. Se acercó a la suplente y estuvieron hablando en voz baja durante un minuto. Luego vi que tomó la fotografía enmarcada que tenía en frente. Creí que la suplente le diría a la señora Gamba que fuera a sentarse en su puesto, ¡pero no! ¡La suplente solo sonreía!

—Es mi nuevo sobrino —le oí decir—. ¿No es un bombón?

Saqué un marcador. ¡NO QUIERO BEBÉS! Me escribí en el brazo.

Me gusta escribirme en el brazo las cosas importantes que debo recordar. Así, no se me pierden —siempre sé dónde está mi brazo—, lo que no sucede con los papeles. Además, se ven como tatuajes. Los domingos por la noche, mamá me quita con estropajo las anotaciones de la semana y yo vuelvo a comenzar. La que me acababa de escribir estaba bien para comenzar la semana.

La señora Gamba recogió una pila de papeles y se dirigió al frente del salón. Ella nunca tenía que decir "Préstenme atención" mientras palmoteaba porque todos la mirábamos como atraídos como un imán. Puede que cuando yo sea grande, asista a la escuela de directores para poder aprender ese truco.

La señora Gamba repartió los papeles. Mi mano quería dibujar algo en el mío, pero le dije que esperara.

—Cada uno de ustedes debe escribir una carta para los jueces de "Aventuras para maestros" —dijo ella—, y explicar por qué su profesor debería ganarse ese viaje. Llévensela de tarea. Volveré mañana para recogerlas y enviarlas. ¿No les parece una buena idea?

Todos aparentaron que era una buena idea. Menos yo, porque no lo era. Una buena idea es atrapar bandidos mientras estos toman cerveza en una taberna, o que un profesor siga siendo tu profesor, si eso es lo que ha prometido.

De regreso a casa, Margarita se sentó a mi lado, como siempre. Yo todo el tiempo estuve mirando por la ventana, pero Margarita se disgusta si no la miro a ella. Me pellizcó hasta que me di la vuelta.

—¿Te pasa algo en los ojos? —me preguntó—. ¿Has estado llorando?

—No —dije, y me volví otra vez hacia la ventana.

Margarita me volvió a pellizcar.

—Bueno, tal vez si he estado llorando un poco. En el baño de las niñas —dije.

—¿Por qué? —preguntó ella.

Entonces le conté todo lo que había pasado.

—Él prometió que sería nuestro profesor y ahora no le importa. Si gana, se irá por el resto del año. Yo ya estaba logrando entender cómo se trabaja en tercero y ahora tendré que comenzar de nuevo. Y la señora Ángel es realmente mala conmigo.

Sentí un hurgonazo el cuello y me di la vuelta.

—La señora Ángel no es mala —dijo Lulú—. Es buena.

Luego, pellizcó a su hermano y le dijo:

—Tutú, dile a Clementina que la señora Ángel no es mala.

Tutú se encogió de hombros.

—No es mala —dijo.

Eso no contaba. Tutú hace todo lo que le dice Lulú.

A veces quisiera tener un hermano gemelo cuyo nombre rimara con el mío y que hiciera todo lo que yo le dijera. Pero en cambio, tengo un hermano que solo tiene tres años y que hace todo lo que le digo que *no* debe hacer.

Además, su nombre no rima con el mío y ni siquiera es el de una fruta, como el mío. Lo que me hizo acordar.

Saqué un marcador y me escribí en el brazo: BUSCAR MÁS NOMBRES DE VEGETALES PARA NABO. Luego, miré a Tutú y a Lulú.

—Ella es mala *conmigo*. Estuve en problemas todo el día.

—Eso es porque estabas *haciendo* cosas —dijo Lulú—. Yo no estuve en problemas hoy. Yo nunca me meto en problemas.

—Probablemente fue culpa tuya, Clementina —interrumpió Margarita, aunque yo N-O, *no* estaba hablando con ella—. Probablemente estabas haciendo cosas raras. ¿Por qué no observas a Lulú y la imitas durante esta semana?

—¡Qué idea tan tonta! —dije.

Tutú me pellizcó el cuello.

–Eso es lo que yo hago –me dijo–. Y yo jamás me meto en problemas.

Me desplomé en la silla.

–Bueno, está bien –dije–. Lo haré.

Capítulo 4

Cuando regresé a casa de la escuela saqué la tarea, la puse sobre la mesa de la cocina y me quedé mirando fijamente la hoja de papel en blanco.

Mamá llegó y me preguntó si quería comer algo.

–No –dije. Dejé los dientes apretados para que sonara como un rugido. Un rugido *feroz*–. Lo que quiero es que mi profesor no se vaya.

De todas maneras, mamá me dio un poco de queso y jugo.

—¿El señor Morcillo se va? ¡Qué lástima! Sé que lo quieres mucho. ¿Quieres que hablemos al respecto?

En ese momento, oímos un ruido en el salón y a mi hermano que se reía. Esto significaba que otra vez estaba en el sitio donde ella guarda sus cosas de pintar.

—¡Ojalá no haya encontrado los marcadores! —dijo mamá, mientras salía de la cocina.

Luego llegó papá. Al verme la cara dejó las llaves a un lado.

—¿Quieres dar un paseo? —me preguntó.

Cuando estoy molesta, papá me deja montar en el ascensor de servicio hasta que me calme.

—No —rugí de nuevo—. Lo que quiero es no tener que hacer esta tarea.

Papá se sentó a mi lado.

—¿Una tarea difícil, eh? ¿Quieres contarme de qué se trata? —me preguntó. Realmente quería contarle, pero en ese momento le sonó el teléfono del trabajo. Cuando regresó, me dijo:

—Lo siento, campeona, tendrá que esperar. El ascensor se ha vuelto a dañar. Hablaremos de eso después.

Papá es el administrador de nuestro edificio. Según él, eso significa que está a cargo de todos los problemas. Pero también está encargado de las cosas buenas.

Como la azotea. Algunas veces, en las noches de verano, mi familia sube a la azotea, que queda a ocho pisos de altura. Desde allí, podemos ver todo Boston. Subimos una pizza extra grande con doble porción de queso y una lámpara con un cable de extensión muy largo, y jugamos un juego de mesa que se llama "Vida", aunque Brócoli no hace más que atiborrar las fichas en los carritos de plástico y jugar a las carreras por todo el tablero. Esto hace sonreír a mis padres; dicen que mi hermano está viviendo la vida por el carril rápido.

En ese momento, mi gatito entró en la cocina y se me sentó en las piernas. Lo consentí y le di trocitos

de queso que tenía. Comenzó a ron-
ronear.

–No te preocupes, Humectante.
Yo no me iré a ningún lado –le dije–.
Puedes contar conmigo. Si *digo* que
estaré aquí, estaré aquí.

Mi hermano también entró en la
cocina.

–¡Juega conmigo!

Le mostré la hoja de papel.

–No puedo, Haba. Tengo que hacer
tareas.

Mi hermano se rio como si le hubiera contando un chiste realmente
bueno y se me sentó encima, junto a
Humectante.

–No es gracioso –le dije–. Ya verás.
En cinco años estarás en tercero,

como yo, y es posible que tengas que hacer una tarea estúpida como esta.

De hecho, no estoy muy segura de eso. Cuando mi hermano se despierta, sostiene un pie en el aire y al verlo le lanza una gran sonrisa, como si su mejor amigo hubiera estado perdido toda la noche. Mueve el pie hacia adelante y hacia atrás y cree que este lo está saludando.

Grita: "¡Hola, pie!", y luego, hace lo mismo con el otro pie.

No creo que alguien que salude a sus propios pies pueda llegar alguna vez a estar en tercero.

Supongo que mi hermano tampoco pensaba que podría llegar a tercero. Me maulló, y luego él y Humectante tomaron turnos para comerse mi queso. Cuando lo acabaron, se bajaron y se fueron a jugar juntos.

–Apreciados jueces de "Aventuras para maestros" –comencé a escribir.

Luego, me quedé mirando fijamente el papel e intenté pensar en algo que decir. Lo intenté y lo intenté hasta que comenzó a oler a humo de cerebro. Me di por vencida y fui al congelador por un helado para enfriarme la cabeza.

Mientras me lo estaba comiendo, papá regresó por una llave inglesa y pasó a mi lado, meneando la cabeza.

—Debería escribir un libro —murmuró.

Papá siempre dice que debería escribir un libro. Dice que ve cosas muy extrañas en su trabajo. La mayoría de estas, dice él, son cosas fascinantes y maravillosas. Pero también dice que por ahí hay más locos de los que nos imaginamos. Y que podría escribir un libro realmente bueno si alguna vez se sentara a intentarlo.

De repente, tuve una idea estupenda.

Fui al sitio donde mi mamá guarda sus cosas de pintar y saqué un cuaderno de dibujo nuevo. En la cubierta, en letra importante, escribí: EL ADMINISTRADOR DEL EDIFICIO, POR PAPÁ. Debajo del título, hice un dibujo de nuestro edificio. En la primera página, escribí la primera frase, para darle un empujón.

Había una vez un administrador de edificios.

Fui a la habitación de papá y mamá y puse el cuaderno en la mesa de noche, en el lado de papá. Luego, llevé la tarea a la recepción a ver si papá me podía ayudar mientras arreglaba el ascensor.

No lo encontré, pero me encontré con el hermano mayor de Margarita,

Miguel. Estaba aceitando su guante de béisbol, y se veía aburrido.

—¿Qué estás haciendo aquí? —le pregunté.

Miguel señaló hacia arriba.

—Margarita está limpiando mi habitación. Tengo que quedarme afuera.

Mi habitación es un poco desordenada. Me pregunté si debería pedirle a Margarita que la limpie para que quede como la de ella.

—¿Cuánto cuesta? —pregunté.

—Tres dólares —contestó Miguel.

—¿Tres dólares? Oh. Yo no pagaría tanto para que limpiaran mi habitación.

—Yo tampoco —estuvo de acuerdo Miguel—. Eso es lo que Margarita me paga *a mí* para que la deje limpiar mi habitación. Estoy ahorrando para comprarme un nuevo bate. De otro modo, no se lo permitiría. Cuando termina, no puedo encontrar mis cosas.

—¿Te las esconde?

—No, solo las pone en orden. Conoces a Margarita y sus reglas... de pequeño a grande, de nuevo a viejo, en orden alfabético. Me toma mucho tiempo volverlas a poner como me gusta.

Miguel se desplomó y yo hice lo mismo para que no se sintiera solo. Luego, le conté todo lo de mi profesor y Egipto.

—¡Él cree que eso es más importante que nosotros! Excavar por todos lados para buscar momias viejas y estúpidos jeroglíficos. ¡Y ni siquiera quiere ir!

—Entonces va a acampar —dijo Miguel.

—Supongo —dije—. ¡Pero se *irá*, Miguel! ¡Después de habernos prometido que estaría aquí todo el año!

Pero Miguel estaba concentrado en el tema de acampar. Estaba silbando.

—Espero que no le toque en la misma carpa con alguien como Fríjoles Martínez.

—¡No me estás escuchando!

Miguel seguía sin escucharme.

—¡Oye! —dijo, moviendo la cabeza como si aún no pudiera olvidar lo mal que le había ido—. ¡Tuve que vivir con él durante dos semanas enteras en el campo de verano!

Me rendí.

—Está bien. ¿Cuál era el problema de Fríjoles Martínez?

—¿Cuál *no* era el problema de Fríjoles Martínez? Bueno, para empezar… ¡sus medias! Nunca se las cambiaba. Y cuando digo nunca, es nunca. Creo que su mamá le puso esas medias desde la cuna y él jamás quiso quitárselas —Miguel se tapó la nariz y fingió desmayarse–. ¡Esas medias casi pelan la lona de nuestra carpa!

–Ay, no exageres –dije–. No pudo haber sido tan malo.

Miguel se quitó la gorra de los Medias Rojas y la sostuvo contra su corazón. Eso significa: "Lo juro por los Medias Rojas".

–Clementina –me dijo–, cuando ese chico salía a caminar, hasta los zorrillos se desmayaban.

No pude evitar reírme con eso. Cuando tenga un novio, que jamás tendré, escogeré a alguien tan gracioso como Miguel. Hice un dibujo en la parte de atrás de la hoja de la tarea para no olvidarme de lo que Miguel había dicho. Aquí está:

Miguel seguía refunfuñando contra Fríjoles.

—Y eso solo fue el *comienzo*. ¡Ese chico debió haber venido con un letrero de advertencia!

—¿Por qué?

—¡Para que la gente supiera que no lo debían dejar entrar!

Y, de repente, ¡tuve una idea genial!

Le di la vuelta al papel de la tarea y lo dejé por el lado de: "Apreciados jueces de 'Aventuras para maestros'".

—Bueno, comienza por el principio —dije—. Dime todo lo que debió haber dicho el letrero de advertencia de Fríjoles Martínez. No olvides nada.

Capítulo 5

El martes, a la hora del desayuno, mamá me preguntó sobre mi profesor y su partida.

—No es grave —le dije—. Regresará el lunes.

Luego, papá me preguntó cómo me iba con la tarea. Le dije que bien.

—Solo necesito una cosa: ¿Cómo se escribe "amenaza para la sociedad"?

Papá lo escribió y luego me preguntó si eso era realmente todo lo que necesitaba.

—Pensé que te estaba dando problemas.

—Nop. Miguel me ayudó y así fue más fácil.

—¡Qué amable de su parte! —dijo papá—. ¿Quieres mostrárnosla?

—Oh… mmm… no. Es una sorpresa, más o menos —le dije. Lo cual era verdad, porque mi carta ciertamente iba a ser una gran sorpresa para esos jueces.

Papá se fue y yo entré a hurtadillas a su habitación para revisar si había trabajado en el libro que yo había comenzado. Había escrito una sola frase. Después de:

Había una vez un administrador de edificios.

Él había escrito:

Era extremadamente apuesto y tenía la fuerza de diez bueyes.

Algunas veces, papá necesita ayuda para concentrarse. Entonces, le volví a señalar el camino correcto.

Escribí.

En el autobús camino a la escuela, le conté a Margarita que estaba ayudándole a mi papá a escribir un libro.

Ella solo gruñó.

—Bueno, ahora tendrás que hacer algo bonito por tu mamá. Esa es la regla. No será justo si no lo haces.

—Tienes razón —dije—. No me gusta cuando le regalan algo a Judía Verde y a mí no. Y mamá también vive en esa habitación, así que se va a dar cuenta de lo que estoy haciendo.

Margarita parecía realmente enojada conmigo.

—Eres tan afortunada —gruñó.

—¿Qué quieres decir?

—Siempre tienes mucha suerte y ni siquiera te das cuenta.

—¿Cómo así que tengo suerte? —me habría gustado que se hubiera enterado de que me iban a regalar un gorila de Navidad. Pero no era eso.

—Bueno, primero, no tienes a Miguel.

—Tengo a Calabacín —dije.

—Tu hermano es tierno —hizo una cara que decía: "¡No te imaginas las cosas que debo aguantarme!".

Yo no le hice ninguna cara porque creo que Miguel no está mal. Lo que N-O, *no* significa que sea mi novio.

—Y segundo, no tienes a Andrés —añadió.

Andrés es el novio de la mamá de Margarita. Cada vez que Margarita dice su nombre hace una cara parecida a la que haría si alguien le pide que acaricie una babosa. Yo le hago la misma cara porque tiene razón con respecto a Andrés.

Comprendí que papá era el que realmente tenía suerte de que mamá no tuviera novio, pero no le dije eso a Margarita. En cambio, le pregunté si había otra cosa por la cual pensara que yo era afortunada.

—Si no lo sabes, no te lo voy a decir —dijo ella.

Y cerró la boca en línea recta, como si fuera una regla. Excepto que eso no le funcionó porque los labios se le quedaron atrapados en los frenillos. Ella lo llama labios de frenillo. Me di la vuelta para no reírme, porque sé lo desagradable que es que se rían de uno.

Bueno, también porque ella es un poco más grande que yo y su libreta de notas tiene los bordes puntiagudos.

–No se te olvide –dijo Margarita cuando bajamos del autobús–. Hoy, haz solo lo que hace Lulú.

Lo intenté.

Tan pronto se sentó, Lulú abrió el morral, sacó la hoja de papel con la tarea, y la puso dentro del pupitre. Yo abrí mi morral, saqué el papel con la tarea y la puse dentro del pupitre.

Hasta ahora, todo iba bien.

Luego, Lulú hurgó a su hermano en la parte de atrás del cuello y le dijo entre dientes que pusiera la tarea dentro del pupitre, al igual que ella. Yo le hurgué el cuello a Tutú –no muy fuerte, porque ya tenía muchas marcas allí– y también le dije eso entre dientes.

Después, la señora Ángel aplaudió pidiendo atención.

Lulú golpeó con las manos el pupitre y se enderezó. Yo también me enderecé para ver mejor. Ella miraba a la señora Ángel como si estuviera hipnotizada. Yo también di un golpe con las manos sobre el pupitre e hice la mirada de hipnotizada. Luego, me deslicé hasta el suelo para ver mejor lo que Lulú estaba haciendo con el resto del cuerpo.

Y no creerán lo que vi: ¡Lulú estaba congelada! No movía nada, ¡ni un dedo! ¡La señora Ángel la había hipnotizado para que se volviera una estatua! Frente a ella, Tutú también estaba congelado.

—Clementina, ¿qué estás haciendo en el suelo? —gritó la señora Ángel. Bueno, en realidad solo lo *dijo*, pero desde el suelo sonó como un grito—. ¿Se te perdió algo?

—No, solo trataba de ver qué estaba haciendo Lulú para imitarla —le expliqué.

—Bueno, aquí en la primera fila hay un espacio libre —dijo—. Tal vez te sea más fácil concentrarte desde aquí.

Entonces, tuve que moverme al frente del salón, desde donde veía su escritorio con todas sus cosas encima, donde tenían que estar las cosas de mi profesor.

Luego, ella recogió nuestra tarea y la guardó en un sobre grande, que puso encima de su escritorio. Eso estuvo bien, porque durante todo el día ese sobre me recordó que nuestro profesor N-O, *no* iba a ganar ese premio de Egipto. Nop, una vez los jueces leyeran mi carta, lo harían regresar al salón el lunes por la mañana. Sería nuestro profesor por el resto del año. Tal y como quería él que fuera. Tal y como lo había prometido. Eso me hizo sentir mucho mejor.

Bueno, no mucho mejor, pero sí un poco.

Cuando llegué a casa, papá y mamá estaban sentados alrededor de la mesa de la cocina. Tenían la mirada fija sobre una pila de correo, de la misma manera en la que yo miraba fijamente la tarea el día anterior. Como si no pudieran creer lo que debían hacer. Esto significaba que era el primer día del mes que es, para mi familia, el día de las cuentas. No me gusta el día de las cuentas, porque ese día papá y mamá me dicen "No" a todo lo que les pido. De todos modos, lo intenté.

—Necesito buscar nuevos nombres para Brócoli. ¿Alguno de ustedes podría llevarme al mercado?

—Primero que todo, tu hermano no se llama Brócoli. Y segundo, NO —dijeron al mismo tiempo. Luego, como si ambos hubieran tenido una idea sospechosamente maravillosa, dijeron al mismo tiempo—: ¡Espera! ¡Sí! ¡Yo puedo! —y se pusieron de pie. Después, se miraron y sus cuatro hombros se hundieron al mismo tiempo y volvieron a sentarse—. No, no podemos —dijeron los dos a la vez.

Volvieron a mirar fijamente la pila de cuentas.

Mamá miró hacia arriba.

—Es martes. Tal vez Miguel pueda llevarte.

Los martes y los jueves la mamá de Margarita trabaja hasta tarde en el banco. A veces le paga a Miguel dos dólares para que le haga diligencias y lleve a Margarita con él, para que al mismo tiempo pueda cuidarla.

—¡No es mi niñera! —grita siempre Margarita si se encuentran con alguien—. ¡Y debería ser yo la que recibe los dos dólares por cuidarlo a *él*!

A veces papá y mamá también le pagan a Miguel para que les haga diligencias y para que no nos cuide a mi hermano y a mí.

Llamé a su casa.

—Campamento de entrenamiento de los Medias Rojas. Casa de Miguel el Guante, futuro jugador estrella.

Miguel está obsesionado con los Medias Rojas de Boston. Dice que son el mejor equipo de béisbol en la historia del mundo. Dice que la única manera como los Medias Rojas podrían ser un mejor equipo es si él estuviera en él. Y pronto lo estará.

Pero solo contesta el teléfono así cuando su mamá no está en la casa. La mamá de Margarita y Miguel no tiene sentido del humor. Papá dice que vivir con Margarita y sus reglas le dañaría el buen humor a cualquiera.

—Hola, Miguel —dije—. Mamá quiere saber si podrías no ser nuestra niñera esta tarde para llevarnos al mercado.

—Claro —dijo él—. Encontrémonos en la recepción.

Mamá y yo sujetamos a Repollo al cochecito y esperamos el ascensor. Cuando Margarita y Miguel bajaron, mamá le dio a Miguel dos dólares por no ser nuestra niñera. Luego, me dio dinero para que le comprara un tubo de óleo en la tienda de materiales para pintar.

—Rosa permanente —me dijo.

A veces, me confundo en la tienda. Todos esos colores hermosos y todos esos nombres hermosos de esos colores hermosos me marean un poco. Alizarina carmesí, azul cerúleo, cadmio limón. Comencé a sentir que me desmayaba con solo pensar en ellos. Le mostré el brazo a mamá.

—Deberías escribirlo.

—No te preocupes —dijo ella—. Lo recordarás. Piensa en el pelo de tu tía abuela Rosa. Ella tiene una permanente. Rosa permanente.

—Rosa permanente —dije—. Lo recordaré.

—Bueno, adiós. Nos vemos en una hora. Acuérdate de los cacahuetes —dijo.

Mi hermano es alérgico al cacahue-te. Esto significa que si se come aun-que sea uno, la cabeza le explotará.

Finalmente salimos. Fuimos a la farmacia, a la lavandería y a dejar un video en la tienda de alquiler de videos. La última parada era la tienda de materiales para pintar.

En la sección de óleos, en la vitrina, había cientos de tubos pequeños de pintura, todos ordenados y limpios. Margarita puso las manos en alto y se retiró, como si los tubos de pintura es-tuvieran a punto de explotarle sobre

el vestido. A Margarita ni siquiera le gusta mirar cosas que puedan ensuciarla.

—¡Rápido, apresúrate al pasillo de los papeles! —le dije—. No dejes de mirar esas pilas limpias de papel.

Miguel se llevó a mi hermano a dar un paseo por la tienda, y yo seguí mirando todos esos colores hermosos. Siena tostado, violeta manganeso, verde veridiano. Comencé a sentirme un poco mareada.

Un empleado se acercó y me preguntó si podía ayudarme a encontrar algo.

—Quisiera un tubo de óleo rosa bigote —le dije.

—¿Rosa bigote? —preguntó él—. ¿Estás segura de que ese es el nombre correcto?

—Segurísima —le dije—. Lo sé porque mi tía abuela Rosa tiene un bigote. Uno pequeño. Debes mirarla de perfil para verlo mejor. Por eso me acuerdo, el color de la pintura se parece al pelo de mi tía abuela.

Miguel llegó detrás de mí y me susurró al oído.

–Oh –dije–. Que sea un tubo de rosa permanente.

El empleado encontró la pintura y fuimos a la caja registradora a pagarlo. Y ahí, sobre el mostrador, había una caja de madera grande y hermosa, con muchos compartimentos adentro. ORGANIZADOR DE LUJO, decía el letrero.

–¡Mira, Miguel! –dije–. Este es como un edificio pequeño para que

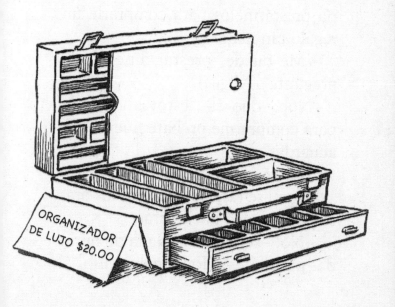

ORGANIZADOR
DE LUJO $20.00

vivan las pinturas y los pinceles y otras cosas. Mamá guarda sus cosas en latas viejas de galletas. Mi hermano siempre quiere sacarlas... ¡Esta caja tiene un candado! A ella le encantaría. ¡Le gustaría tanto que no se sentiría celosa de que le ayudara a papá a escribir un libro!

La etiqueta del precio decía que costaba veinte dólares. Busqué en los bolsillos. Dos monedas de veinticinco centavos y una de cinco. El empleado me entregó el cambio de mamá. Tres dólares y once centavos. Probablemente, a ella no le molestaría prestármelos para comprarle un regalo tan maravilloso.

—¿Me puedes prestar dinero? —le pregunté a Miguel.

—Nop —dijo él—, estoy ahorrando para comprarme un bate nuevo. ¿Te acuerdas?

Lo miré fijamente.

Miguel se tapó la cara con los brazos y tambaleó hacia atrás.

—¡No! —se quejó—. ¡Nada de miradas punzantes! ¡Todo, menos eso!

Mi mirada punzante es extremadamente poderosa. La uso solo en caso
de emergencia. La subí a su máximo
poder.

—¡Aaaaaahhhhhhhh! ¡Me rindo!
—gritó Miguel.

Sacó todo su dinero: los dos dólares
que le había dado mamá y dos billetes nuevos de un dólar. La mamá de
Margarita y de Miguel trabaja en un
banco. Ella cambia todos los billetes
de dólar que tiene por billetes nuevos
y jamás usados, para que Margarita
no se preocupe por los gérmenes.

Ahora, tenía siete dólares y sesenta
y seis centavos.

—Margarita —grité—. Ven acá, por
favor.

Margarita vino, mirándome con
ojos bizcos.

—¿Cuánto dinero tienes? —le pregunté.

—Un dólar —respondió ella—. Voy a
comprar un jabón desinfectante para
las manos.

—Ya no, ya no lo vas a comprar.
Te devolveré el dinero pronto, pero

tengo que comprarle esto a mamá. Tú misma lo dijiste. Es para que ella no vaya a sentir celos de lo que estoy haciendo por papá.

Margarita apretó los dedos contra su cartera y negó con la cabeza. Yo la miré con la mirada punzante. Pero ella me la devolvió, haciéndome la de ella. A veces pienso que habría sido mejor no haberle enseñado a hacer esa mirada a Margarita. Por suerte, nunca le enseñé el nivel más alto, y entonces lo activé, y finalmente ella se dio por vencida y me entregó su billete nuevo y jamás usado de un dólar.

Ocho dólares y sesenta y seis centavos.

—Todavía necesito once dólares y treinta y cuatro centavos —les dije a todos.

—No entiendo cómo haces eso, Clementina —dijo Miguel—. Eres asombrosa.

Luego, empujó el cochecito hacia la puerta.

–Vamos. De prisa.

–Está bien –dije mientras le daba palmaditas a la caja de madera–. No la venda todavía, ¿bueno? –le dije al empleado–. Porque voy a regresar por ella.

Capítulo 6

Afuera, le recordé a Miguel que todavía teníamos que ir a un mercado.

–Pero no a uno normal –dije–. Necesito nombres *nuevos* de legumbres.

Él señaló al final de la calle.

–¿Qué te parece ese?

Miré y había un mercado. MERCADO CHINO DEL SR. ALIUGNA, eso decía el aviso encima de la puerta. ¡Y en el andén había cubos repletos de legumbres! Corrí por la calle. Había legumbres que jamás había visto.

–Col china, tirabeques –leí en los avisos–. Rábano daikon, brotes de bambú.

–¿Tienes un bolígrafo? –le pregunté a Miguel cuando todos me alcanzaron en el mercado–. Quiero escribir algunos nombres.

Miguel no tenía nada en los bolsillos excepto una pelota de béisbol.

No me tomé la molestia de preguntarle a Margarita, porque ella nunca lleva consigo algo que pueda mancharle la ropa.

Entonces, decidimos entrar. Estaba a punto de pedirle al tendero un bolígrafo cuando el increíble rabillo de mi ojo divisó algo. Corrí hacia allá.

Y no creerán lo que vi. Anguilas en un tanque. Anguilas y anguilas y anguilas. Las anguilas estaban nadando, haciendo nudos y bucles en el agua, enredándose y luego desenredándose, como haciendo magia.

–¡Guau! –dije.

–Guau –dijo Miguel.

–Guau –dijo Col China.

Capítulo 6

Afuera, le recordé a Miguel que todavía teníamos que ir a un mercado.

–Pero no a uno normal –dije–. Necesito nombres *nuevos* de legumbres.

Él señaló al final de la calle.

–¿Qué te parece ese?

Miré y había un mercado. MERCADO CHINO DEL SR. ALIUGNA, eso decía el aviso encima de la puerta. ¡Y en el andén había cubos repletos de legumbres! Corrí por la calle. Había legumbres que jamás había visto.

–Col china, tirabeques –leí en los avisos–. Rábano daikon, brotes de bambú.

–¿Tienes un bolígrafo? –le pregunté a Miguel cuando todos me alcanzaron en el mercado–. Quiero escribir algunos nombres.

Miguel no tenía nada en los bolsillos excepto una pelota de béisbol.

No me tomé la molestia de preguntarle a Margarita, porque ella nunca lleva consigo algo que pueda mancharle la ropa.

Entonces, decidimos entrar. Estaba a punto de pedirle al tendero un bolígrafo cuando el increíble rabillo de mi ojo divisó algo. Corrí hacia allá.

Y no creerán lo que vi. Anguilas en un tanque. Anguilas y anguilas y anguilas. Las anguilas estaban nadando, haciendo nudos y bucles en el agua, enredándose y luego desenredándose, como haciendo magia.

–¡Guau! –dije.

–Guau –dijo Miguel.

–Guau –dijo Col China.

—Voy a vomitar —dijo Margarita.

—Son peces, Margarita —le dije—. No pueden evitar ser extra largos y resbalosos.

Pero Margarita ya estaba un poco verde.

—¡Rápido! —le dije—. Corre al pasillo de los arroces. No dejes de mirar las cajas de arroz limpio y bonito.

Margarita salió corriendo y yo volví a mirar las anguilas.

A veces, en los días cálidos de verano, me gusta hacer dibujos de agua sobre el andén del callejón de atrás de nuestro edificio. Así es

como se hacen: se toma un buen pincel grande, se sumerge en el agua y luego se dibujan líneas en forma de espiral sobre el concreto. Las líneas en forma de espiral se evaporan casi tan rápido como las haces, entonces parece como si se movieran. Al igual que estas anguilas.

Oh, me olvidé de decir una cosa: hay que preguntarle primero a mamá antes de usar su pincel.

Señalé a la más pequeña que se escondía en una esquina.

—Mira lo triste que se ve.

—Las anguilas no pueden ponerse tristes —dijo Miguel—. Son anguilas.

—Está llorando —dije—. Es difícil notarlo bajo el agua.

Miguel hizo una cara incrédula, pero vi que miraba el tanque de reojo para ver si esto era cierto.

—Especial: cinco dólares y noventa y nueve centavos por medio kilo —leí en el letrero—. Es un buen precio por una mascota —dije.

—Esta no es una tienda de mascotas, Clementina —dijo Miguel—. Es

un mercado. Las anguilas son para comer.

—Silencio —callé a Miguel por decir eso frente a ellas.

Miguel se encogió de hombros.

—Bueno, es la verdad. La gente se las come, o se las fuma.

Margarita debía estar escuchando desde el pasillo de los arroces porque la oímos gritar:

—¡No dejes que Andrés se entere de eso! Su pipa ya es bastante asquerosa.

Una parte pequeña y muy secreta dentro de mí quería ver a alguien fumándose una anguila. Pero no hoy. Y no estas anguilas. Me dirigí al mostrador.

—Disculpe —le dije al tendero—. ¿Podría prestarme un bolígrafo?

El tendero me prestó uno y me escribí en el brazo los nuevos nombres de legumbres para mi hermano.

—Disculpe —le dije de nuevo al devolverle el bolígrafo—. ¿Es usted el señor Aliugna?

—Sí, soy yo —dijo él.

—Bueno, Aliugna es anguila al revés. ¿No es genial? Si yo tuviera un mercado y vendiera cosas que fueran mi nombre deletreado al revés, no seguiría vendiéndolas.

Tuve que detenerme un minuto para pensar qué sería eso.

—Síp, si tuviera Anitnemelc en mi mercado, las regalaría como mascotas.

El señor Aliugna sonrió, como si le hubiera acabado de contar un buen chiste.

—¿Ves? —me dijo Margarita al oído—. Él piensa que eres rara. Siempre estás haciendo cosas raras, Clementina.

Miré fríamente a Margarita y salí, empujando el cochecito de Brote de Bambú.

Margarita me siguió y señaló los apuntes en mi brazo.

—Eso también es raro —dijo.

Me di la vuelta y miré a Miguel.

—¿Tú crees eso? ¿Crees que hago cosas raras?

—Claro que sí —dijo él—. Por eso es que te dejo andar conmigo.

Eso lo dijo porque estaba tratando de ser mi novio. No le dije que no quería un novio, porque no quería romperle el corazón, como pasa en las películas. En cambio, le pregunté si tenía alguna idea de cómo podía ganar veinte dólares para comprarle el regalo a mamá. Solo se le ocurrió una: podría convertirse en un jugador de béisbol famoso y volverse rico y regalarme todo ese dinero. Le di las gracias, pero le dije que eso tomaría mucho tiempo.

Cuando regresé a casa, mamá estaba sentada frente a la mesa de dibujo.

Saqué el cambio y el tubo de rosa permanente del bolsillo.

Ella levantó las manos, que tenía cubiertas de polvillo.

—¿Podrías guardarlo?

Abrí la lata de galletas que mamá usa para guardar los óleos. Todos los tubos estaban mezclados. A mí me parecía hermoso, pero no era nada comparado con las vitrinas de la tienda de materiales para pintar. De repente, me di cuenta de algo: la gente de la tienda había ordenado todas las pinturas de acuerdo con una regla. No era una regla tonta, como las de Margarita, sino una realmente buena.

—¿Quieres que te arregle las pinturas por colores? —le pregunté.

—¡Eso sería estupendo, querida! —dijo mamá.

Entonces puse todos los tubos de pintura en un arco iris circular, como estaban en la tienda. Cuando terminé, mamá se inclinó y lo observó.

—Eso es maravilloso —dijo—. Ahora, no perderé tiempo buscando un color.

¿Podrías hacer esto también con las acuarelas y los lápices de color?

–¿En serio? –le pregunté–. ¿Puedo tocar todas tus cosas?

–Claro que sí.

–¿Incluso los marcadores especiales?

Mamá me miró durante un minuto, y pude ver que estaba acordándose de cuando le pinté el pelo a Margarita con ellos.

–Claro. Sé que ahora sabes las reglas de mis utensilios de pintura. Entonces, cada vez que tengas ganas de ordenarlos, puedes hacerlo.

Entonces, ordené todas sus cosas en el arco iris de color y sonreí en secreto, pensando en lo feliz que se iba a poner mamá cuando le regalara ese organizador de lujo.

Después, entré a la habitación de papá y mamá para ver cómo le estaba yendo a papá con el libro. Debajo de,

¡Veía muchas cosas interesantes!

Él había escrito:

Y además, tenía una esposa hermosa y dos hijos extraordinarios.

Le di la vuelta al cuaderno para ver si había escrito algo más sobre las cosas interesantes en la página siguiente. Nop. Entonces, debía hacerlo yo.

Un día, ¡el administrador del edificio vio algo súper interesante!

Escribí.

Después, fui a dejar el cochecito en el depósito. Camino hacia allá, pasé por el cuarto de basura y reciclaje. Ahí, vi algo *realmente* súper interesante: ¡la solución al problema de los veinte dólares para el organizador de lujo de materiales para pintar!

Capítulo 7

—Clementina, esta es la tercera vez que te veo mirando el reloj hoy —dijo la señora Ángel el miércoles por la mañana—. ¿Estás esperando que algo suceda?

Comencé a sentir que las orejas me ardían. La señora Ángel no paraba de mirarme. Entonces, aunque no quería decir lo que estaba haciendo, lo hice.

—Solo estoy jugando a ganarle al reloj —dije.

—¿Cómo se juega? —preguntó Juan.

—Miro el reloj, después miro hacia otro lado mientras cuento los segundos en mi cabeza y luego vuelvo a mirar el reloj para ver si estuve cerca. Estoy mejorando mucho. Si alguna vez participo en un concurso en el que deba adivinar cuántos segundos han pasado, creo que ganaré. Y no voy a escoger premios tontos.

—Bueno, ¡suficiente! —dijo la señora Ángel.

Y tenía razón: ya había explicado lo suficiente. Todos comenzaron a jugar a ganarle al reloj. Gritaban: "¡Dos segundos menos!" y "¡Dieciocho segundos exactos!" y "¡No es verdad, vi que mirabas el reloj!", hasta que la señora Ángel pegó un pedazo de cartulina sobre el reloj.

Me miró como diciendo: "¡Tu profesor se enterará de esto!".

Yo no le devolví la mirada, pero si lo hubiera hecho, mi mirada habría dicho: "Bien, porque mi profesor sabe qué significa ganarle al reloj. Entiende que contar los segundos con una parte de mi cabeza me ayuda a prestarle atención a él con la otra parte. Tenemos un pequeño arreglo. Y además, cuando mi profesor quiere decirme que deje de jugar ese juego, no lo hace frente a toda la clase. Hace una P mayúscula con los dedos, que significa "en privado". Después, yo voy hasta su escritorio y él me dice que pare de jugar. Y en este momento, extraño mucho a mi profesor. Menos mal que no va a estar mucho tiempo por fuera".

Eso era demasiado para una sola mirada, de todos modos.

El resto de la mañana fue peor. Cuando sonó la campana para salir a recreo, apuesto que ya había oído cientos de "¡Clementina, presta atención!". Y cada vez ¡*estaba* prestando atención!

Claro que no a la señora Ángel, porque había pasado de ser aburrida a ser súper aburrida. En lugar de eso, le estaba prestando atención a la idea increíble que me había venido a la cabeza cuando pasé anoche por el área de basura y reciclaje. Esa idea era lo opuesto a aburrido, créanme.

"¡Veinte dólares, llegarán pronto!", escribí en el trabajo de matemáticas.

La escuela terminó después de cien horas. El recorrido del autobús tomó otras trescientas horas. Todos querían hablar de lo fabulosa que era la señora Ángel, lo que probaba que había logrado hipnotizarlos a todos menos a mí. Finalmente, llegué a casa.

Mamá estaba a punto de irse con Brote de Soja para la biblioteca a la hora del cuento. Me dio un vaso de yogur y una manzana. La manzana me recordó el experimento de ciencia del lunes, lo que me hizo sentir un poco mal. Me la metí en el bolsillo.

Mamá se inclinó para mirarme la nuca.

—¡Oh, por Dios! —dijo. Luego, me miró los brazos—. Voy a tener que hablar con la mamá de Margarita.

—No todos son pellizcos —dije—. Algunas son marcas de cuando me hurgan con el dedo. Las de la nuca son de Lulú. Las del lado izquierdo son de Fabián-Floirán-Sebastián y las del brazo izquierdo son de…

–Un niño no es una almohadilla para alfileres. ¿No les enseñan eso en la escuela?

–No es grave. Ahora me siento al frente de Juan y de María. Juan es muy bajito para alcanzarme por encima de su pupitre y María es una debilucha y no puede hurgarme –en ese momento, se me ocurrió algo–. Espera. Ahora que lo pienso, María tiene dedos extra duros y puntiagudos. ¿Y qué pasa si Juan usa el pincel? Podría herirme en los pulmones o algo así. Supongo que es mejor que no vaya a la escuela durante un buen tiempo… como hasta el lunes…

–No seas tontita. Solo tendré que escribir una nota… ¿Cómo dijiste que se llamaba la suplente?

–¡No, mamá! ¡No le escribas!

–¿Por qué no?

–Empeorarás las cosas.

–¿Empeoraré qué cosas?

Entonces, tuve que contarle sobre todos los problemas que estaba teniendo con la señora Ángel. Y sobre la idea de Margarita de hacer todo lo que hacía Lulú, que no funcionó y por eso tuve que cambiarme de puesto.

Mamá se sentó a mi lado.

—Bueno, no creo que ese haya sido un buen consejo, de todas maneras —dijo—. Nunca es buena idea hacer algo solamente porque alguien más lo hace. Cuéntame por qué crees que estás teniendo tantos problemas.

Le quité la tapa al yogur y la lamí.

—No le caigo bien a la profesora.

—Oh, eso no puede ser cierto —dijo mamá. Eso lo tenía que decir porque es mi mamá—. Debe de haber otra razón. Si pudieras encontrarla, de pronto podrías solucionar las cosas.

Mamá atrapó a Castaña de Agua mientras pasaba

e intentó ponerle el saco. La observé durante un rato y vi que no lo estaba logrando.

—Está jugando a que es un chico espagueti —le expliqué a mamá.

—Juega a que eres un chico árbol —le dije a mi hermano—. Pon los brazos como una rama.

Mi hermano se dejó engañar con esto y mamá pudo vestirlo.

Le subió el cierre.

—Gracias, Clementina. ¿Ves lo que quiero decir? A veces, tienes que darte cuenta de cuál es el problema antes de encontrarle una solución.

Eso parecía ser algo que valía la pena recordar, así que me lo escribí en el brazo. Mamá alzó a mi hermano y lo cargó hasta la puerta, porque él seguía jugando a que era un árbol.

—Papá está atrás. Está con los albañiles, porque están comenzando a construir la nueva pared de ladrillo en el jardín. ¿Quieres ir a observarlos?

Dejé caer la cuchara. Había estado esperando esto todo el mes, porque me encantan los ladrillos. Me encanta la manera como se ve la argamasa blanca junto a la arcilla roja. Me encanta la manera como cada ladrillo está puesto justo en el medio del que tiene debajo, y hace que cada hilera termine en un ladrillo completo o en uno cortado a la mitad. Me encanta lo uniforme que es, hasta que se acaba la pared, incluso si esta tiene cien pisos de alto.

Me gustan tanto los ladrillos que, cuando mi familia hizo una casa de galletas de jengibre la Navidad pasada, le hice las paredes con barritas de chicle, como si estas fueran ladrillos, y usé clara de huevo batida como argamasa. Esa cantidad de chicle me costó dos semanas de mesada, pero valió la pena.

Pensé en lo mucho que me agradaría observar a los albañiles. Y luego pensé en el regalo para mamá.

—No, gracias —dije—. Tengo cosas que hacer esta tarde.

Antes de llevar a cabo mi idea, fui a la mesa de noche de papá para ver

cómo le estaba yendo con el libro. No muy bien, debo decir. Debajo de,

Un día, ¡el administrador del edificio vio algo *súper* interesante!

Él había escrito,

Y se lo mostró a su hija.

Levanté el bolígrafo y escribí:

Lo hizo porque a veces el administrador del edificio necesita que ella lo ayude.

Después, me dirigí al cuarto de basura y reciclaje.

A veces, papá y mamá ven un programa de televisión sobre cosas viejas. Las personas se reúnen en un gran salón con sus cosas. El presentador, que es un experto en esos cosas viejas, se acerca a cada una de estas personas y les dice cuánto valen sus cosas. A veces, el presentador dice: "Oh, lamento que hayas arreglado esto, porque ahora no vale nada". Y con eso, las personas actúan como si no les importara y dicen: "Todavía me encanta y eso es lo que cuenta". Esto lo dicen porque están avergonzadas de haber cometido el gran error de arreglarlas.

Pero algunas veces, el presentador dice: "¡Santo cielo! Esto es increíble. Este es un trasto extremadamente valioso y ahora, ¡eres millonario!" y las personas aplauden y se llevan las manos a las mejillas y hacen bocas grandes en forma de O, como si estuvieran muy impresionadas para hablar. Y luego, el presentador mira hacia la cámara y dice: "¡Usted también podría tener tesoros en el ático o en el sótano!", y ese es el final del programa.

Cuando sea grande, no veré el programa de cosas viejas, porque es A-B-U-R-R-I-D-O, *aburrido*. Pero me dio una idea extraordinaria.

En medio de los barriles de basura y las cajas de reciclaje, había un montón de bolsas. Y las bolsas

estaban llenas de... ¡cosas viejas!
Una corbata tejida con lana amarilla.
Cuatro individuales que parecían
cuatro alfombras trenzadas pequeñas.
Un figurín de porcelana de un gallo
con un sombrerito de paja. Y otras
baratijas.

Ese presentador de televisión tenía
razón: ¡yo también tenía tesoros en
el sótano!

Encima de las bolsas, había un
letrero: COLECTA DE CARIDAD. DONE A
UNA BUENA CAUSA LOS ARTÍCULOS QUE
NO NECESITE.

PRECIO:
LO QUE USTED
CREA QUE
VALGA.

Darle un regalo a mamá era definitivamente una buena causa.

Arrastré las bolsas y una mesa de juego hasta la recepción, y le pegué un letrero a la mesa: PRECIO: LO QUE USTED CREA QUE VALGA.

Capítulo 8

La señora Jacobi llegó mientras yo sacaba la primera cosa: el juego de individuales trenzados.

—¡Pero qué individuales tan encantadores! —dijo—. La señora Fernández viene esta tarde a tomar el té. ¡Se verán hermosos con las tazas de té!

Me dio un dólar.

Organicé el resto de cosas. La señora Fernández llegó después.

—Voy a tomar el té con la señora Jacobi esta tarde —me dijo—. Me gustaría llevarle un detalle.

Escogió el gallo de porcelana y también me dio un dólar.

El siguiente, fue el señor del sexto piso. Compró la corbata tejida. Cincuenta centavos.

Todos mis vecinos vinieron y todos compraron algo.

Andrés fue la última persona en venir. Escogió una pipa.

–¡Este es mi día de suerte! –dijo. Su cara era exacta a la que ponía el presentador del programa de las cosas viejas al descubrir un tesoro–. ¡La semana pasada perdí una pipa igual a esta! ¡Era mi favorita!

Y me dio dos dólares y se guardó la pipa en el bolsillo. Todavía tenía la cara de "¡Santo cielo!".

Conté el dinero… ¡veintidós dólares! Guardé la mesa de juego y subí en el ascensor hasta el quinto piso para devolverles a Margarita y a Miguel el dinero que me habían prestado el martes.

Miguel tomó el dinero y me dio las gracias.

Margarita miró por ambos lados el billete de un dólar que le entregué.

—¿A dónde lo has llevado? —me preguntó.

—A ningún lado. Ha estado en mi bolsillo. ¿Ves? Todavía está limpio y nuevo.

Margarita gruñó. Lo tomó con dos dedos y fue a lavarlo.

Como ya era muy tarde para ir a la tienda de materiales para pintar, fui a ver trabajar a los albañiles. Margarita tenía razón: ¡tuve suerte esta semana! Ellos ya estaban terminando el trabajo del día, ¡y me regalaron los ladrillos rotos y la argamasa que había sobrado!

Se me ocurrió, entonces, una idea excelente. Saqué la manzana que tenía en el bolsillo, me la comí hasta que llegué a la parte de las semillas y luego escogí algunas. Abrí un pequeño hueco en la tierra al lado de la pared de ladrillo y las sembré. Después, construí una pequeña pared de ladrillo alrededor del lugar, para proteger al manzano cuando este creciera. Y, aunque los ladrillos estuvieran rotos, todo se veía hermoso.

Sonreí, porque si el árbol llegaba a crecer, tendría todas las manzanas que quisiera. E invitaría a todos mis conocidos y les diría: "Sigan, utilicen algunas manzanas para hacer un experimento de ciencia, si quieren. O denle algunas a su hámster si está hambriento. Hagan lo que quieran con ellas. Siempre habrá manzanas".

Después entré corriendo al edificio para llamar a papá y a mamá y mostrarles mi pared.

Cuando entré a mi apartamento, papá estaba al teléfono.

—No, claramente yo no le di esas cosas. Me acabo de enterar del asunto.

Se veía bastante enojado. Pero mi pared de ladrillo lo animaría. Tan pronto colgó, le pregunté si quería venir conmigo a ver lo que había hecho.

—No, no quiero —dijo—. Ya sé lo que has hecho. ¡Un desastre! ¡He estado oyendo al respecto durante la última media hora!

—¿Qué quieres decir?

—Estaba al teléfono con la señora Fernández; cuando llegó a la casa de la señora Jacobi a tomar el té, vio los individuales que les había dado a los Suárez en su aniversario. Aparentemente, ellos los habían botado. Ahora, la señora Fernández no les habla.

–Oh –dije.

–Y eso no es todo –continuó papá–. La señora Jacobi llamó hace unos minutos. La señora Fernández le llevó de regalo un pequeño gallo de porcelana. La señora Jacobi lo reconoció porque era el mismo gallo que le había dado al señor del sexto piso en su cumpleaños. Entonces, está molesta con él. Cuando él fue a su apartamento para disculparse, los Suárez estaban ahí, dándole explicaciones sobre los individuales. El señor del sexto piso tenía puesta una corbata amarilla, que la madre de la señora Suárez le había tejido a su marido, la señora Suárez no le habla al señor Suárez y el señor Suárez no le habla al señor del sexto piso. Clementina, temo preguntarte, ¿pero cuántas personas te compraron cosas?

–Todos –le dije.

Papá se dio un golpe en la frente.

—Entonces esto podría ser solo el comienzo. Y me están culpando por todo.

—No te preocupes, Lucas —dijo mamá—. Cuando todos se hayan calmado, se darán cuenta de que no es tu culpa. Y de que tampoco es culpa de Clementina —se detuvo a pensar por un momento—. Bueno, no es *completamente* su culpa. Después de todo, ¿cómo podía saberlo?

Papá no dijo nada.

—¿Qué opinan si mañana, después de la escuela, me disculpo con todos? —les pregunté.

—Supongo que ese es un comienzo, campeona —dijo papá—. Y tendrás que decirles que volverás a comprarles de vuelta todo lo que les vendiste.

Eso N-O, *no* era justo. Pero como papá todavía se veía bastante enojado, no se lo pude decir.

Más tarde esa noche, mientras intentaba no pensar en lo enojado que se veía papá, él entró a mi habitación. Se sentó en mi cama con el cuaderno.

—Por eso lo hice —dije, señalando el cuaderno—. Quería comprarle un regalo a mamá para que no se sintiera mal porque había tenido un detalle contigo.

Papá me miró por un rato. Luego, me dijo:

—En eso estás equivocada, campeona. Mamá jamás se sentiría mal porque hayas tenido un detalle conmigo.

—Margarita dice que es una regla: si tienes un detalle con alguien, también debes tenerlo con la otra persona.

—Puede que esa sea la regla de Margarita. Pero no es nuestra regla. Yo me alegro cuando haces algo por mamá y ella se alegra cuando haces algo por mí. Cuando quieres a alguien quieres que esa persona sea feliz, ¿no es cierto?

Pensé en eso durante un momento y luego asentí con la cabeza.

Papá me pasó el cuaderno.

"A veces la hija del administrador del edificio era muy impulsiva", leí. "A veces hacía las cosas sin pensar más allá. Sin pensar en las consecuencias. Eso la metía en muchos problemas. A veces, hasta metía a su padre en problemas".

Tomé mi bolígrafo y escribí en el cuaderno,

Ella sentía mucho lo que había pasado.

Le iba a pasar el cuaderno a papá para que leyera, pero lo retuve y añadí:

Lo sentía muchísimo.

Y pensé en otra cosa:

¡Entonces él la perdonó!

Papá tomó el bolígrafo.

El administrador del edificio sabía que su hija lo sentía y como la amaba tanto, <u>siempre</u> la perdonaba. Pero se preocupaba por ella. Le preocupaba que se pudiera sentir mal por meterse en problemas al ser tan impulsiva. Esperaba que pensara las cosas un poco más. Que pensara lo que podría pasar <u>antes</u> de hacer las cosas.

Miré ese párrafo durante algún tiempo. Luego, escribí:

La hija del administrador del edificio estaba tan contenta de que su papá la hubiera
perdonado, que prometió pensar un poco
más las cosas de ahora en adelante.

Papá tomó el bolígrafo de nuevo.

*Eso lo hizo sentirse realmente
orgulloso de ella.*

Me acerqué y lo abracé.
–Creo que es un libro realmente
bueno –le susurré.
–Yo también lo creo –me susurró
él–. Creo que puede llegar a estar
entre los más vendidos.

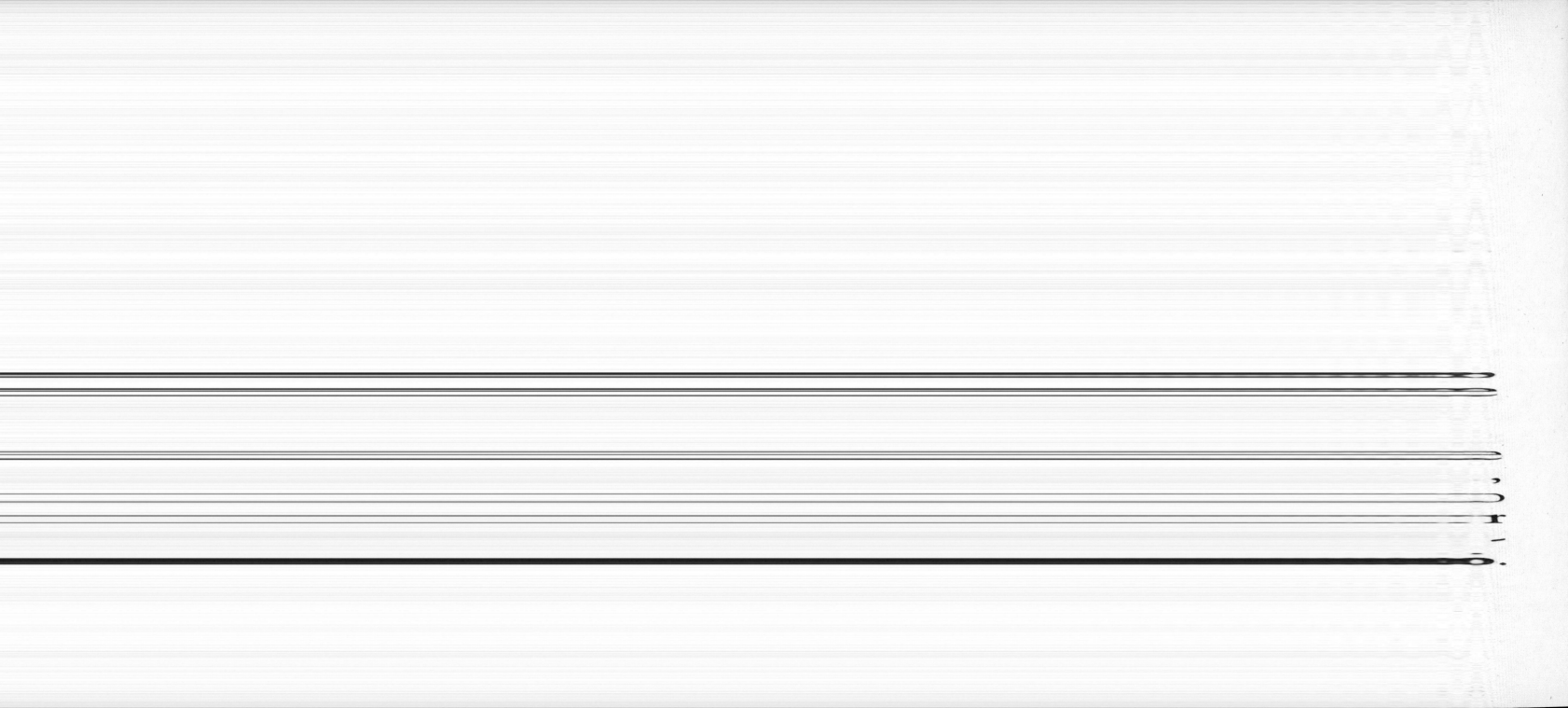

Y lue
se secó
aunque
de gérm
–Mi p

La actri
resfriad
puede c
lo fabul
tener la
encontr
nuevo.
–Lo si
tía. Mar
visita de
No habl
–Eres
zando–.
ta!
–¿De q
soy afort
–Porqu
días.
–Pero t
–dije–. C
da una se

La hija del administrador del edificio estaba tan contenta de que su papá la hubiera perdonado, que prometió pensar un poco más las cosas de ahora en adelante.

Papá tomó el bolígrafo de nuevo.

Eso lo hizo sentirse realmente orgulloso de ella.

Me acerqué y lo abracé.

–Creo que es un libro realmente bueno –le susurré.

–Yo también lo creo –me susurró él–. Creo que puede llegar a estar entre los más vendidos.

con él. Él no trabaja cuando viene a verte, y es como unas vacaciones. Mi papá siempre está trabajando.

—Supongo que sí —dijo Margarita.

—Y puedes quedarte con él en el hotel y pedir que te traigan comida a la habitación y quitarle las envolturas a los vasos del baño. Y el inodoro tiene una cinta por encima que dice: "Desinfectado para su protección". ¡A ti te encanta eso!

Margarita asintió y se alegró un poco.

—Y a veces puedes ir a Hollywood, California, ¡y ver cómo se hace un comercial! Creo que eso es tener suerte. Y un día, ¡tu papá podría dejarte aparecer en un comercial!

Nos quedamos ahí sentadas por un minuto, pensando en cuál de las dos era la verdaderamente afortunada.

—Creo que las dos lo somos —dijo Margarita al fin—. Solo que de diferente manera.

Excepto que yo no fui tan afortunada al llegar a la escuela.

Durante la clase de matemáticas, la señora Ángel escribió un problema difícil en el tablero y luego preguntó si alguno sabía la solución. Yo levanté la mano y le di la respuesta.

Si mi verdadero profesor hubiera estado ahí, se habría tocado la nariz con el dedo índice y luego me habría señalado, sonriendo. Esto significa: "¡Lo tenías frente a las narices! ¡Bien hecho!".

En cambio, la señora Ángel dijo:

—Eso es correcto, Clementina. Pero yo no pedí la respuesta, solo pregunté si alguien la sabía.

Lo que prácticamente fue equivalente a decir: "Nunca serás una estudiante exitosa".

Luego, borró el tablero, y apuesto a que lo borró tan fuerte que casi le quita el color verde.

En clase de escritura, nos hizo leer en voz alta lo que habíamos escrito en el diario.

—Nuestro profesor no nos hace leer en voz alta lo que escribimos —le dije.

–Pero el señor Morcillo no está aquí –me recordó. Y yo no lo había olvidado–. Así que hoy lo leeremos en voz alta.

Entonces, tuve que leer lo que había escrito en mi diario, que era sobre por qué me gustaban tanto los ladrillos, y dejó de ser un secreto.

La señora Ángel fue mala conmigo otras tres veces. Lo único bueno fue que al fin pude comprender por qué estaba teniendo tantos problemas. Levanté la mano y le dije que necesitaba ver a la directora.

Ella dijo:

–Anda a verla.

Con esto probablemente quiso decir: "Por fin podré trabajar un poco con los estudiantes exitosos". Lo que hizo que me enfureciera aun más. Caminé por los corredores pisando tan fuerte que probablemente rompí el sótano de la escuela. Y no me importó.

La señora Gamba me vio la cara cuando entré y dijo:

—¿Quieres decirme qué te está molestando hoy?

—Todavía no —dije—. ¿Le gustan los tatuajes?

—No, no mucho. ¿A ti?

—Sí —dije. Respiré profundamente—. Bueno, ahora sí quiero decírselo. No entiendo las reglas de la señora Ángel. Son diferentes de las de mi profesor y solo las dice cuando ya es demasiado tarde y estoy en problemas. Eso no es justo. Así que quería saber si usted podría pedirle a mi

profesor que vuelva antes de tiempo. Por ejemplo hoy. ¿Podría llamarlo y decirle que no se prepare más para Egipto durante lo que queda de la semana? De todos modos, él no quiere ir allá.

—Lo siento, Clementina, pero no voy a hacer eso. De hecho, acabo de hablar con él y me dijo que la estaba pasando de maravilla.

Crucé los brazos sobre el pecho y sentí que me ponía más y más furiosa.

—Clementina, ¿crees que la señora Ángel podría estar sintiendo lo mis-

mo que tú? ¿Que no puede adivinar las reglas? Es difícil ser suplente y tener que aprender las reglas de una escuela. Tal vez debas ayudarla y explicarle cómo se hacen las cosas en tu salón.

–No –gruñí–. No creo.

La señora Gamba se quedó mirándome quieta y sentada, hasta que finalmente hipnotizó mi boca para que dijera:

–Bueno, está bien. Tal vez *alguien* deba hacerlo.

La miré fijamente mientras decía "alguien", pero ella solo me devolvió la mirada.

Negué con la cabeza.

–Tal vez alguien de sexto. Yo no.

La señora Gamba se recostó en el espaldar de su silla.

–Bueno, eso es una pena. Creo que harías un muy buen trabajo.

Se puso de pie.

–Regresemos a tu salón. El señor Morcillo me pidió que les dijera lo mucho que le habían gustado las tarjetas que le escribieron. También me dijo que les contara lo que ha estado haciendo esta semana —me entregó un diccionario—. Si buscas la palabra "momificación", puedes ayudarme a explicar lo que él ha estado aprendiendo.

Busqué la palabra y regresamos al salón.

La señora Gamba les dijo a todos lo mucho que el señor Morcillo había agradecido nuestras tarjetas. Dijo que había pasado una semana maravillosa y que hoy había aprendido un poco más sobre la momificación.

—Y ahora, Clementina les va a explicar lo que significa esa palabra.

—Primero, le sacan las entrañas al señor con una cuchara grande —dije—. Luego, le sacan el cerebro por la nariz. Si la momia estornuda mientras hacen eso, habrá pedazos de cerebro por todas partes. Tendrían que rasparlos del techo con una pala...

A mi lado, la señora Gamba se aclaró la garganta.

—Bueno, no. Supongo que esto no sucede con frecuencia. Pero sí es algo asqueroso. Y además –dije–, ¡las momias están *desnudas* debajo de las vendas!

La señora Gamba suspiró un suspiro muy fuerte.

–Clementina, gracias por esa explicación tan clara de lo que es la momificación.

Cuando regresé a casa de la escuela, me guardé los veinte dólares en el bolsillo y me dirigí al último piso.

–Hola-señora-Jacobi-lamento-haber-vendido-lo-que-usted-dejó-para-la-caridad-aquí-está-su-dinero-¿quiere-que-se-lo-devuelva?

La señora Jacobi me miró como si yo estuviera loca.

–Me encantan los individuales –dijo–. No quiero que me devuelvas el dinero.

En el siguiente piso, pasó lo mismo. Y en el siguiente. Y en el siguiente. Todos me miraron como si estuviera loca. Todos estaban contentos con lo que habían comprado. Nadie quería que le devolviera el dinero. Por último, fui al apartamento de Margarita y Miguel, porque Andrés no llega sino hasta las cuatro de la tarde.

Miguel abrió la puerta.

—¡Hola, Clementina! —dijo. Tenía una sonrisa inmensa en la cara.

—¿Está Andrés? —pregunté.

—¡Nop! —gritó. Su sonrisa se agrandó aun más.

—¿Por qué no?

La cara de Miguel casi se parte por la mitad.

—¿Te acuerdas de la pipa que le vendiste? ¿La que dijo que se parecía a la que se le había perdido? Pues *era* la de él. No se le había perdido, ¡mamá se la había botado! Así que está enojado con ella y no va a venir. ¡Gracias, Clementina!

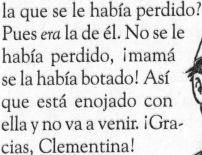

Normalmente, me siento bien cuando alguien

me da las gracias, pero, esta vez no me sentí bien. De todos modos dije: "De nada".

Después caí en la cuenta de algo: ¡Todavía tenía el dinero para el regalo de mamá!

—Debemos regresar a la tienda de materiales para pintar de inmediato —le dije a Miguel.

—Bueno —dijo él.

Esto es algo que me gusta de Miguel: jamás pregunta por qué, solo hace las cosas.

Si le hubiera pedido eso a Margarita, ella me habría hecho cientos de preguntas y luego me habría dado cientos de razones por las que pensaba que mi idea era estúpida y luego me habría dicho que ella tenía una mejor.

Miguel no era así. Él solo decía: "Bueno". Si alguna vez tengo novio, que jamás tendré, podría ser él.

—Llevemos a tu hermano —dijo Miguel. Esto también me gusta de Miguel: le agrada mi hermano. Y a mi hermano le agrada él.

Así que bajamos a mi apartamento y amarramos a Cebolleta al cochecito. Miguel se inclinó hacia delante.

—¿Carrera de cochecitos? —le preguntó Miguel a mi hermano.

Mi hermano dio un alarido, que es su manera de decir "sí" cuando está muy emocionado para poder hablar.

Da muchos alaridos cuando está con Miguel.

Miguel salió corriendo con mi hermano, pero no aplastó a nadie por el camino. Cebolla siguió dando alaridos todo el tiempo porque le encantan las carreras de cochecitos y porque le gusta oír cómo le tiembla la voz cada vez el coche se da un topetazo. Yo tuve que correr para alcanzarlos y llegamos a la tienda en pocos minutos.

Una vez allí, arrojé el dinero sobre el mostrador. Me había quedado sin aire.

–Volviste –dijo el empleado. Después, me preguntó cómo estaba mi tía abuela Rosa.

–No lo sé –le dije–. No la he visto esta semana. Pero supongo que está normal.

Después, le pregunté cómo estaba *su* tía abuela.

–No lo sé –dijo–. Tampoco la he visto esta semana. Pero también supongo que está normal.

Después, terminamos con las cortesías y él empacó el regalo de mamá. Yo amarré el paquete a la parte de atrás del cochecito de mi hermano y nos dirigimos a casa.

—Esta vez no habrá carrera —le advertí a Miguel.

Miguel y mi hermano me miraron como si les hubiera partido el corazón. Pero yo me mantuve firme en mi posición.

—Lo siento —dije—. No con algo tan valioso en el cochecito.

Esto es "ser responsable".

Capítulo 10

Mamá había dejado una nota:

Fui a entregar las pinturas.
Papá está afuera con los albañiles.

Como Rábano estaba agotado de tanto gritar, lo llevé afuera en el cochecito y lo senté en la banca al lado de papá.

—¿Qué hay en la bolsa? —preguntó papá, tomando a mi hermano en brazos.

Saqué la caja de madera.

–Es para mamá. Es para sus cosas de pintar. Le va a encantar, ¿no crees?

Papá tomó la caja.

–Guau –dijo–. Con seguridad le va a encantar. Pero ya hablamos de esto. Sabes que no tienes que…

–Lo sé –dije–. No pude dejar de pensar en lo feliz que la haría. Quería ver su cara de "¡Guau, debo estar soñando!".

Papá sonrió.

–A mí también me gusta cuando hace esa cara. Bueno, creo que eso mejora las cosas. Lo que hiciste. Es una buena razón… querer hacer feliz a alguien.

–¿La gente del edificio continúa enojada? –pregunté.

Él asintió.

–Digamos que hoy el aire en el ascensor estaba un poco frío.

–No querían que nadie supiera lo que habían regalado para la colecta de caridad –dije.

Papá asintió de nuevo.

–Por eso lo habían puesto en bolsas.

—Pero yo no lo sabía.

—Lo sé.

—Me gusta conocer las reglas antes —dije.

—Entiendo —dijo papá.

Y luego, nos quedamos callados por un momento, observando a los albañiles terminar la pared. Esto me dio una buena idea y se la conté a papá.

—No veo por qué no —dijo él—. Hay ladrillos de sobra y suficiente dinero en el presupuesto para mejoras en el edificio.

Entonces, les preguntamos a los albañiles si podían construir una pequeña pared de ladrillo alrededor del área de la colecta de caridad y dijeron que sí.

Cuando terminaron, papá y yo le hicimos una tapa de madera con una puertita para que la gente pueda meter sus regalos adentro. Yo hice un letrero que decía:

¡PRIVADO!
¡Prohibido sacar las cosas y venderlas!

Luego, escribí "Lo siento" por todo el letrero y puse adentro los dos dólares que me habían sobrado de todo lo que había vendido.

—Eso resolverá el problema —dijo papá—. Eso hará que todos los del edificio se sientan bien.

Casi todos.

Le pregunté a papá si podíamos cenar en la azotea del edificio, y jugar "Vida" e invitar a Margarita y a

Miguel. Le expliqué que su papá no podría venir este fin de semana y que Margarita había llorado.

—¿Y podrías ser el padre suplente de ella?

—¿Suplente? No lo sé. Margarita parece ser un poco… particular frente a las cosas. No sé si yo podría entender sus reglas.

—Bueno… creo que no deberías preocuparte por las reglas de Margarita. Tan solo sé el papá que eres siempre.

—Bueno —dijo papá—. Lo haré.

Llevamos a mi hermano adentro, y llamé por teléfono a Margarita y le pregunté si ella y Miguel podían comer pizza con nosotros en la azotea.

—¡Gracias al cielo! —dijo ella—. Mamá está cocinando una cena de "lo siento" para Andrés. Pastel de carne con cebollas extra. Y probablemente ¡va a besarla!

En ese momento, mamá llegó y se veía un poco triste. Tomó los dibujos y dijo:

—No le gustaron. Dijo que no eran suficientemente modernos. Que les faltaba color.

Yo le dije que estaban perfectos y que no les faltaba color.

—¡Pero tengo algo que te hará sentir mejor!

Hice que se sentara.

—¡Cierra los ojos! —le dije, y luego fui por su regalo y se lo puse sobre las piernas.

Cuando abrió los ojos, se emocionó tanto no que podía terminar las frases, lo que usualmente es una mala señal, pero en este caso no lo era.

—¡Mira todas las... para mis pinceles... y tiene una... ahora él no podrá...! —y todo el tiempo hizo la cara de "¡Guau, debo estar soñando!", que tanto me gusta y que algún día voy a dibujar.

En ese momento mi hermano se despertó y todos esperamos hasta que saludara a sus pies y nos los mostrara como si nunca antes los hubiéramos visto. Luego, mamá lo alzó, lo sentó en sus piernas y le dio un par de latas de galletas desocupadas.

—También es tu día de suerte —le dijo—. ¡También te dan regalos!

Mi hermano sonrió y comenzó a golpear las latas de galletas. Mamá me miró.

—Oh, espera. Clementina, ¿quieres unas también?

Y en ese instante, sin pensarlo siquiera, dije:

—No, dáselas todas a él. ¡No hay problema!

¡Y esa era la verdad! Papá me guiñó el ojo y eso hizo que la cara se le viera tan bonita que algún día también haré un dibujo de ella.

Luego, ordenamos dos pizzas, recogimos a Margarita y a Miguel en el quinto piso y subimos todos a la azotea. No jugamos "Vida", porque teníamos muchas otras cosas que hacer ahí.

El sol se estaba poniendo, y yo hice una lista de todos los colores que podía ver sobre las nubes de Boston. Conté treinta y tres.

Luego, Miguel señaló hacia la dirección en la que quedaba el Fenway

Park, el estadio de los Medias Rojas. Nos contó de todas la bolas que se habían precipitado fuera del estadio durante la última temporada y también quién las había bateado, la distancia que habían recorrido y quién había ganado.

Luego, desviamos la luz de la lámpara hacia Margarita y ella actuó cada uno de los comerciales de su papá. Papá aplaudía como loco y decía: "¡Voy a comprar *ese* producto!" después de cada comercial. Esto hizo que Margarita sonriera tanto, que los frenillos de los dientes brillaban bajo la luz de la lámpara.

Hasta Espinaca hizo algo: gritaba cada vez que Miguel le guiñaba el ojo.

Mientras empacábamos las cosas para regresar, Miguel me preguntó por mi profesor.

—Entonces, ¿se fue a acampar?

—Ya no va a ir. No va a romper su promesa. De todas maneras, no quería ir.

—Bueno, es bueno saber que cambió de opinión.

—No cambió de opinión, exactamente —le expliqué lo de la carta a los jurados.

Miguel se detuvo y me miró fijamente.

–¿Escribiste esas cosas terribles que te conté sobre Fríjoles Martínez? ¿Y qué pasa si tu profesor las lee?

–No lo hará. Es una carta para el jurado.

–¿Estás segura?

–Claro que sí –pero de repente...

Bueno, no estaba tan segura.

De vuelta en nuestro apartamento, papá y mamá fueron a la habitación de mi hermano para acostarlo y arroparlo y yo fui a la habitación de ellos y abrí el cuaderno de papá. Encontré la página en la que él había escrito sobre lo orgulloso que se sentía el administrador del edificio porque su hija había prometido pensar antes de hacer algo, y escribí:

Pero ella podría no ser muy buena para esto.

Capítulo 11

El viernes por la mañana, me levanté contenta: hoy era el último día que tendría que aguantar a la señora Ángel. También estaba un poco preocupada, como si algo malo fuera a suceder, pero no sabía qué era.

Me enteré en la escuela.

—Partiremos para el capitolio después de almuerzo —anunció la señora Ángel—. La invitación dice que la ceremonia comienza a la una en punto, con la lectura de las cartas.

–¿Qué quiere decir con la lectura de las cartas? –pregunté–. ¿En voz alta?

–No lo sé –contestó ella–. Lectura de cartas; anuncio del ganador; discurso. Eso es todo lo que dice.

Sentí que me iba a dar un ataque, pues el corazón me daba golpes. Me quedé sentada allí toda la mañana, como congelada en la silla. Estuve tan callada, que no escuche ni un solo "Clementina, ¡debes prestar atención!". Eso era un nuevo récord para mí. Supongo que eso es lo bueno de los ataques.

Y luego, llegó la hora de partir. Mientras todos alistaban las mochilas y las chaquetas, yo me quedé de pie en un rincón.

–¿Estás bien, Clementina? –preguntó la señora Ángel.

–Me está dando un ataque –le dije–. Creo que debería irme a casa.

Ella me miró con los ojos entrecerrados durante un minuto.

–Dudo que eso sea lo que te está sucediendo. Probablemente estás emocionada porque vas a ir al capitolio.

Así que tuve que caminar hacia la salida con la señora Ángel y cuando me senté en el autobús, ella se sentó a mi lado.

–Me alegra que tengamos la oportunidad de hablar –dijo ella, cuando el autobús comenzó a andar–. Me temo que tú y yo no tuvimos una semana muy exitosa.

Decidí que, como iba a morirme pronto, podía decirle la verdad de una vez.

—No pude entender ninguna de sus reglas —le dije.

—¿Qué quieres decir?

Respiré profundamente.

—Sus reglas son diferentes de las de mi profesor. Me tomó mucho tiempo aprenderlas, pero lo hice. El lunes, cuando vi las tajadas de manzana, recordé nuestra regla de "Alimentar a los hámsteres primero", pero no adiviné su regla de "No tocarlas porque es un experimento de ciencia". Ayer, cuando escribió el problema de matemáticas en el tablero, recordé nuestra regla de "No copiar el problema con marcador mágico", pero no adiviné su regla de "No dar la respuesta en voz alta". Cuando nos entregó la hoja de papel el primer día, recordé nuestra regla de "Escribir su nombre arriba, al lado derecho de la página", pero no adiviné su regla de "No dibujar nada en ella".

Respiré profundamente, otra vez.

—Me gustaría conocer las reglas de las cosas al principio. Antes de que pueda cometer un error.

—Oh —dijo la señora Ángel y luego se quedó callada durante un minuto.

Después dijo:

—Eso tiene sentido. Me habría gustado que tú y yo hubiéramos hablado el lunes.

—A mí también —dije—. Pero el lunes no sabía cuál era el problema.

Luego le mostré mi brazo lleno de letreros.

La señora Ángel lo miró por un momento, luego sacó un bolígrafo ¡y se escribió lo mismo en el brazo! ¡No estoy bromeando! A VECES, TIENES

QUE DARTE CUENTA DE CUÁL ES EL PRO-
BLEMA ANTES DE ENCONTRARLE UNA
SOLUCIÓN.

–Gracias por el buen consejo –dijo.

Yo la miré fijamente durante un minuto. Luego, recordé mis buenos modales.

–De nada.

–Y otra cosa –dijo–: si tu profesor se gana el viaje, estaré aquí el resto del año. Entonces, ¿crees que el lunes podrías indicarme las reglas que tienen para el salón de clase? Porque yo no las conozco.

Yo dije que sí, aunque sabía que mi
profesor no se iba a ganar el viaje.
Pensar en eso hizo que el ataque me
doliera aun más. Cuando llegamos al
capitolio, estaba a punto de morir.

Los otros dos cursos ya estaban en
el vestíbulo. Uno, era un grupo de
estudiantes de bachillerato que estaban empujándose los unos a los otros.
El otro grupo era un curso de niños
de preescolar. También se estaban
empujando y muchos se habían caído
al suelo. Antes de que nuestro curso
pudiera comenzar a hacer lo mismo,

nos dijeron que podíamos entrar al auditorio.

Los de bachillerato llegaron en fila y se sentaron al lado derecho de la sala. Después, entraron los de preescolar y se sentaron al lado izquierdo. Pero entonces hubo un problema.

Los de preescolar eran tan pequeños que cada vez que se recostaban en el espaldar las sillas se cerraban y los mordían como cocodrilos locos en un charco de ranas. Por un momento las cosas se salieron de control, con diecinueve niñitos que se caían entre las sillas y gritaban como si alguien se los estuviera devorando. Y probablemente eso era lo que sentían.

—Caramba —oí que le susurraba la señora Gamba a la señora Ángel—. ¡Ojalá que nuestros niños sean lo suficientemente pesados! De otro modo, ¡la Asociación de Padres y Maestros va a llevarse un susto!

Finalmente, alguien trajo diecinueve libros de derecho para hacer más peso sobre las sillas de los de preescolar. Luego, nuestro curso entró y nos. sentamos justo en el medio.

Frente a nosotros, en una mesa muy larga con un letrero que decía COMITÉ DE JUECES, había cuatro personas. Una de ella tenía una placa y una cara seria, lo que quería decir que era el jefe.

Detrás de ellos estaban sentados los tres profesores que competían por el premio. Yo desvié los ojos para no tener que mirar al señor Morcillo.

El juez jefe se puso de pie.

—Vamos a oír la carta de un alumno sobre cada profesor —dijo—. Luego, anunciaremos nuestra decisión.

La maestra de preescolar fue la primera. Le hizo señas a una niñita a la que le faltaban todos los dientes del frente. La niña parecía estar aliviada de que la alejaran de la silla mordedora, probablemente porque ella no podía hacerle lo mismo a la silla. Como los de preescolar son muy pequeños para escribir cartas, ella solo les dijo a los jueces por qué creía que su maestra debía ganar.

—Mi pofesoa esh la mejó —comenzó a decir. Después de eso, no entendí nada de lo que dijo; y creo que los jueces tampoco, aunque siguieron sonriendo y asintiendo.

Luego fue el turno de los de bachillerato. Un chico con púas moradas en el pelo se puso de pie y fingió un bostezo para demostrar que no estaba nervioso por leer su carta.

Tampoco entendí mucho de lo que dijo, aunque él sí tenía todos los dientes. Dijo algo sobre los exámenes finales y algo sobre la atmósfera académica y algunas palabras más complicadas que esas. Estaba segura de que se las estaba inventando.

Sin embargo, los jueces también sonrieron y asintieron durante toda la lectura de su carta.

Luego el señor Morcillo se puso de pie. Los jueces le entregaron un sobre grande, del cual sacó una hoja de papel.

—Clementina, ¿podrías subir acá y leer tu carta por favor?

Desde mi asiento, moví la cabeza para decir "no" y lo miré fijamente con los ojos entrecerrados.

Él asintió con la cabeza para decir "sí" y me miró con más insistencia.

Yo lo miré de nuevo fijamente.

Claro que no usé la mirada punzante, aunque no habría importado. Porque él me miró con su mejor truco: ¡la mirada láser!

La mirada láser es la mirada más poderosa de todas. Me hipnotizó para que me pusiera de pie y caminara hasta el podio. El señor Mor-

cillo me entregó la carta y yo se la recibí. Y comencé a leerla.

–Tengo que contarles algunas cosas sobre mi profesor. Si se van a acampar con él, y tienen que preparar fríjoles…

Y luego miré disimuladamente… a mi profesor.

Porque quería verlo por última vez, antes de que me odiara para siempre.

Y cuando vi que la cara le estaba brillando con una sonrisa feliz que decía: "Me iré a Egipto y Clementina me está ayudando".

El papel se me cayó de las manos. El jefe de los jueces lo recogió y me lo pasó de nuevo.

Yo lo aparté y negué con la cabeza.

–Está bien –le dije–. No lo necesito. Sé lo que quiero contarles sobre mi profesor.

Y comencé otra vez.

Pero no con lo que había escrito el lunes.

–Si van a acampar con él y tienen que preparar fríjoles, no se preocupen. Porque, incluso si jamás los han preparado, no tendrán problemas. Mi profesor nunca diría: "¿Cómo así que no sabes preparar fríjoles? ¡Te enseñé a hacerlo la semana pasada!". No. Él diría: "Mira, veo que vas a preparar fríjoles. Sé que lo harás bien porque tú eres buena para muchas cosas. Probablemente empezarás por abrir la lata, luego tomarás un tazón limpio". Y sin que se hayan dado cuenta, les enseñará a preparar fríjoles. Y aquí va la parte misteriosa: de alguna manera, ¡pensarán que aprendieron solos! Además, pensarán que preparar fríjoles es la cosa más interesante del mundo, porque mi profesor hace que todo sea interesante. ¡Hasta las cosas que otros piensan que son raras!

"Y todas la mañanas, cuando vayan a la escuela... quiero decir, cuando vayan a acampar con él... se morirán de ganas de saber qué planeó para ese día. Y cuando sea hora de regresar a casa, se sentirán un poquito tristes, porque se divirtieron muchísimo. Pero no tienen por qué preocuparse,

porque él tiene muchísimos proyectos excelentes y estará ahí al día siguiente. Y…

Sentí una mano sobre el hombro y miré hacia arriba. La señora Gamba asintió con la cabeza y dijo:

–Gracias, Clementina –como si yo hubiera terminado.

–Pero hay más –dije–. Quiero contarles más cosas.

–Lo sé –dijo ella–. Pero por ahora es suficiente.

Luego me acompañó a mi asiento, lo que estuvo bien, porque el ataque se me había subido a los ojos y los había puesto un poco borrosos.

Después los jueces se pusieron de pie y se acercaron a... mi profesor. Sonrieron y le estrecharon la mano. Después, se dirigieron hacia los otros profesores y también les sonrieron y les estrecharon la mano. Después, los cuatro jueces regresaron a su mesa y el jefe tocó el micrófono.

–El ganador del programa "Aventuras para maestros" de este año es...

Y en ese momento sabía que iban a decir el nombre de mi profesor por todo lo que yo había dicho sobre él. Lo que me hizo sentir muy, muy, muy triste y muy, muy, muy feliz a la vez. Esto debió confundir a mis oídos, porque lo que oí fue:

–...¡La señorita Gladis Herrera!

La profesora de preescolar debió haber oído lo mismo porque caminó hacia el podio con una enorme sonrisa de "¡No puedo creer que sea yo!", en la cara. Los de preescolar comen-

zaron a saltar y a aplaudir como locos.
Esto no fue una buena idea porque los
libros de derecho se cayeron al suelo
y las sillas comenzaron a morderlos
de nuevo.

–Muchas gracias no lo habría logrado sin mis maravillosos alumnos –dijo
con afán la señorita Herrera frente al
micrófono–. ¡Y creo que ahora debo
regresar a rescatarlos!

Y ese fue el final del programa.

Mi profesor fue al lugar donde estaba nuestro curso y se inclinó frente
a mí.

–Muchas gracias por esa increíble
carta de recomendación, Clementina.

–Pero no ganó –dije–. Lo siento
mucho.

Y de repente, ¡lo sentí mucho!
Bueno, un poquito.

–No lo sientas –dijo–. Yo no lo
siento.

–¿No?

–No –repitió él–. Realmente quería
ganar, pero cuando leíste tu carta,
pensé… que había extrañado mucho

a mis alumnos esta semana. Todo lo que dijiste en tu carta me recordó lo mucho que me gusta enseñarles. Hemos comenzado muchos proyectos y no quiero irme dejándolos a medio terminar. Mi plan era estar con ustedes este año, y no quiero incumplirles. Tenías razón en eso. Así que, si hubiera ganado, les habría dicho que lo sentía, pero que no podía aceptar el premio.

Miró a la profesora de preescolar.

—Me alegra que se lo hayan dado a ella. ¡Me imagino que una excavación arqueológica le parecerá unas vacaciones!

Me toqué la nariz con el dedo índice y lo señalé: "¡Lo tenías frente a las narices! ¡Bien hecho!".

Y él me sonrió.

—Estoy muy orgulloso de ti, Clementina —me dijo.

De repente, quería que él supiera la verdad.

—No debería estar orgulloso de mí —dije—. No sabe lo que realmente decía mi carta.

–Sí, lo sé –dijo–. Las leí todas esta mañana.

–Oh, no. No pudo haber leído la mía –le dije.

El señor Morcillo me miró y levantó las cejas.

–"El olor de sus medias le haría caer las vendas a una momia. Si pasara frente a la Esfinge, esta se desplomaría".

–Entonces… ¿por qué…? ¿cómo supo que yo…?

–¿Recuerdas la historia de la mamá pájaro?

No hice cara de "¡Otra vez con lo mismo!", porque en ese momento quería escuchar la historia. Pero el señor Morcillo no me la contó. A cambio, me apretó la mano y dijo:

–Sabía que podías volar, Clementina. Y sabía que volarías.

Mientras estaba sentada ahí, apretándole la mano a mi profesor, el ataque se desvaneció. ¡Y no creerán lo que sucedió después! Sentí una picazón por toda la piel.

¿Y saben qué era?

¡Plumas!
Bueno, en realidad era piel de gallina.

NOT
A SAFE
GOD

Also by Tim Riter

Strong Enough to be a Man: Reclaiming Biblical Masculinity (2005)

Twelve Lies Husbands Tell Their Wives (2005)

Twelve Lies Wives Tell Their Husbands (2005)

Twelve Lies You Hear about the Holy Spirit (2004)

Twelve Lies You Hear in Church (2004)

Just Leave God Out of It (2004)

A Passionate Pursuit of God (1999)

Deep Down: Character Change through the Fruit of the Spirit (1995)

WRESTLING WITH THE
DIFFICULT TEACHINGS OF JESUS

NOT
A SAFE
GOD

TIM RITER

BROADMAN
& HOLMAN
PUBLISHERS

Nasville, Tennessee

Ten-digit ISBN: 0-8054-4298-7
Thirteen-digit ISBN: 978-0-8054-4298-4

Published by Broadman & Holman Publishers,
Nashville, Tennessee

Dewey Decimal Classification: 248.84
Subject Heading: SPIRITUAL LIFE \ DISCIPLESHIP \
JESUS CHRIST—TEACHINGS

1 2 3 4 5 6 7 8 9 10   10 09 08 07 06

Dedication

Two friends played essential roles in the development of *Not a Safe God*.

My pastor, Greg Sidders, continually challenges me to confront the clarity of Jesus' radical demands. He increases my spiritual discomfort level, which I desperately need. He also suggested the title's link to C. S. Lewis and The Chronicles of Narnia series. Thanks, my friend.

Suzanne Rae Deshchidn, poet, editor, and intriguing thinker, gave of herself to improve the manuscript. But even more, she encouraged me to share my own battles with Jesus' words in a more transparent manner. I don't do that easily, so thanks, I think.

Contents

Introduction

In C. S. Lewis's classic children's tale for adults, *The Lion, the Witch and the Wardrobe*, Mr. and Mrs. Beaver tell the children about Aslan, a mighty lion who serves as a Christ-figure. Feeling somewhat leery of a lion they ask, "Then he isn't safe?"

"Safe? Don't you hear what Mrs. Beaver tells you? Who said anything about safe? 'Course he isn't safe. But he's good."

Contemporary Christianity has focused so much on God's goodness that we've forgotten that he's a lion. He's not safe; not safe at all. He demands much of us and throws down the gauntlet to the fatal disease of complacency that infects us. We've made God comfortable for us. But if we take him seriously, he'll overturn our current lifestyles.

Symptoms of complacency abound in the lives of those who claim to follow Jesus. Church attendance continues to decline. Sharing our faith has become rare. Prayer has all but faded out of the daily practice of most Christians. The ethical and moral behavior of Christians doesn't stray too far from that of unbelievers in general, whether we look at divorce rates, pornography consumption, or premarital sex. Churches struggle to get enough members to serve in Sunday school and other ministries. Congregations find themselves in competition for the best worship services, with people flocking to those with the music they favor. We've evolved into a church full of self-serving people, with little desire for commitment or sacrifice.

Perhaps worst of all, we've grown comfortable with this. We've made it the norm for the Christian life. We love God, but not passionately. We change, but not radically. We give, but not sacrificially. We've relied so heavily on being saved by grace (Eph. 2:8) that we've forgotten we're saved to do good works (v. 9). And we think that God rejoices to have us on these terms.

Does he? God is good. But he's not soft, and only at our peril do we think of God as a tame lion. Jesus came with a radical agenda: Transform the world. Knowing his followers didn't have that natural bent, he gave us some apparently impossible demands. Demands that stretch us far out of our comfort zones. Essential demands. Let's explore them together.

Risky Faith

Jesus makes high demands of his followers,
requirements that push us out of our comfort zones.
How do we respond to what he requires?
Let's explore the death of complacency.

He's Not Safe

Warning labels abound in our litigious society. Cigarette packets caution that smoking can kill us. Food packages inform us of the fat and carbohydrates they contain. Many stores have signs indicating the presence of cancer-causing agents. Construction sites advise: "Wet Paint: Do Not Touch."

Typically, we read these warnings and blithely proceed with what we had planned. We still smoke, we still eat unhealthy food, we still enter stores with carcinogens, and we always test the wet paint. These warnings strike little or no fear into most of us because the dangers don't seem imminent.

Too many of us read the Bible in the same way that we read these signs and labels. We read the admonitions, warnings, demands, and instructions in God's Word, only to pass them off as inconsequential or irrelevant to our lives. But such an attitude might prove perilous.

We like to think of God as a safe harbor, a loving father figure who only wants to help us reach our goals. We misread him, with grave consequences.

God is not safe. His demands will disrupt our carefully planned lives. The journey of faith includes risks to our safety, comfort, possessions, and self-determination. Early believers never saw follow-ing Jesus as the pathway to success, prosperity, self-actualization, or ease. Jesus never spoke casually about the cost of discipleship. We never hear him say, "Well, just hang out with me and the guys for a while, and see if it resonates with you. We don't want to put any pres-sure on you. We're here to answer any questions you may have."

Instead, Jesus confronted seekers with the most difficult area in which they personally would have to change. He told the rich young ruler to sell all he had (Matt. 19:21). He told Nicodemus, perhaps the primary teacher of Israel, to start all over like a young baby (John 3:1).

We read passages such as these and we typically choose one of two options. Either we ignore what Jesus said, claiming he exaggerated to make his point, or we turn these into rules for everyone to keep. The first option disregards Jesus' teaching; the second establishes rules impossible to follow. Both options lead us to lies and bondage.

A third alternative exists. Take Jesus seriously. Realize that he meant what he said. He fully intends to seriously disrupt our lives. We face risks when we follow him, and we should know that going in. Listen to just some of what Jesus *requires* of those who follow him.

- "Anyone who does not carry his cross and follow me *cannot be my disciple*" (Luke 14:27).
- "If anyone comes to me and does not hate his father and mother, his wife and children, his brothers and sisters—yes, even his own life—he *cannot be my disciple*" (Luke 14:26).
- "Any of you who does not give up everything he has *cannot be my disciple*" (Luke 14:33).
- "For I tell you that unless your righteousness surpasses that of the Pharisees and the teachers of the law, you will certainly *not enter the kingdom of heaven*" (Matt. 5:20).

- "I am the vine; you are the branches. If a man remains in me and I in him, he *will* bear much fruit; apart from me you can do nothing. If anyone *does not remain* in me, he is like a branch that is thrown away and withers; such branches are picked up, *thrown into the fire and burned*" (John 15:5–6).

Jesus asked for total commitment from his followers, and the apostles echoed that call for radical change.

- "No one who is born of God will continue to sin, because God's seed remains in him; he *cannot go on sinning*, because he has been born of God" (I John 3:9).
- "Be joyful *always*" (I Thess. 5:16).
- "Pray *continually*" (I Thess. 5:17).
- "Give thanks in *all circumstances*" (I Thess. 5:18).
- "*Do not worry* about tomorrow, for tomorrow will worry about itself" (Matt. 6:34).

The demands from Jesus, and the apostles' description of the Christian life, all express absolutes. Unless we do these we cannot fulfill our calling as a disciple. Why? Disciples always do this. The conclusion? God disrupts our lives. He defines the authentic Christian life, and he's strongly opinionated about it. He requires major changes in us.

God is not safe if we want to live in spiritual complacency. We'll explore the risky faith described by Jesus and the apostles. We won't whitewash their teachings, and we won't spiritualize them away into comfortable platitudes. We must address them squarely if we want to fully follow Jesus.

This chapter will briefly survey some of these demands to highlight the degree of disruption God intends. Then each will be explored more in-depth in its own chapter. What unites these? What do they share in common? Each is absolute. To be a disciple, we *must* . . . A disciple *always* . . . God is good. But he's not soft.

God Intimidates

Jann discovered an intimidating God. A European who immigrated to the U.S. in his teens, he dedicated himself to career success. Then a cousin gave him a copy of Josh McDowell's *Evidence That Demands a Verdict*. His analytical accountant mind grappled with what he read, and came to these logical conclusions: The Bible accurately recorded the life and claims of Jesus and, as the Son of God, only Jesus could provide access to God.

Jann became a follower of Jesus and started to explore his new life, beginning with some deep study of the Old Testament. When I asked what he'd learned about God, he pondered a moment and said, "God is one tough guy. You don't mess around with him."

Too many of us have overlooked that truth. We take God lightly, and minimize the passages that reveal the hard edge of God. But those tough passages demand our attention and they refuse to fade into insignificance.

The Old Covenant recognized the intimidating side of God. Just before presenting the Ten Commandments, Moses warned the people of the consequences of lightly entering into covenant with God:

> Be careful not to forget the covenant of the LORD your
> God that he made with you; do not make for yourselves an
> idol in the form of anything the LORD your God has forbidden. For the LORD your *God is a consuming fire*, a jealous God.
> (Deut. 4:23–24)

Moses might have said, "If you don't carry through, you'll get burned." Six other times the Old Testament writers refer to God as a "consuming fire" (Exod. 24:17; 2 Sam. 22:9; Ps. 18:8; Isa. 30:27, 30; 33:14). But the image spills over into the New Testament as well. The author of Hebrews revives that powerful image to encourage the followers of Jesus to live the transformed life: "for our God is a consuming fire" (12:29).

This concept appeared earlier in Hebrews 10:30–31, as the author urged Christians to persevere, to help each other grow, and to avoid sin. Why? "The Lord will judge his people. It is a dreadful thing to fall into the hands of the living God."

Why should we dread God? In part, because his nature intimidates us. He is nobody's fool. When sin encounters holiness, or disloyalty clashes with faithfulness, or selfishness meets selfless love, then confrontation ensues, not consolation. Apathy repulses Christ.

God is a consuming fire. His nature surpasses ours. He's 220 volts and we're only wired for 12. Experiencing God in his fullness would blow our circuits. That's why God told Moses that no one could look on him and live (Exod. 33:20). It's an awesome experience to find ourselves in the overwhelming presence of God. The disciples discovered the same thing when they saw Jesus calm the gale on the Sea of Galilee. Previously in fear for their lives from the storm, they now became terrified, intimidated by the presence of a person with power over the storm (Mark 4:35–41).

When angels appear to people, they usually begin by saying, "Don't fear." Even angels intimidate us. But God intimidates angels, as Isaiah testified:

> In the year that King Uzziah died, I saw the Lord
> seated on a throne, high and exalted, and the train of his
> robe filled the temple. Above him were seraphs, each with
> six wings: With two wings they covered their faces, with
> two they covered their feet, and with two they were flying.
> (Isa. 6:1–2)

Not even angels could look directly at God. But God also intimidates us because his demands push us out of our comfort zone and into radical transformation.

God Demands Total Transformation

Several times the apostle Paul exhorted believers to experience radical transformation. He wrote to the Galatians that what really matters is "a new creation" (Gal. 6:15). Later he wrote to the Corinthians that if anyone follows Christ they become "a new creature" (2 Cor. 5:17). Our old self disappears and we become a new person. God's goal for us falls nothing short of total transformation.

Paul wrote "flee from sexual immorality". So, have we really grasped the radical principle behind it?

> Flee from sexual immorality. All other sins a man commits are outside his body, but he who sins sexually sins against his own body. Do you not know that your body is a temple of the Holy Spirit, who is in you, whom you have received from God? You are not your own; you were bought at a price. Therefore honor God with your body.
> (1 Cor. 6:18–20)

God can demand our transformation because we have transferred ownership of our lives to him. "You are not your own; you were bought at a price." Since God saved us and paid the price for us, we no longer own our lives. We belong to him. Therefore, each act must bring honor to God. We live to glorify God, not ourselves. This ownership issue changes our core identity. Rather than valuing God as a peripheral option in our lives, we place him at the very center. Each decision we make must be based on the simple question, "Which option will bring the greatest honor to God?"

This ownership change results in the radically different life that Paul described in Romans 12:1–2: "Therefore, I urge you, brothers, in view of God's mercy, to offer your bodies as *living sacrifices*, holy and pleasing to God—this is your spiritual act of worship. Do not conform any longer to the pattern of this world, but *be transformed* by the renewing of your mind."

To state the obvious: A sacrifice involves sacrifice. We lose something; we give it up. And we sacrifice our lives to God. We live for him, not ourselves. But Paul's last phrase adds to this radical dimension: transformation. We are transformed from being a natural person to a spiritual one; from self-centeredness to God-centeredness; from gaining honor for ourselves to gaining it for God. We become a different person and choose to live differently. Our values change. Our choices expand. Our goals shift. Our purpose in life becomes freshly defined.

Let's eliminate the notion that God exists to help us reach our goals, maximizing our potential and talents. God offers a radical agenda. We serve his goals. We honor him. We use our talents for his purposes. It's not about us, but about him. Discipleship is not about striking a deal that will be good for us, but surrendering to the one who has graciously reached out to transform our lives.

TOTALLY NEW PRIORITIES

Consequently, very specific admonitions fill the New Testament. Jesus and the apostles expressed a number of radical requirements for believers. We'll explore each of these in depth in the following sections, but we want to scan them now to provide an overview of how truly radical a life for Christ could be. Again, we tend to either turn them into impossible and legalistic requirements, or to completely minimize their meaning. But Jesus meant what he said, and his teachings reveal crucial truth about the Christian life. When we discount his call to radical discipleship, minimizing the depth of transformation he desired, then we ignore the warnings at our peril.

Let's survey some of these radical demands. For now, simply allowing them to percolate within, permitting the sheer number of demands to pound against the hardened rock of our lives like waves against the shore, turning it into sand.

Disciples Must Die. Changing from a life without Christ to a life for Christ is more radical than those diet posters promising that 300 pounds of blubber can change to 180 pounds of chiseled muscle. Listen to Jesus: "And anyone who does not carry his cross and follow me *cannot be my disciple*" (Luke 14:27). Jesus was utterly emphatic. The cross symbolized death, so we *cannot* be a disciple unless we die. Jesus didn't leave very much room for compromise.

To follow Jesus, we must put our old life to death. Period. Nothing less.

Disciples Must Imitate Jesus. We yearn for role models. I patterned much of my ministry after Herb Read, the senior pastor where I reentered the vocational ministry. Not that I copied all that Herb did, but I learned great practical insights from him.

We read books on mentoring, how to find and act like mentors, to share the wisdom gained by others. But Jesus gave another pattern: "A disciple is not above the teacher, but everyone who is fully qualified will be like the teacher" (Luke 6:40 NRSV). Notice the little phrase *will be*. Not that disciples *should be* like Jesus, or *may be*. The Master expects that his followers will most definitely imitate him.

Do we use Jesus as our pattern for the spiritual life? Do we, like Jesus, use our talents, resources, and time for God's purposes? Are we prepared to die for God's cause, like Jesus? That's part of what being a disciple means.

Disciples Must Hold to Jesus' Teaching. A book David Timms and I wrote explored how easily we embrace the values of our culture rather than the values of the kingdom of God. Josh McDowell has produced statistics claiming that 75 percent of Christians don't accept the concept of absolute truth. But the counter-cultural teaching of Christ leaves little room for the rampant relativism of our day.

We tend to craft our values based on our experiences, family teaching, preferences, and the culture that surrounds us.

But Jesus called for absolute and uncompromising allegiance when he said: "If you hold to my teaching, you are really my disciples" (John 8:31). If we don't hold to Jesus' teachings, we're really not his disciples. We may hold the name and play the game, but we just don't qualify. Authentic disciples must hold onto Jesus' teaching. We don't have the right to craft our own values and claim to live as a disciple of Jesus.

Disciples Must Give Up Family. God created the family as the centerpiece of society. He intended a safe environment in which to bring children into the world and to prepare them for it. In the set of covenant standards called the Ten Commandments, the first to deal with interpersonal relationships told us to honor our father and mother. That came with a promise of long life to those who obeyed.

But Jesus turned that upside down in Luke 14:26: "If anyone comes to me and does not hate his father and mother, his wife and children, his brothers and sisters—yes, even his own life—he *cannot be my disciple.*"

Once again, strong words. Did Jesus literally mean we must hate our blood family? We can't doubt the seriousness of the call to be his disciples.

TOTALLY NEW LIFESTYLE

We begin with a radical restructuring of our priorities, but that leads to a radical change in our lifestyle and behavior. Again, let's survey some of the demands.

Disciples Must Pursue Purity. Authentic grace and forgiveness do not allow us to continue in impurity when we choose to follow Jesus. "No one who is born of God will continue to sin, because God's seed remains in him; *he cannot go on sinning,* because he has been born of God" (1 John 3:9). Do we continue to sin? Disciples cannot.

Disciples Must Rejoice. We all face difficulties. Few people see their dreams develop into reality. Yet, followers of Jesus must respond consistently to these frustrations with joy. Very simply, Paul tells us: "Rejoice in the Lord always. I will say it again: Rejoice!" (Phil. 4:4). Paul could have stopped with that word *always;* that's absolute enough. But then he repeats himself to place even more stress on our always rejoicing.

Not sometimes. Not when we receive good things. Always.

As we tremble at the seeming impossibility of Jesus' demands, we can be tempted to rationalize them away. They can feel overwhelming.

The only conclusion we can draw, then, is that God isn't safe. He desires the total transformation of his people. When we embark on the Christian journey, God warns us of the risks we face. Losing our lives. Losing our families. Handing over ownership. Being utterly changed.

So, together, let's explore those impossible, radical demands that Jesus made. Let's explore how we can become the person Jesus wants. Let's take God seriously, and enjoy the unsafe ride he takes us on!

But He's Good

Not long after our family moved to Long Beach, California, a black and white cocker spaniel chose us as his new family. The new tract homes didn't have side or back fences, so Bob roamed from house to house at dinnertime, sharing his affection with others, and receiving the table scraps he loved so much in return. At a mere ten years of age, I thought I could have some fun with Bob's passion for people food.

I held a piece of scrap meat just out of his reach. Bob would jump for it, and just miss it. And jump again. And again. And again. After realizing how meanly I'd treated him, I held the meat within his reach, and he almost took some fingers with the meat. I deserved that.

At times, I've felt toward God like Bob must have felt toward me. Teased. God held out the ideal Christian life, which I desired like Bob did table scraps. But again, like me, God held it just out of my reach. What kept it out of my reach? The impossibility of those commands. "Unless you . . . , you cannot be my disciple." I desperately wanted the godly life, but couldn't attain it, at least not with those conditions. Could I hate my family? Could I accept crucifixion? Could I continue sinless in Christ? Could I accomplish all those demands?

Absolutely not. So the prize remained just beyond my grasp, causing frustration. Guilt possessed me every time I failed at one of those impossible tasks. And *if* I could have reached one of those demands, I would have been sorely tempted to nip God's fingers as my dog did with me.

How dare Mr. and Mrs. Beaver proclaim God's goodness, when he gives us impossible requirements? Unsafe? Absolutely. But part of that lack of safety involved giving me impossible requirements. I knew I wasn't good to Bob, and I doubted that God was good to me. Did I commit blasphemy if I thought that God acted in meanness?

I can't stress enough how critical this issue is to every follower of Jesus. Should we even attempt to follow those demands that merely breed failure and frustration? Will we go to hell if we don't follow them? Must we follow them fully to go to heaven? Why did Jesus give such harsh terms?

Unless we can wholeheartedly see God's goodness, we can't begin to address the specific demands. We must interpret them in the light of God's love for us. These demands represent essential targets for followers of Jesus. Essential: because Jesus expressed them in that manner. Targets: because no one can fully do them. First, let's eliminate some options.

Mere Suggestions?

Some read these passages, see their impossibility, and rationalize them away. They interpret them as hyperbole: an intentional overstatement in order to grab attention. "I've told you a million times to not exaggerate!" Or, more biblically: "If your right eye causes you to sin, gouge it out and throw it away" (Matt. 5:29). Commentators agree that Jesus didn't mean that literally, instead he wanted to make a dramatic statement about the urgent need to avoid sin.

Others will just ignore them, since they don't easily fit them into their interpretative grid. They realize that God inspired all Scripture, and that we need all Scripture to make us complete, but they classify them with the confusion of end times and Revelation, and conveniently close their eyes to them.

Others we may superspiritualize these impossible demands. They assume they represent general good things that all should do, but they reflect spiritual attitudes, not concrete behavior. After all, since we can't do them, they can't reflect Jesus' real desires for us. Jesus would never speak in such a cruel fashion as to require the impossible of us.

However, these approaches do serious injustice to what Jesus repeatedly said. He used some form of absolute language too often for it to have no meaning. These approaches don't match the clear understanding of the text, words, and grammar. If we ignore these, then language itself has no meaning, like Humpty Dumpty said in *Through the Looking Glass*, "When I use a word, it means just what I choose it to mean, neither more nor less."

Without a common base of understanding, communication becomes impossible. Any of us can make any passage mean anything we want it to mean. We can disregard the original meaning God wanted to give us.

So, let's eliminate the option of these demands as mere suggestions, or something we can ignore.

Legalistic Requirements?

Most people seem to interpret these as legalistic demands, as more rules that we have to follow. I teach writing at a Christian college prep high school, and it amazes me how many students define Christianity as a set of behaviors. "I really struggle to do all the things

I should do as a Christian," one remarked. Now, I did the same at that age; that can represent a lack of knowledge, an inability to think more deeply, or a convenient way to disregard Christianity entirely.

Yes, what we do as Christians has great importance. Jesus said that if we love him, we will obey him (John 14:15), and that we need results, or fruit, in our lives (John 15:1–8). His half brother James agreed, saying that faith without action is dead (James 2:17). Paul coupled the truth that faith saves us (Eph. 2:8–9) with the truth that God created us to do good works (2:10).

The New Testament gives a number of physical acts associated with receiving salvation, even though they don't earn that salvation. We should confess with our mouth (Rom. 10:10), and be baptized (Mark 16:16; Acts 2:38).

Physical acts don't earn our salvation, let's be clear on that. A passage we just referred to affirms that: "For it is by grace you have been saved, through faith—and this not from yourselves, it is the gift of God—not by works, so that no one can boast" (Eph. 2:8–9). Even so, we can't divorce what we do (actions) from what we believe (faith).

But, didn't Jesus at least *sound* like he gave these as entrance requirements? "If anyone comes to me and does not hate his father and mother, his wife and children, his brothers and sisters—yes, even his own life—he *cannot* be my disciple" (Luke 14:26).

Now, let's go to the next step. I think we all would say we can't fully and perfectly live out these commands. That adds another brick or two to the wall of the frustration and guilt in my life. How about yours? But does God share that perspective? Does he view these as impossible, or difficult? We need to move beyond our opinion to gain his view on this.

Speaking to followers of Christ, John the apostle provided the slant: "If we claim to be without sin, we deceive ourselves and the truth is not in us" (I John 1:8). To sin means "to miss the mark." Jesus gave a target, a good number of them, actually, and we miss them. Frequently. God himself said we can't live up to them.

So we can logically eliminate them as legalistic entrance requirements to heaven. After all, some will make it to heaven, but no one has done these fully. That means that we must find another way to interpret these absolute demands.

Essential Targets

This concept combines the impossibility of doing them fully and the importance of what Jesus commanded us to do. As we said earlier, we call them essential to honor the seriousness of Jesus words, and we call them targets because no one can fully live up to them. But we *must* aim for them to follow Jesus. These *must* represent our sincere desire as followers of Jesus.

Doesn't that reflect what it means to follow Jesus: we follow his commands? We can't follow Jesus unless we follow him! That takes us beyond the multiplicity of meanings in our culture for the term *believe*. I believe Ford is the best American truck, but one of my students gave a speech that suggested that Chevy is the best American truck. Did I flunk him for his immature beliefs? No, because he presented a pretty good case. But even though I believe Ford is the best, I don't own one. My belief in this area has little to do with my behavior.

That matches many believers. Too often, we *believe* in Jesus, but it doesn't impact our behavior. Something like 80 percent of Americans believe in Jesus, but many act like their Lord is themselves. That's why I prefer the term *follower of Jesus*, it moves belief into the realm of actions. Following requires doing something.

Followers of Jesus, then, want to live like Jesus has a higher priority than their blood family. Followers of Jesus, then, want to place

Jesus above the accumulation of stuff. Followers of Jesus, then, want to know and obey his teachings. Followers of Jesus, then, want to express joy in the most difficult circumstances they face. And so on.

And, we pursue these with passion. We acknowledge when we fall short, we don't deny the truth. We build structures and disciplines into our lives to best help us reach these targets. We don't rationalize that "we're only human," and prone to fail. We don't become content in partial success. We don't sit back, thinking we've arrived, once we've made a little progress. We continually press on to make each of them more imbedded in our lives and character.

Rule out these as cruel and impossible demands, which require what we cannot reach, as I did with Bob. God does not treat us as I treated Bob. But this merely makes God neutral. Not good, not bad. Now, we need to continue developing the thought that not only is God not cruel, but that these demands represent his goodness.

A Good God Provides the Power

I edit our church's e-zine, which has five departments, including a book review, a news commentary, a question and answer column, a story about a Christian acting with courage, and one about living the Christian life. Check it out at http://news.go2cornerstone.com if you'd like to see it. I want to be a good editor of a good e-zine, so each month I let our writers know what articles we need for the next issue, and then I go a step further. For this upcoming month, I suggested someone cover the recent Supreme Court decision on posting the Ten Commandments in public buildings, and that another write an article on one of our associate pastors who left a well-paying job to enter the ministry in midlife. Why? I want to do what I can to help our writers do their best.

God does something similar. He truly acts with goodness when he makes these impossible demands. When God gives a command, he also provides us with the ability to make some progress. No, we won't perfectly carry them out instantly, but we begin the growth process. As we survey the following verses, apply them in your mind to our impossible demands by Jesus.

Philippians 1:6 gives the general principle that God will continue to work in our lives: "And I am sure that God, who began the good work within you, will continue his work until it is finally finished on that day when Christ Jesus comes back again" (NLT). Notice first that God did begin a good work in us. Second, realize that God will continue to work in our lives until we become complete when Jesus returns.

We can look back at our lives, at the changes that following Jesus has made in us, and see both God's goodness and his continual work in us. He wants to complete it, and that includes those impossible demands. But this verse just gives the broad brush strokes; now let's see the details of how God accomplishes that. Move one chapter later.

We find the means by which God enables us to follow these commands in Philippians 2:12–13:

> Therefore, my dear friends, as you have always obeyed—not only in my presence, but now much more in my absence—continue to work out your salvation with fear and trembling, for it is God who works in you to will and to act according to his good purpose.

We receive salvation when we enter a relationship with Christ as Savior and Lord; we don't earn it. But we then begin a lifelong process of working that salvation into each area of our lives. The areas that Jesus talked about, remember. But we don't do that alone, or under our power. Our power made those demands look impossible, didn't they? Now comes the good news.

God also works in us. He provides the power we need to make legitimate transformation. Again, this doesn't happen instantly, but the process begins. I learned that early on, as we all need to. Although

I grew up in church and developed a genuine relationship with Christ, the questions of college life took their toll. I spent four years searching, questioning, and sinning. In that time, I saw a trait in me that I didn't like: an intense self-absorption. I learned to treat people nicely, since I got my way more often like that.

I tried to change that, and couldn't. That failure devastated me. I finally turned to God, recommitted my life to him, and gave him the freedom to change anything, including my selfishness. What most amazed me? Within days, friends remarked on the change. A change I knew I couldn't make. I'd tried.

Now, have I perfectly acted in a selfless manner the rest of my life? My wife, along with others, would say no, and I would readily agree with them. But God broke the back of my self-centeredness in February 1971. Together, we still work salvation into that area. I deeply appreciate the goodness of God to both let me know I had to change, and to work with me on continuing the change.

We can see God's goodness as he works with us to accomplish these impossible demands.

A Good God Blasts Us Out of Complacency

But even deeper, the very impossibility of those demands reveals God's goodness. Perhaps the greatest enemy of spiritual growth is complacency, that deadly disease that lies to us by saying that once we've made some progress, we can rest easy.

I received pretty good grades in high school, except for physical education. At Millikan High School in Long Beach, California, you only received an A if you were an exceptional athlete in a regular PE class or if you participated in a sport. As an average athlete, I got a B, and Dad razzed me about it. We then bet five dollars that I could get an A in PE, so as a senior I joined the cross-country team. The top ten ran varsity, the next ten ran JV, and if I couldn't make them,

I could run with the "hamburger" squad and still get the five bucks. But I thought that if I worked hard, I might make the junior varsity.

We had a great coach, Bucky Harris, and a great team that consistently finished as league champs. After a few days of practice, the coach took me aside. "Tim, keep up the training, and you can make our varsity." That stunned me. I'd never run competitively before, and only ran in PE class when the teacher made us. A great coach thought I could run varsity? That goal appeared impossible, but it intrigued me.

So, I began to put more effort into the daily training runs. Rather than just going through the work out, I worked out, full out. I ran some on my own. Rather than slowing down when the pain of distance running invaded my mind, I pushed through the agony.

Beginning in practice and continuing into the meets, I looked on each runner ahead of me as a target to pass. I discovered how to run, the body posture and movement that maximized my speed. I learned to pace myself through the race, leaving enough energy for a closing kick, and to finish with little left in the tank.

That year, our varsity team went undefeated in league. In one meet, all ten of our varsity runners beat every runner from the other school. We finished third in CIF, the largest high school athletic association available. Me? I ran as sixth man, varsity. No, that didn't change my athletic life. I didn't go to college on a cross-country scholarship and I never ran in the Olympics. I ran one year in college as a walk on, and realized I couldn't compete at that level. But I did learn something significant that has changed my life.

Impossible goals keep us from taking the easy road, from becoming complacent. I originally planned to do just enough to make the squad and earn my five dollars. If I had kept that goal, I could have taken it easy and felt content. But Coach Harris gave me a goal I had considered impossible. He did a good thing and taught me that impossible goals blast us out of complacency.

God's goodness acts in the same way. He gives commands that we can never fully live up to, and that causes us to not stop along the way, content and complacent. Otherwise, we'd make a little progress, and our lazy carnal natures would tell us to relax and enjoy the level we've attained. We would get something good, but miss the best.

That nearly happened with my selfishness. I noticed the progress, as did others. At one point I felt like relaxing spiritually. I had grown. But God silently whispered, "Tim, you've done well. I'm proud of you. But have you seen how the self-centeredness impacts how you treat fellow students at college?"

I honestly hadn't considered that. Yes, I'd grown, but not to the level God demanded. He still demands more growth in that area, thirty-five years later.

Think of these absolutes like this. They address the issues that work most effectively against the spiritual life. We prioritize our family, so Jesus tells us we must hate them. We prioritize material things, so Jesus tells us we must give them up. We prioritize life, so Jesus tells us we must die. We prioritize getting our desires, so Jesus tells us we must follow him. This applies to each absolute, which we'll explore in following chapters.

But since Jesus phrased each as an absolute, we can't ever quit. Jesus made these absolute to blast any complacency out of us. We don't confuse valid progress with completion. We know we can't arrive, so we press on. We shoot for the varsity, not the junior varsity.

A Good God Leads Us into Godliness

Growing up, I idolized John Wayne, the epitome of manhood, courage, and strength. Every Saturday, *The Three Mesquiteers* played on TV, featuring a young Wayne and two cowboy companions as they rode through mesquite-covered hills to stop the evil actions of guys wearing black hats. Wayne became famous for a line from one of his movie characters. He set his body at an angle, looked down from his height, and drawled, "Well, pilgrim, I wouldn't want you to do anything I wouldn't do myself."

Does God act heroically, like John Wayne? Or does he tell us, "Do as I say, not as I do?" With these impossible demands, does he require of us what he cannot or will not do himself?

God shows his goodness when he simultaneously requires and enables our growth. Let's take it a step further. The impossible demands also reflect God's goodness because they help us develop God's character. We can't limit following Jesus to providing fire insurance to escape hell. Obviously, we do go to heaven! But following Jesus means we desire the life and character of Jesus—we become Christlike.

2 Corinthians 3:18 provides an astounding promise: "And all of us, with unveiled faces, seeing the glory of the Lord as though reflected in a mirror, are being transformed into the same image from one degree of glory to another; for this comes from the Lord, the Spirit" (NRSV).

In chronological order, when the Spirit comes into our lives, we see the glory of Jesus. We see his identity, his nature, his involvement in our world and the majesty of his creation, and that naturally attracts us. Or, we see a goal. But grab this next part. Then, the Lord transforms us, one step at a time, into the image of Christ. That represents God's goal for us: Christlikeness.

Personally, Christ is a much better person than I am by nature, so I would gladly make the exchange! I drive a ten-year-old Mustang convertible, with a V6 engine. I didn't buy it as the original owner, and although I greatly enjoy the car, I don't have a huge emotional attachment. So, if I had the chance to get, free, one of the new Mustang GT convertibles, with a powerful V8 and based on the classic '67, I'd make the trade in a flash. In the same way, why wouldn't I trade in the old me for a new me, one like Christ?

Those impossible demands play a critical role in developing the character of Christ. When we accept them as essential targets, we begin the process. How? Each expresses a key trait or action of God. Good acts, by a good God, to increase the goodness of his followers. God doesn't ask things of us that he himself hasn't already done.

When Jesus requires that we hate our family, didn't he do pretty much the same when he left his heavenly home with the Father to take on the sin of all mankind? When Jesus told us we must take up our cross, didn't he do that himself? When Jesus commanded us to give up all our stuff, didn't he wander around with no income and just one set of clothes? When Jesus told us we must obediently continue with him, didn't he continually obey the desires of the Father?

We can, and will, apply this dimension of each command in the relevant chapters, but I think we can all easily grasp the principle: obeying each demand helps us imitate the Father and Son. They first did what they ask of us. We take on their character. So, God genuinely acts in love when he requires such impossibly godly acts.

God Is Good

The conclusion seems inescapable. God is good. He provides essential targets, but gives us the power we need to make some progress. Those targets work to blast us out of spiritual complacency into Christlikeness. He consistently acts out of an innate, pure goodness.

Many times in Christian books, we reason deductively. We start with a general principle that the audience accepts. From that, we pull out specific applications. For instance, God tells us not to allow greed in our lives. Most Christians would accept that concept. From it, we can reason that tithing, or giving ten percent of our income, can effectively combat greed. If the action logically connects to the general principle, then the reasoning works.

In this chapter, we've worked in the opposite direction. We call that inductive reasoning. With it, we begin with specific examples, and from them we reach a general conclusion. As an example, we notice that we stick our finger in the fire on the stove, and get burned. Another time we pick up a burning branch in a campfire, and again get burned. From these specifics, we develop the general principle that fire will burn us.

What we've tried to do here is to look at a number of examples that demonstrate God acting in goodness. From that, we hope that all can reach the general conclusion that God is good. Even though we may at first view these commands as impossible tasks that tantalize us, we can see them as expressions of God's goodness. Now, to wrap up the chapter, let's look deductively at some general principles from Scripture that affirm this.

GOD HAS A GOOD NATURE

In Mark 10:17, a young man came up to Jesus, "Good teacher, what must I do to inherit eternal life?"

The question had a deeper component, however: Did Jesus have the authority to answer such a question about eternal life? Jesus addressed that in the next verse. "Why do you call me good? No one is good—except God alone."

When I first remember reading this, I thought Jesus disassociated himself from the Father. Actually, he didn't deny his own goodness, he just meant that only a person equal to the Father could be called good. Jesus taught that only God has a truly good nature. We've worked up to this general principle from the opposite direction, but Jesus just stated it as truth. We can find more deductive truths about God's goodness.

GOD CARES ABOUT OUR GOOD INTERESTS

In a passage we covered earlier, Paul the apostle talked about the partnership of God working with us in our lives. Let's review the last part of that, which gave God's goal: "for it is God who works in you to will and to act according to his good purpose" (Phil. 2:13). Or, deductively, God has a good purpose when he works in our lives. That includes giving us these impossible requirements. He doesn't act in an arbitrary manner; he doesn't intentionally tease us, as I once wondered about.

He has a clear goal: that we become changed to look like Christ, and he works in us so we can reach that good goal.

Yes, I did think of God as cruel, earlier in my life. But I've learned, and I hope that you have as well, that although we cannot call God safe, we can call him good. Now, let's check out those good demands, one at a time, in more depth.

Section II

The No-Option Clauses

In the "No-Option Clauses," Jesus describes following him in imperative terms, what we *must* do to qualify as a disciple. These essential targets focus on how we must value God and our relationship with him above all else in our lives.

Disciples Must Die: We Embrace the Cross

Most of us today recognize the name of Charles Colson. We know him as the founder and leader of Prison Fellowship, a ministry that focuses on prisoners, their families, and prison reform. We know him as a bestselling author, beginning with the story of his conversion in *Born Again,* and more recent works that center on establishing a Christian worldview, such as *How Now Shall We Live* (1999) and *Lies That Go Unchallenged in Popular Culture* (2005). We may also know him as a central leader in Evangelicals and Catholics Together, where he played a central and continuing role in enhancing unity between various branches of the Christian family.

But we would have to be either a reader of political history, or in our fifties, to know the beginning of the story. Back in the sixties, Colson established a successful law practice and became involved in politics. In late 1969, President Nixon asked him to work in the White House as special counsel to the president. Colson soon developed a reputation of getting things done. The classic line, "I'd walk over my own grandmother to reelect Richard Nixon," illustrates his commitment to do whatever it took to serve his president. Colson rarely hesitated to use dirty tricks and lies to advance Nixon's agenda.

Then, in 1972, along came Watergate, the break-in of the offices of the Democratic National Committee. That "third-rate burglary" led to a cover-up that involved nearly everyone in the Nixon White House, a multitude of convictions and prison terms, and the resignation of President Nixon. And although Colson didn't participate directly, the brush of Watergate tarred him hard.

In the midst of the turmoil in 1973, he visited with Tom Phillips, president of Raytheon, a large defense contractor. After a long conversation, Phillips gave Colson the book *Mere Christianity* by C. S. Lewis, which led Colson to accept Christ. Colson then became involved with a fellowship of Christian men who helped guide him into a deeper relationship with Jesus Christ. Later, he described the process, as given by Jonathan Aitken in *Charles W. Colson: A Life Redeemed*.

> Once I had accepted that gift [salvation] by making a commitment, which I did not then understand, a process began. It was driven by a conviction of sin and wanting to change into a better person, just as Tom [Phillips] had changed . . . I now realize that God was stripping me of my worldly pride and values in order to raise me up as his servant. It made no sense to me at the time, but now it makes total sense. All I could do when the blows were raining down on me was to hang on to my faith and to trust God.[1]

That stripping process began with one major article of clothing at a time; he first received a five-year sentence for obstruction of justice. Then, Colson's father passed away while packing for a trip to visit his son in prison. But the pace and severity soon increased. In January 1975, Judge Gesell, who had sentenced him, indicated he wouldn't consider an early parole. Next, prison officials transferred him to a much tougher prison in Alabama, and then Virginia barred him from practicing law, a career that had provided his livelihood. The next blow came when his attorney told him that his eighteen-year-old son, a college freshman, had been arrested for narcotics possession.

Finally, Colson gave up. At this, the lowest point in his life, shattered emotionally, facing financial ruin, his family battered, he fully surrendered, "Lord, if this is what it is all about, then I thank you. I praise you for leaving me in prison, for letting them take away my license to practice law—yes, even for my son being arrested. I praise you for giving me your love through these men [his fellowship partners], for being God, for just letting me walk with Jesus."[2]

That total surrender turned the corner for Colson. He continued to battle his old nature; he sometimes slipped into his old prideful and controlling ways. But he knew a major change had just taken place. "In the hours that followed I discovered more strength than I had ever known before. This was the real mountaintop experience. Above and around me the world was filled with love and beauty. For the first time I felt truly free."

In prison and apt to remain there, his son arrested, his father recently deceased, his career gone—and he felt free? That doesn't make sense. Or, perhaps Colson discovered the reality of death bringing freedom. Jesus talked about that.

The Impossible Demand

Many Christians feel torn in numerous directions. People make requests and demands on us, from family members to bosses to neighbors. We have some interest in God, and he encourages us to do certain things. Then we try to make room for at least some of our own desires, what we'd like to achieve, to have a chance to relax and enjoy life. No wonder we feel pressure and stress, we just cannot meet all these demands. We try to juggle them, but we drop as many as we catch.

And then Jesus comes along and makes it worse with the most impossible demand he gives: "And anyone who does not carry his cross and follow me cannot be my disciple" (Luke 14:27). But why did Jesus say that? What did he mean by it? Does he truly mean that unless we accept crucifixion we cannot follow him?

Let's explore the context along with a similar passage to discover how radically Jesus confronted us, but first I'll tell a brief story.

I've now conducted over 150 wedding ceremonies, and I always require premarital counseling. Over the years I've modified some of the content, but one primary purpose hasn't changed. I always try to talk the couple out of getting married. Honest. I don't tell them reasons they personally shouldn't get married, they have to decide that. But when we discuss the permanence of the commitment they will soon make, the depth of interaction that two becoming one involves, the practical and sacrificial dimensions of love, and the difficulty of making marriages work today, it forces them to think ahead.

Some people turn pale (usually the guys!), and some haven't come back for the next session. Only once, with Michelle and Tony, did I have to decide that I couldn't in good conscience go on with it, but they came to the next session to tell me they'd cancelled their plans. If I can get them to change their minds, then they're not ready for marriage. Jesus operated the same way.

To demonstrate that, let's return to the passage which begins: "Large crowds were traveling with Jesus" (Luke 14:25). Awesome! Today, when we attract a large group to our church, we write a book, contact a speakers' bureau, and purchase a sports arena to handle the growing crowds. Jesus did it differently.

> Suppose one of you wants to build a tower. Will he not first sit down and estimate the cost to see if he has enough money to complete it? For if he lays the foundation and is not able to finish it, everyone who sees it will

ridicule him, saying, "This fellow began to build and was
not able to finish." Or suppose a king is about to go to war
against another king. Will he not first sit down and consider
whether he is able with ten thousand men to oppose the one
coming against him with twenty thousand? If he is not able,
he will send a delegation while the other is still a long way
off and will ask for terms of peace. (Luke 14:28–32)

Jesus did what I do in premarital counseling, but in a much
bolder manner. He didn't keep his purpose private, but slapped potential followers in the face with it. "If you want to follow me, you better
know what I require before you start. Otherwise, you'll look like an
idiot for starting and then bailing out."

In just this one section, he gave three of our indispensable costs.
We've read the one about the cross, but he said more: "If anyone comes
to me and does not hate his father and mother, his wife and children,
his brothers and sisters—yes, even his own life—he cannot be my
disciple" (v. 26), and "In the same way, any of you who does not give
up everything he has cannot be my disciple" (v. 33).

What did Jesus mean we must carry our cross? A parallel passage
in Luke 9 makes that pretty clear and very scary. Many wondered just
who this traveling preacher was, and how he fit into God's plan. So
Jesus asked his followers what the crowds thought.

They replied, "Some say John the Baptist; others say
Elijah; and still others, that one of the prophets of long ago
has come back to life."
"But what about you?" he asked. "Who do you say
I am?"
Peter answered, "The Christ of God." (vv. 19–20)

Jesus rarely brought out a truth unless he revealed the implications and applications. When Peter identified Jesus as the Christ, or

Messiah, notice how Jesus then gave the implications: "The Son of
Man must suffer many things and be rejected by the elders, chief
priests and teachers of the law, and he must be killed and on the third
day be raised to life" (9:22). Jesus told us that the role of the Christ
was to give his life for the sins of the world. The specific means of
death was crucifixion on a cross. Or, the implication of Jesus' identity
was that he would die for us.

Now, look at how Jesus applied this to us, in verse 23, "If anyone
would come after me, he must deny himself and *take up his cross* daily
and follow me." Notice the absolute tone, followers *must* do this.

Just as Jesus accepted the cross, so do those who wish to follow
him. The next few verses show the importance of this:

> For whoever wants to save his life will lose it, but
> whoever loses his life for me will save it. What good is it
> for a man to gain the whole world, and yet lose or forfeit
> his very self? If anyone is ashamed of me and my words, the
> Son of Man will be ashamed of him when he comes in his
> glory and in the glory of the Father and of the holy angels.
> (9:24–26)

Or, if we try to avoid the cross, we'll lose eternal life. But if we
accept the cross, we'll gain eternal life. Sounds like a pretty good trade
to me, much like the old Mustang for the new one I mentioned earlier!
Jesus gives a nonnegotiable cost of following him: to do what he did,
to accept the cross. But what does it mean to accept the cross?

PHYSICAL DEATH

For Jesus, taking up his cross literally meant to die. All those
who have viewed Mel Gibson's film, *The Passion of the Christ* have seen the
terrible physical agony that Jesus experienced on the cross. But Jesus
also took on all the sin and guilt of all people for all time. The cross

represents total surrender. Total surrender, like Colson did in January 1975.

But what is *our* cross? Some groups draw lots each Easter to determine which one of them will be crucified that year. Literally hung on a cross, and they consider it a great honor. Some even survive! But notice that in both Luke 9 and 14, a follower must take up *his* cross. Not the cross of Jesus. Jesus' acceptance of the cross paid for our sins, once for all time (Heb. 9:26 NLT), so we humans don't have to hop on that cross. Others may put us there, as later happened to Peter, but we don't have to volunteer.

As we examine the context of Luke 9, Jesus speaks literally. In verse 20, he was literally the Christ of God. In verse 22, he literally suffered, was rejected, killed, and rose on the third day. So when it comes to our cross, why would we change the interpretive grid from literal to symbolic? If the cross meant death to Jesus, then Jesus meant death when he said we must take up our cross. We cannot exclude this possibility.

The early followers apparently took Jesus literally. All of the apostles except one died for their faith, and quite a few followers had the same experience, beginning with Stephen in Acts 7. Continuing that example, more followers of Jesus died for their faith in the last century than all the previous centuries combined. Not many in America, granted, although Cassie Bernal would certainly fit into this category. At Columbine High School, a gunman walked into the library and asked her if she believed in God. She said yes, he asked why, and before she could answer, he shot and killed her.

Following Jesus must include a willingness to die for him. If we have nothing worth dying for, we have nothing worth living for. And Jesus promised that if we lose our physical life for him, we'll gain eternal life. But if we seek to save our physical life, we can lose eternal life.

Some say we can't know until the actual moment if we would give our life for God. We fear we may not have the courage Cassie did. That statement has a lot of truth, *if* we wait until the moment to decide. However, we can make that decision right now. Each of us. Will we commit our lives to following Jesus in this, if needed?

SPIRITUAL DEATH

We may never have to physically die to take up our cross, but we certainly must die to our old life. Colson chose the term "born again" for the title of his first book, and it well represents the magnitude of change that we experience when we follow Jesus. "What this means is that those who become Christians become new persons. They are not the same anymore, for the old life is gone. A new life has begun!" (2 Cor. 5:17 NLT). Colson's entire emphasis on worldview comes from his realization that we need new values, priorities, behaviors, and relationships when we come to Christ.

Megan understood that well. Our church had a joint Thanksgiving service with another church, and we opened up the microphone for all those who wanted to thank God for something. Her words touched every heart.

"You couldn't really call me a whore, because I didn't charge. I gave it away. To almost anyone. For almost any reason. I drank too much, way too much, and I did my share of drugs." A sad, almost smile slipped across her face. "It's hard to believe I did all that, because I was raised differently. I knew about God. But I never really knew Jesus; I certainly didn't follow him. So when I started to date Warren and he told me about Jesus, and grace, and forgiveness, it resonated inside. I saw the direction my life was heading, and it scared me. But I really never believed Jesus could love me, or forgive me. I thank God so much for the new life he's given me."

At this, a few tears slipped down her cheek, and the cheeks of more than a few of us. We hadn't known the details of her past life until then, just that she'd lived in darkness. But we all saw the light of God shining through her life, we saw that she had died to that old life. She and Warren later married, they opened their home to a Bible study, and couldn't help but graciously telling everyone they could about new life in Christ.

A nice story, true, and a pattern for us all. But let's delve deeper into the connection between the cross and dying to our old lives. This next verse by Paul convicts me on a regular basis. I want to serve God, but as I desire. I want to call the shots of what I do for God. Maybe you tend to do the same, but this verse destroys our wiggle room. "Do you not know that your body is a temple of the Holy Spirit, who is in you, whom you have received from God? *You are not your own; you were bought at a price.* Therefore honor God with your body" (I Cor. 6:19–20).

When Jesus accepted his cross, he paid the penalty for our sins. He bought us from Satan. So, who "owns" our lives? Do we, or does God? Paul says that because we accepted Christ's death on the cross as the payment for our sins, we belong to God. We don't own our lives, God does. So we die to our old life where we called the shots, and begin a new life where God calls them.

I hate that. It means I can't justify looking at porn on the computer. I can't justify being rude in return to a surly checker at the market. I can't justify ignoring the needs of my wife. I can't justify doing good things for God, but in my timetable and the manner I desire.

That's what it means to take up our cross. The question Jesus has for us: Will we commit our lives to becoming a totally new person spiritually?

God's Mission for Us

Jesus' cross represented the mission the Father gave him, a mission Jesus took on regardless of the cost. Our cross represents the mission the Father gives us, one we must also take on regardless of the cost. Then come two questions. First, what mission does God give us? Second, will we take up our cross as Jesus did?

Listen carefully to God's call. He's uniquely crafted each of us for a ministry no one else can do. But I'm convinced we don't struggle as much in identifying our mission as giving ourselves wholeheartedly to it. Many who hear God call us to our cross resist.

God called Moses to free the people of Israel, and Moses fought it tooth and nail. He couldn't speak well, he faced a murder rap back in Egypt, and he just flat out didn't want to do it.

God called Gideon to lead the fight to free his people from the Midianite oppressors. Gideon also resisted. He questioned God's presence with his people, considered himself a coward, and twice required God to grant him a sign.

God called Saul to take the good news of Jesus to the Greek world, and Saul objected to the point of killing the followers of Jesus.

And I can't count the number of times God has called me to do something, whether to forgive someone who's wounded me, to get more involved in world missions, or other acts of obedience. And I fight it. Colson fought that full surrender to God, until God stripped away nearly everything that he held dear.

Let's make no mistake: taking up our cross and following God's mission for us can be difficult. It can lead to our physical death, and it certainly leads to the death of our old person. It leads to painful, costly, and difficult service. But that's what a follower of Jesus does, takes up their cross. Yes, let's count the cost before. Let's know what we're getting into. But just do it.

Complacent Faith and Self-Will

What causes us to drag our feet when we face our cross? Why, when we know that eternal life accompanies it? I've become convinced that this issue of taking up our cross identifies the key battleground between complacency and commitment. If we can win this battle, we've made significant progress in following Jesus. But until we fully surrender, like Colson, we'll continually battle complacency and mediocrity in our faith.

The history of humanity shows repeated struggles with self-will, our desire to get what we want from life. Who's boss in our lives? Taking up our cross, in all three dimensions we've discussed, directly attacks this. Jesus isn't safe, because he directly attacks our selfishness. We cannot remain complacent. But he is good, because he blasts us out of the old life dedicated to getting our own way.

I'm convinced that self-will is our greatest barrier to knowing God, since it strikes at the heart of our relationship with him. So look back at some examples of how we battle over the ownership of our lives. What caused Eve to sin in the garden? The self-driven opportunity to be like God, to determine right and wrong (Gen. 3:1–5). What caused Abram to twice lie about his wife being his sister? A fear that if he spoke the truth, he could lose his life. He chose self-protection over reliance upon God (Gen. 12:10–20; 20:1–18). What caused Ananias and Sapphira to lie about the price of some land they sold? Their selfishness in wanting to get credit for generosity without fully surrendering (Acts 5:1–11).

And don't we do the same? Don't we respond, too often, to a call of God for action or purity by, "Yeah, God, I'm sure that would be a good thing, but . . ." and we fill in the reasons that we think we know more than God about this. We think we can make a valid argument for an exception, just for us. Not for everyone, mind you, just us. We have a good reason.

Because the concept of taking up our cross involves full surrender—of our physical life, our spiritual life, and acceptance of God's will for our lives—Jesus' demand directly challenges the area that we typically find most difficult. When we resist the cross, we resist following Jesus. When we accept the cross, we strike a blow at the most dangerous deterrent to a vibrant Christian life. That's why Jesus required that his followers each take up their cross.

Understanding Radical Discipleship

Personally, it helps me to know that Jesus already lived this out as a pattern for us. That gets me away from the "tease" aspect we covered in the second chapter, where God requires something we absolutely cannot do, and sits back and laughs. I did that with my dog Bob. Rather than sounding like, "Do as I say, not as I do," God did it first, through his Son. That's what Jesus meant when he told us to *follow* him; we merely copy what he already did.

Let's review some of the material we explored in Luke 9. In verses 18–20, Peter revealed the identity of Jesus as the Christ, the Messiah, the Son of God. Jesus then revealed his purpose: to give his life to serve the mission God had for him. That purpose involved his physical death, and although he didn't embrace it gladly, he did accept it. Only then did Jesus tell his followers to do the same. But this total surrender opens the doors for God to deeply work in our lives.

Let's go back to Colson. Soon after he fully surrendered everything to the Lord, things began to change. His attorney went to Judge Gesell and asked for a ten-day furlough for Colson to visit his son who had just been arrested. Out of the blue, Gesell replied, "I'll release Colson for good today."

That began a trail of service to God that continues to astound many. The former master of dirty tricks became a champion of absolute moral values. The ex-con began a prison ministry that has lasted thirty years and has touched millions of prisoners, their families, and volunteers. He has approximately ten million copies of his books in print, in eleven languages. The partisan Republican politico has led efforts to unite the various wings of Christianity, including Protestants and Roman Catholics.

What allowed such radical following of Jesus? Total surrender. Taking up his cross.

A Radical Following

How does this work? At the beginning of "The Impossible Demand" section, we discussed how we get pulled in a variety of directions. Self, family, work, leisure, relationships, and God all want things from us. How do we balance them? By denying our ownership of our lives, and by placing all other calls under those of the one who owns us.

When we face a decision, we simply ask, "What would the owner of my life want me to do?" We place our desires, and the desires of others, under that umbrella. Will we always do this successfully, in practice? No, we've covered that before. But we must accept taking up our cross as an essential target.

Now, let's glance at four practical steps in following Jesus in such a radical manner. We take all of them from our central verse, Luke 9:23, "If anyone would come after me, he must deny himself and take up his cross daily and follow me."

DAILY SURRENDER

Recovery groups such as Alcoholics Anonymous have pioneered the "One Day at a Time" process, where they approach their sobriety one day at a time. They don't commit to stay sober the rest of their lives, just today. That gives a pattern for us, because Jesus demanded that a follower "take up his cross *daily.*"

Why? For most of us, we struggle to build deep-seated habits. I've heard that we must repeat an act seven times to make it a habit. Others say fourteen. Some say forty days of repetition will do the job. But in my life, I only have to do a bad act four or five times for it to embed itself in my life, but good habits take continual upkeep.

About seven years ago, I allowed myself to get caught up in soft internet porn for almost a year. Then, thankfully, my wife caught me. I read a lot of books, established several accountability relationships, installed a filter on my computer, changed some behaviors that made me more vulnerable, and regularly attended Sexaholics Anonymous meetings. The next year went pretty well, and I thought I had some good habits built up. But I relaxed my vigilance some, thinking my new habits had become strong enough, and the desire to start viewing again almost overwhelmed me.

Why? Thinking my habits were solid, I didn't pay attention to the little, daily issues. I kept my sobriety, but I battled. And since then, I've seen that when I don't surrender daily to God's best, the temptation increases. I now print out a phrase to remind me, and tape it to my computer monitor. My current one, done around the turn of this year, reads, "A new year, a new man; in a battle for the soul." But by now it has almost become part of the landscape; I often don't notice it. I need to get a new phrase, tape it to a new location on my monitor, so it can again catch my attention.

Building strong habits requires daily maintenance, since we can so easily fall back into a rut of self-will. So, every day, surrender. Totally. Daily devotions can be a great tool to do this. Years ago, my grandson gave me a glow-in-the-dark cross. I now dangle it from the rearview mirror on the Mustang, as a quick reminder that I belong to Jesus. But let's not rely on a one time commitment that we don't regularly refresh.

DENY SELF

Jesus said that denying self takes us through the first step in following. This means that we deny that we own our own lives. We deny that we have the right to do what we desire with our lives. Remember, "You are not your own; you were bought at a price. Therefore honor God with your body" (I Cor. 6:19–20). The more often we repeat this to ourselves, the more deeply it grows into our value system. But let's do it daily.

Back in my early twenties I seriously considered retreating into the wilderness to become a mountain man. That may not have been practical, but even today, if I could, I'd get lost in my office. Writing. Reading. Surfing the Internet. Lost within myself. But God won't let me, he wants us to impact others for the kingdom. I have to deny some parts of me that don't advance God's cause.

Take Up the Cross

On that daily basis, declare to God that we'll face physical death, today, if necessary. Declare to him that we want to continue to die to our old self, and will continue to grow into Christlikeness. Declare to him that we will accept his mission for our life, regardless of the cost. William Barclay said it well, "The Christian must realize that he is given life, not to keep it for himself, but to spend it for others; not to husband its flame, but to burn himself out for Christ and for men."[3]

I really don't want to minimize this, or to spiritualize it away. This commitment is huge. But it helps me to remember that Jesus didn't eagerly embrace God's will either! The evening before he took up his cross he asked the Father for a way out. He would go through with it, if the Father really wanted it, but he'd rather not.

We can fight against our cross, and we probably will. But let's accept after that battle.

Follow

Very simply, this means we do it. We don't think about it. We don't discuss it with others. We don't make plans for it. We do it. We continue to do it. Nike has made a fortune with the advertising slogan "Just Do It," but if Jesus had copyrighted it, the church would be wealthy! Because Jesus gave that as an essential target: acting on what we say we believe.

The Payoff

A good friend, Darrell Dement, often uses this anonymous quote: "If we don't find something greater than ourselves to serve, we end up serving ourselves." Taking up our cross provides something greater than us. We can break the back of serving ourselves, only because Jesus gave such an impossible demand. But, he gave us a great pay off in Luke 9:24–25: "For whoever wants to save his life will lose it, but whoever loses his life for me will save it. What good is it for a man to gain the whole world, and yet lose or forfeit his very self?"

Not a bad trade, taking the cross now in exchange for eternal life. I'll make that trade, and pray you'll accept that essential target as well.

Notes

1. Jonathan Aitken, *Charles W. Colson: A Life Redeemed* (Colorado Springs, CO: WaterBrook Press, 2005).

2. Ibid.

3. Source unknown.

4. Source unknown.

Disciples Must Imitate Jesus: We Choose an Impossible Mentor

I've used a lot of mentors in my life. Some involved formal relationships, like my senior pastor when I served as an associate. Others I merely observed, and they probably never knew I studied their example. You've probably never heard of any of them.

As a follower of Christ, I've used two apostles as primary mentors: Peter for his impulsiveness, both to affirm some of mine and to see the dangers of it run amok, and Paul for his analytical traits and deep concern for truth. As a husband, I've tried to pattern myself after my dad. His firm, moral, and sacrificial example has consistently challenged me to go beyond my natural self.

As a pastor, I looked to Herb Read for his practical wisdom, Phillip McClendon for his ability to inspire and motivate, and Ron Keller for his style of preaching. As a professor, I'd love to more fully copy Chuck Boatman for his thoughtful and fresh approach to Scripture. As a fisherman, Dad has to be the top example; I've never found anyone better at pulling wild trout out of a stream, nor anyone who loved the mountains more than he.

As an author, I appreciate the lyrical quality of Phillip Yancey, the practical analysis of Chuck Colson, the convicting content of J. I. Packer, and the encouragement of Robin Jones Gunn.

In thinking about mentors, I noticed that each of them had a trait that significantly exceeded my abilities in that area. But I also thought I could at least come close to doing the same. Why choose an impossible task? Perhaps that's why my list of mentors has a conspicuous absence.

Did you see Jesus there?

I left him out. Intentionally.

Why? I can't come close to being like him.

The Impossible Demand

Yet Jesus demands that very accomplishment. Luke's account of the Sermon on the Mount begins in chapter 6, verse 17 He includes much of Matthew's version, but he gives an impossible and new demand in verse 40: "A student is not above his teacher, but everyone who is fully trained *will be like his teacher.*"

Note the very definite terminology. Not that we *should* be like our teacher, not that we *might,* but that we *will.* I can at least come close to my human mentors, but not to Jesus. My friend and pastor Greg Sidders describes Jesus as "God in a bod." I have the bod part down, but I'll never reach the God part. Nor will you. Nor will Greg.

Does Jesus tease us once again, with an impossible demand? When I think of Jesus, three primary traits come to mind that I cannot possibly achieve.

GOD

John calls Jesus "the Word," and notice how he described him: "In the beginning was the Word, and the Word was with God, and *the Word was God.* He was with God in the beginning. Through him all things were made; without him nothing was made that has been made. In him was life, and that life was the light of men" (John 1:1–4).

Deity lies at the very heart of Jesus' identity, but not ours. I realize God has given us a favored role. He created us in his image so we could rule over creation (Gen. 1:26). He gives us the authority to judge angels (1 Cor. 6:3). But the original sin came when Eve thought she could become like God: "For God knows that when you eat of it your eyes will be opened, and *you will be like God,* knowing good and evil" (Gen. 3:5).

So, can I choose Jesus as a mentor and hope to become divine like him? Absolutely not. Another impossible demand.

SINLESS

Remember Greg's description of Jesus as "God in a bod"? Jesus combined that full deity with full humanity, with one glaring exception. Although he faced temptation, he never gave in like we do. Never. "For we do not have a high priest who is unable to sympathize with our weaknesses, but we have one who has been tempted in every way, just as we are—*yet was without sin*" (Heb. 4:15).

Don't think that Jesus resisting sin came merely because of his deity. Notice that clause that he was tempted in every way like we are, yet resisted. As a human, Jesus avoided sin.

Can I live up to that example? Not really. I can resist any single temptation, and I may resist most. Paul gives the excuse breaker in 1 Corinthians 10:13: "No temptation has seized you except what is common to man. And God is faithful; he will not let you be tempted beyond what you can bear. But when you are tempted, he will also provide a way out so that you can stand up under it."

So, we can resist temptation. But can we resist all temptations, to the point of not sinning at all? Not even close. "If we claim to be without sin, we deceive ourselves and the truth is not in us"

(I John 1:8). So, can I choose Jesus as a mentor and hope to become sinless like him? Absolutely not. Another impossible demand.

THE SACRIFICE

The fact that Jesus lived a righteous life, facing temptation yet remaining sinless, allowed him to give himself for our sins. "For Christ died for sins once for all, the righteous for the unrighteous, to bring you to God" (I Pet. 3:18).

We can't repeat that once-for-all act. First, once is enough. Second, we're not righteous enough to die for anyone's sins but our own. So, can I choose Jesus as a mentor and hope to offer myself as a sacrifice for others sins? Absolutely not. Another impossible demand.

This demand passes improbability into the realm of impossibility. Literally and absolutely, we cannot live up to any of these traits of Jesus. But we can look at a deeper dimension of each, which although improbable, lies within our grasp.

NOT GOD, BUT CHRISTLIKE

Consider God's goal for his people, and the process he uses to accomplish that.

> For those God foreknew he also predestined to be
> conformed to the likeness of his Son, that he might be the
> firstborn among many brothers. And those he predestined,
> he also called; those he called, he also justified; those he
> justified, he also glorified. (Rom. 8:29–30)

God's goal: that followers of Jesus look like Jesus. To accomplish that, God justified us (he looks on me "Just as if I'd" never sinned), and he glorified us (making us Christlike in our attitudes and behaviors).

This hurts. I might be able to come close to Herb in some things, or Ron, or Dad. But this goal of conforming to the likeness of

Christ will stretch me far beyond my comfort zone. Yours too, so don't look down on me! But at least I don't have to do this instantly.

Those two concepts of justification and glorification give some broad brush strokes. Justification happens when we accept Jesus as Savior and Lord; the glorification begins as we conform to Christ. We see that lifelong process in 2 Corinthians 3:18: "And all of us have had that veil removed so that we can be mirrors that brightly reflect the glory of the Lord. And as the Spirit of the Lord works within us, we become more and more like him and reflect his glory even more" (NLT).

The closer a mirror is to the source, the better the image. As we progressively follow Jesus more closely, we get more glory.

We'll explore this process later in the chapter, but we can see that when we accept Jesus as a mentor, we become more like him.

NOT SINLESS, BUT SIN LESS

Perhaps I like the Sierra mountains so much because they remind me of my spiritual journey. Ragged. Characterized by sharp peaks and drop-offs. Often each success gets balanced by a fall. The longer I follow Jesus, the more issues I discover that he cares about, which seems to make the journey even more difficult. In the early days, I never dreamed he cared about some of the things he insists on now.

But if I look back over the last five years, or ten, or twenty, I really do see some progress. So, at times I need to take the long view. I will never eliminate sin from my life, we saw that already in 1 John 1:8. But I can decrease the frequency. Let's go to the next chapter of 1 John to discover the purpose of the letter, "My dear children, I write this to you so that you will not sin. But if anybody does sin, we have one who speaks to the Father in our defense—Jesus Christ, the Righteous One. He is the atoning sacrifice for our sins" (1 John 2:1–2).

John wants us to eliminate sin. He knows we still will, but even then we rely on Jesus' sacrifice for our sins. Now, go to the next chapter.

"No one who is born of God will continue to sin" (I John 3:9). At least, we won't continue to sin the way we used to. We'll sin, but it should become less.

So, when we accept Jesus as a mentor, we can sin less than we did before.

NOT THE SACRIFICE, BUT SACRIFICIAL

We follow Christ when we give ourselves to meeting the needs of others when they need help. Look at how it describes the role of Jesus.

> Christ loved the church and gave himself up for her
> to make her holy, cleansing her by the washing with water
> through the word, and to present her to himself as a radiant
> church, without stain or wrinkle or any other blemish, but
> holy and blameless. (Eph. 5:25–27)

As followers of Jesus, we willingly sacrifice our desires and preferences when we can impact another's spiritual life, just like Jesus. We give ourselves to increase their glory. And as we do, we ourselves take on the glory of Jesus. So, when we accept Jesus as a mentor, we begin to sacrifice ourselves for God's kingdom.

In my office, I do the work that pays our bills. I love my office. My desk, computer, and pictures all lie within sight or reach. But Sheila sees love by yard work getting done. So, in the summer months, as the hot summer day slides into the evening, I leave my nice air-conditioned office and work in the yard. I'd rather stay in my office. But I choose this minor sacrifice to demonstrate love to Sheila.

Complacent Faith and Reachable Targets

Choosing mentors reveals the greatest problem of mentoring. I did the choosing. I could choose targets as easy or as difficult as

I desired. I took control of the process. And for those of us with an innate resistance to great change, that subverts our call to be like Jesus.

Choosing our mentors has two major difficulties.

Low Targets

I truly did want someone who could teach me. I wanted to grow. I wanted to move beyond where I was. But deep down, I didn't want to move too far from there. So each choice represented a reach, but not a real stretch. I knew going in I could at least come close. I chose no one who would blow my doors off, no one that would push me to the very edge of my abilities, effort, and desire.

Targets that we can reach too easily flow from the innate laziness that many of us have. Then, once we achieve it, we rest easy, congratulating ourselves that we have grown and developed. We've extended our skills. We've deepened our faith. But have we done enough of these? A phrase I heard years ago continues to haunt me with its conviction, "The good is the enemy of the best."

Do we choose good mentors, and ignore the best? Do we choose human mentors, and ignore Jesus? Whenever we choose our mentors, we run the risk of choosing too low. Not that the mentors represent less than the best, but do they stretch us to our utmost?

Too easily do we get a false sense of attainment. We get stuck in complacency. Because we reached our goal, we think we've arrived. But we didn't get stretched enough.

When I began writing, I dreamed of getting a book published, which would hit my target dead center. I used to place authors on a par with angels—until I met them. Authors, I mean. I haven't knowingly run into an angel, but I have since discovered authors tend to be just about the same as normal people. Obviously, I wanted people to see my writing as competent and I wanted to touch people with the content. I chose some mentors in writing that would help me do that.

But I've had to stretch that originally fairly low target. I've since formed a mission statement: "To help people build a passion to know God."

I desire to write more books in that line. I've had to raise my sights, and target new mentors. Then, just yesterday, Suzanne Rae Deshchidn, a writing friend/poet/editor/goad gave me a bigger challenge, one that would require a new set of mentors, style, and depth of writing. Very honestly, I don't think I can do what she suggested.

"When are you going to write that deep, contemplative book? That is the one I'm waiting for. I keep seeing glimmers of your depth coming through and it *kills* me that you don't go there. The contemplative book I think you can write is a meshing of Richard Foster and Brennan Manning, with some John Eldredge and John Piper thrown in."

Who *wouldn't* like to write like that? Who can? Not many, and I sincerely doubt I'm in that group. I see myself as a competent writer who has some idea of the spiritual struggles of others because of my own, and a person who wants to see God's solutions expressed in the public arena. But, with writing this chapter, I must be willing to explore if God *may* be using a human voice to give an impossible target. I don't know yet. But I must be open.

PAPER TARGETS

Other chosen mentors look good on paper, but when viewed close up, they only have two dimensions. They lack depth and have significant character defects, enough that we shouldn't use them as a mentor. Often, we only discover those defects after some time.

Way back at the age of eighteen or so, I worked for two summers at a church camp in our local mountains. I loved the spiritual stimulation of listening to the speakers, sitting in on some workshops, and just discussing the Christian life with people living it on a regular basis. Gordon especially impressed me. The youth pastor of a solid church, he seemed to have a clear grasp of vital Christianity. He con-nected well with the kids, and I started to pattern some of my style after him.

In my naiveté, I discounted some controlling traits. I merely saw him as a strong leader. He soon left that church to plant a new one, and gathered a lot of young people around him. One friend of mine, Steve, became a part of the group, and he rejoiced in the level of accountability and discipleship that Gordon required.

But the strong leadership became dominating; he wouldn't allow anyone to question his decisions. The church hit a plateau, and Gordon grew frustrated. His anger slipped to the surface regularly and without warning. Along with most of the others, Steve drifted away. Several decades later, Steve still has not gotten deeply involved in a church. He doesn't trust many pastors now.

Mentors like this keep us from stretching ourselves. We choose one with too much imperfection, and we might give up the quest entirely. With both cases, choosing a human mentor alone, without Jesus as our primary, we run the risk of not stretching ourselves long enough and deep enough.

Understanding Radical Discipleship

Only in writing this chapter did I discover the great spiritual lessons of racquetball. I'd played a little back in college, and then gave it up until I became the associate pastor at a church in Lawndale, California. Merle Blankenship and I began to play each week. Both competitive and pretty equally matched in skill, we battled every week, pretty much splitting victories.

One week, though, Merle outclassed me. My shots didn't fall; I'd aim for a low corner and bounce it off the floor to lose the point. Or I'd try a ceiling shot to put him in a corner, and I'd set him up for an easy kill. We played to twenty-one points, and he had about eighteen to my three. A fleeting thought whispered, "Concede the game," but I knew Merle would razz me mercilessly when we stopped for coffee and a doughnut after.

Although I knew I couldn't win the game, I determined to not give it up. I got the next point, and the next. Merle got one, and I slipped into a zone I'd never felt before. The utter impossibility of winning brought something out in me. I always played hard, but it increased. My concentration became more focused. I thought of each physical movement a split second before I moved. I visualized where the shot would go, and it did.

Merle didn't slack off in his playing, but I came back to tie it, 20-20, and you have to win by two. I did. Now, I must admit that the same thing occurred in the other direction. More than once, I had a huge lead on Merle, and he ended up winning.

Even though I didn't then know the name, I discovered *flow*. Mihaly Csikszentmiayi presented the concept in his book *The Psychology of Optimal Experience* in 1991. Fourteen years later, on the day I write this, it still ranks #528 on the Amazon list of best sellers. After thousands of case studies of artists and athletes, he realized that sometimes a person can slip into a zone. The rest of the world fades away, time becomes unimportant, and a sense of mission takes over.

He defines flow as the state of a person, such as an artist, athlete, or everyday person, when their experiences are the most enjoyable. Intriguingly, flow doesn't occur during relaxation or leisure, but only when we get actively involved in a difficult task that stretches our mental and physical abilities. Flow only comes with an activity that challenges us. In a review, Rob Kall says, "One key ingredient of flow is a challenge that can be reasonably responded to with existing resources."

Csikszentmiayi gives two essential dimensions for flow. First, a person must narrow their focus on a clear goal, which he defines as happiness. Second, flow results in personal growth.

Doesn't that all sound like the racquetball game I played with Merle? But more so, doesn't it sound like focusing on the impossible goal of being like Jesus? Accepting Jesus as our mentor means we can never fully achieve our goal: it remains an ongoing challenge. That stretching that Jesus does to us can put us in the flow. The mere fact of accepting the challenge lets us grow closer to our mentor, doesn't it?

I think this may help explain the lack of logic in the Beatitudes (Matt. 5:3–12), where Jesus turns typical values upside down. We don't usually feel blessed when we experience poverty of spirit, or when we mourn, or hunger and thirst, or face persecution; we struggle with those, don't we? Our spirit rebels at having to endure them. We can easily become bitter and resentful. So why does Jesus say we're blessed?

Because each of these challenges us. They stretch us out of our comfort zone, and into the flow zone.

I shared earlier about my struggle for about a year with online porn. I built new habits, established boundaries, and the temptation almost disappeared—for a year. I thought I could relax, and the temptation came back. Honestly, this struggle has been the most difficult I've ever faced. I get a sense that I've conquered the temptations, but they only wait to return until I let down my guard.

As I researched and outlined this section, the temptation to click onto an inappropriate site almost overwhelmed me. Why? I don't have a clue, for sure. Possibly to distract me from this very important principle. But as I resisted the temptation, and as I focused on the chapter, the flow began. I experienced a huge sense of satisfaction, goodness, and doing what mattered. Or, I felt Christlike.

The radical discipleship that Jesus commands, especially on imitating him, challenges us like nothing else can. But accepting that will flow us into more Christlikeness.

Radical Following

In practical terms, how do we get into the flow of following Jesus as our mentor? We begin with realizing we get more Christlike step by step, not all at one time. Sorry for you instant freaks! We've looked at 2 Corinthians 3:18 several times; it beautifully expresses the incremental nature of the process. "And all of us, with unveiled faces, seeing the glory of the Lord as though reflected in a mirror, are being transformed into the same image from one degree of glory to another; for this comes from the Lord, the Spirit" (NRSV). Transforming ourselves into the glorious image of Jesus will happen, but not instantly.

Let's also go back to our key verse, Luke 6:40, for a vital phrase, "A pupil is not above his teacher; but everyone, *after he has been fully trained*, will be like his teacher" (NASB). Different translations yield different slants. The King James Version has "that is perfect," the New International Version renders it "who is fully trained," and the New King James Version gives us "who is perfectly trained," while the New Living Translation has "who works hard."

Each of them talks about the training process. The passage of time. This shows the goodness of God: he doesn't require instant perfection. He gives us a couple of weeks! Actually, he gives us a lifetime to reach this essential target. A dozen lifetimes wouldn't allow us to become fully like Christ, but we must be in the process.

That process has two primary steps. First, we intentionally, deliberately, and repeatedly commit ourselves to Christlikeness. We choose Jesus as our primary mentor, rather than humans. Yes, Paul encouraged the Corinthians to imitate him: "Follow my example, as I follow the example of Christ," (1 Cor. 11:1). But the Corinthians lived with Paul, they saw him directly. He was an apostle. We don't have those advantages.

Yes, let's continue to use human mentors. Let's benefit from their experience and wisdom. But let's also choose Jesus as our primary, broad-based, long-term mentor. He'll continue to challenge and stretch us beyond our self-perceived limits.

Second, target specific Christlike qualities. Let me suggest these can be very different from what we typically call spiritual growth qualities. Spiritual growth helps us become more spiritually mature, and we can feel falsely complacent when we grow. If I target patience, then I can rest easy when I act more patiently than I had acted before. We can apply that to just about any maturity trait.

Targeting the traits of Christ won't allow that satisfaction, because we can never fully reach the goal. Let's explore some traits that the New Testament refers to as either Christlike or godly. They pretty much mean the same. They represent some of these essential targets for followers of Jesus, since they'll challenge and bring us closer to his image. As we go over each, think how Christ wants to stretch you in that area.

CHRISTLIKE OBEDIENCE

Bill and Melissa had just accepted Christ and joined our church, but they had absolutely no spiritual or church background. I dropped by a garage sale at their house, and Melissa shared one of the many questions that popped into her new life. "Pastor Tim, can you give me some reasons I shouldn't have an affair? I know you gave a verse that said we shouldn't, and I'd do that, if it made sense to me."

We obey, usually. We obey, when it makes sense to us. We obey, when it doesn't cost or inconvenience us too much. We obey, when we want to. That falls short of Christlike obedience.

Jesus made a connection between obedience and love: "If you obey my commands, you will remain in my love, just as I have obeyed my Father's commands and remain in his love" (John 15:10). So, to remain in Jesus' love, we must obey what he commanded. But does Jesus give us any wiggle room on how much we must obey?

If we follow Jesus' example, we need to obey to the point of death. "And being found in appearance as a man, he humbled himself and became obedient to death—even death on a cross!" (Phil. 2:8). Christlike obedience involves doing whatever Jesus said, at whatever cost. One of those essential targets.

CHRISTLIKE SUFFERING

Showing that human nature doesn't change too much, a few centuries ago Duc De La Rochefoucauld said, "Our minds are as much given to laziness as our bodies." We tend to go for the easiest path, the one that seems to require the least amount of effort and struggle, and the greatest pleasure and reward.

Christ provides a radically different example. Ten times in the Gospels he told his followers that he must suffer. Not to take the path of ease and comfort, but to embrace the path of pain. And remember, followers of Jesus must follow his example. 1 Peter 4:1–2 connects us to Jesus:

> Therefore, since Christ suffered in his body, arm
> yourselves also with the same attitude, because he who has
> suffered in his body is done with sin. As a result, he does
> not live the rest of his earthly life for evil human desires, but
> rather for the will of God.

Jesus' suffering encompassed death, sacrificing his own ease for the sake of others. We follow that example, but we must continue. In this next account, the authorities had arrested the apostles. One of the Sanhedrin warned the others about possibly opposing the work of God, so "They called the apostles in and had them flogged. Then they ordered them not to speak in the name of Jesus, and let them go. The apostles left the Sanhedrin, rejoicing because they had been counted worthy of suffering disgrace for the Name" (Acts 5:40–41).

Not only did the apostles accept suffering but they rejoiced in it, because it demonstrated they had passed beyond evil human desires for ease and into the flow of living for the radical will of God. Another essential target for followers of Jesus.

CHRISTLIKE REPENTANCE

This one gets a little dicey. Did Jesus ever repent, or need to? Obviously not. But a certain type of repentance in us leads us to godliness. "Godly sorrow brings repentance that leads to salvation and leaves no regret, but worldly sorrow brings death" (2 Cor. 7:10).

Worldly sorrow makes us grieve over the pain we've caused, or perhaps the fact we got caught. But it doesn't bring any permanent change. Godly sorrow causes us to change. When Sheila caught me viewing internet porn, she saw a great deal of sorrow, but she didn't have a clue if I felt worldly or godly sorrow. I knew my sorrow had a depth I'd not experienced before, but she only heard the words. It took months and years of changed behavior for her to determine which category my sorrow fit into.

A changed life makes us Christlike. Another essential target.

CHRISTLIKE SERVICE

This one brings us full circle, so let's read our key verse again: "A student is not above his teacher, but everyone who is fully trained will be like his teacher."

So, if we imitate our mentor Jesus, what does our mentor do? He teaches. He gives his life to impact others. What do his followers do? They teach. We impact others.

At my first writers' conference, I heard a line that changed my life. "We write for two reasons: therapy or impact." Some write to clarify their thoughts, to write as they desire, to express their feelings, to not submit their art to the vagaries of editors and audiences. That's therapy, and we need it at times. Quite often.

But we can also write to impact people for Jesus' sake. When we choose that, we must deal with frustration from editors, readers, public relations people, sales people, and a whole host of others that will change what we write and how it gets out. Maybe we could call that our cross?

One of the most gifted poets I know has had her work manhandled, and resists that whole process. But I've tried to encourage her to get her thoughts out to a broader audience, to put up with the garbage, to make a greater impact. She has a lot of good stuff to share. She can impact people for Jesus. Like he did.

Don't make the mistake of thinking we must become a small group teacher, preacher, etc. Jesus gave his life to impact others. We need to be about the same business. Another essential target.

The Payoff

Accepting Christ as our mentor forces us to aim higher. Since we can never fully imitate him, we have a model that stretches us, that pushes us beyond the limits we thought we had, and puts us in the flow.

This destroys our attempts to set goals we can reach and then rest. This destroys our selective goals that challenge us in just one area, leaving other more critical issues ignored. This destroys our ability to pick and choose our mentors for our personal advantage. A line by Robert Browning expresses this, "A man's reach should exceed his grasp, or what's a heaven for?"

Let's aim for Christlikeness—and heaven.

Disciples Must Continue in Jesus: We Abide in Him

We tend to regard our parents as the definition of the straight life and guardians of our morality. That certainly matched my view of my mom. Born and raised in Bradyville, a small farming community southeast of Nashville, Tennessee, she grew up in a small church where her grandfather served as lay leader. The church couldn't afford a paid pastor, so he kept things going, and his wife baked the communion bread for each Sunday. Faith played a key role in Mom's early life.

Her mom insisted that each of the daughters have a profession "to fall back on," and Mom became a registered nurse. Not long after Mom graduated from nursing school, World War II broke out, and a nursing friend and her husband got stationed in southern California. When the friend's husband got shipped out, she asked Mom, still single, to move out to San Pedro and stay with her, since nursing jobs abounded. Mom soon moved to Santa Monica, and worked in private practice for a doctor in Westwood, near the UCLA campus.

From brief comments that we couldn't get her to expand on, we knew that she didn't always walk with God during this period. Then she met the son of a neighbor, they fell in love, and several months later ran away to Las Vegas to get married. I arrived nine months after that; in another fifteen, my sister, Jane, joined us.

Although Dad never attended church, marriage and children brought Mom back to God. My earliest memories came from going to church and getting involved in the church's youth groups. As long as I knew Mom, she'd always walked with God. Only those few hints indicated otherwise. I saw Mom as godly, good, and a lot of fun. Somehow those seem like they should go together.

By the time she reached her mid eighties, Dad had been gone for over twenty years, and her body and mind began to fail her. She moved in with my sister and her husband, and often remarked that she was ready to check out. Jane then asked if she had talked to God about it and she said, "No, when he is ready for me he will come and get me."

Although I don't want to speak for God, I think I might know why he delayed. Although Jane had grown up in church, for decades she'd wandered spiritually. On Sunday, August 27, 2000, Mom had a massive stroke. On Monday we brought her back to Jane's house with hospice care, and she passed into heaven on Tuesday morning in the most holy passing I've ever experienced. That played the central role in Jane and her husband coming back to Christ. Sheila and I invited them to church with us the next January, and they've amazed me with their spiritual growth since then. I suspect that God wanted Mom to spend more time with Jane so that Jane would be spiritually primed.

Mom exemplified our next absolute demand by Jesus: disciples must continue.

The Impossible Demand

Jesus' next demand may present our most controversial one: we must continue in him to get to heaven. "Remain in me, and I will remain in you. No branch can bear fruit by itself; it must remain in the vine. Neither can you bear fruit unless you remain in me. . . . If anyone does not remain in me, he is like a branch that is thrown away and withers; such branches are picked up, thrown into the fire and burned" (John 15:4, 6). Withered, thrown in the fire, and burned all give pretty vivid pictures of hell as the destination for those who don't remain in Jesus. But what did Jesus mean when he said we must remain?

CONTINUE IN A FAITH RELATIONSHIP

Let's begin by taking Jesus at the clear meaning of his words. To qualify as a follower of Jesus, we must continue in him. If we don't remain in a faith relationship with Jesus, we don't follow Jesus. In the overall passage of John 15:1–17, we find the word *remain* used eleven times, and implied once more. Each use refers to staying in a vital relationship. Can we dare claim that merely saying the words, "Jesus, I believe in you, forgive my sins and be my Savior" will by itself match the demand of Jesus? A man named Bill made that claim.

I never knew him, only his son Randall. Anyone who knew Randall very long could see the hurt and pain he carried toward his dad. During the years his parents had remained married, Randall rarely saw his dad. He either left for business travels or to play around. Feel free to interpret play in the broadest sense possible. He played golf, he played the horses, and he played with other women. About the only playing he didn't do was with his kids. Finally, he left the family, leaving only his name. No support, no presence.

Yet, he loudly proclaimed his faith in Jesus. Years later, after Randall developed an intimate walk with God, he asked his dad about that on one of their rare talks.

"Dad, you've got me puzzled. You've always said you believed in Jesus, but you never took us to church. You didn't much live like a Christian. But you always tell people you are one. How can you justify having Jesus as your Savior and not your Lord? I can't understand that."

"Randall, you've always looked at life as cut and dried, either/or. Life's more complex than that, and so is faith. Somewhere in Romans it says that if we believe in our heart and confess with our lips, then we're saved. I confessed that when I was just eighteen, that's all it takes. I don't have to keep doing things; I did that stuff once."

In no observable way did Bill show the fruit of an ongoing relationship with Christ. In the next section we'll see specific acts that Jesus connected to remaining in faith, and Bill had none of them. But Jesus did insist that his followers remain in him, and that theme continued through the New Testament.

At least twenty-four different passages tell Christians to continue, to not fall away. Hebrews 3:12–14 may give us one of the clearest examples.

> See to it, brothers, that none of you has a sinful,
> unbelieving heart that turns away from the living God. But
> encourage one another daily, as long as it is called Today,
> so that none of you may be hardened by sin's deceitfulness.
> We have come to share in Christ if we hold firmly till the
> end the confidence we had at first. (See also Ezek. 18:26;
> 33:12–20; Mark 13:13; Luke 8:5–15; John 15:4–6;
> Rom. 11:22; I Cor. 8:9–13; 9:24–27; 15:1–2; Gal. 5:4;
> Col. 1:21–23; I Tim. 1:18–20; 4:1; 2 Tim. 2:11–13;
> Heb. 2:1–3; 3:12–4:1; 6:4–6; 10:26–39; James 5:19–20;
> 2 Pet. 2:20–21; 3:17; I John 2:24; and 2 John 1:8–9.)

We can't turn away from a place we haven't been, can we? Did Bill make a genuine beginning? We can't judge that, only the lack of evidence of continuing. And let's notice the final sentence: We share in Christ if we finish with him. That merely matches what Jesus already said.

Jesus gave the essential target that we must continue to follow him. Despite Mom's period of not walking with God, she finished strong. Despite Bill's initial confession, he gave little evidence of remaining in a faith relationship with Jesus. Whatever else we may believe on this subject, Jesus clearly said we need to finish in a relationship with him.

But, if we start in a genuine relationship, can we voluntarily leave it? Christians disagree on this. Some believe that a genuine profession of faith will last forever, and quote verses such as I John 2:19: "They went out from us, but they did not really belong to us. For if they had belonged to us, they would have remained with us; but their going showed that none of them belonged to us."

Others think we retain the ability to choose or reject God, and refer to some of the verses mentioned above that warn us to not depart from the faith.

Both sides can make a good case, and nearly all would agree that people who finish in a relationship with Christ are saved, but those who don't finish won't be. One side says the profession was genuine, the other says it wasn't. I'm willing to leave that in God's hands, but I'd rather err on the side of caution. I want to guard my faith to insure that I remain faithful.

Even then, we can rest secure in our walk. "Therefore, dear friends, since you already know this, be on your guard so that you may not be carried away by the error of lawless men and fall from your secure position" (2 Pet. 3:17). Relationship saves us. I know if I'm married to Sheila, and I know if I follow Jesus. As long as I do both, I can feel secure.

But let's focus on Jesus' insistence that we remain.

Continue in Productivity

What you've just read covered how I first thought this topic would play out. We'd focus on our need to stay in a faith relationship. But as I explored the greater context of John 15:1–15, I discovered that Jesus crammed a lot more into that package than I had ever seen before. If we had questions about the sincerity of Bill's profession of faith, the elements Jesus mentioned here should clear them up.

In the twelve uses of the word *remain*, Jesus connects *remain* to six behaviors that can help us identify if we truly remain in him. Basically, Jesus says we will have productive lives, that remaining in Christ will change how we live. And, we don't stop doing these at some point. These six behaviors reflect dimensions of the essential target of remaining.

Fruitfulness. When we genuinely follow Jesus, we impact others spiritually. Mom did that to the very last day of her life, at age eighty-six. Her faith influenced me my entire life. Her love of God allowed the grace of her passing. Jesus described this process: "I am the vine; you are the branches. If a man remains in me and I in him, he will bear much fruit; apart from me you can do nothing" (John 15:5). Bearing fruit means we actively and intentionally help others follow Jesus. That includes helping them decide to follow and helping them follow more closely, and Jesus linked it directly to remaining.

If we examine the fruitfulness in our lives, what does it say about our remaining?

Effective Prayer. In talking to people over two decades of pastoral ministry, more followers of Jesus feel inadequate in this area than any other. Yet Jesus placed it as a central part of remaining in him: "If you remain in me and my words remain in you, ask whatever you wish, and it will be given you" (John 15:7).

Why? Very simply, prayer lets us converse with God. Prayer means we slow down and listen to him. How can we have an intimate relationship if we don't communicate?

If we examine the effectiveness of prayer in our lives, what does it say about remaining?

A Love Affair with Jesus. Remaining with Jesus embarks us on a love affair with him that should last until eternity: "As the Father has loved me, so have I loved you. Now remain in my love" (John 15:9).

Rather than Christianity having a lot of rules that we must follow, Jesus wants a personal love relationship as part of remaining. Author Andrew Greeley suggests that marriage at its best pictures the connection God desires with us.

If we examine the level of intimacy with God in our lives, what does it say about our remaining?

Obedience. But what we do impacts our love. Husbands and wives know this, if they treat their mate inconsiderately, it changes their relationship. "If you obey my commands, you will remain in my love, just as I have obeyed my Father's commands and remain in his love" (John 15:10). Jesus patterned this for us with the Father, but he also emphatically stated the clear link between obedience and a love relationship. If we love, we will obey.

If we examine the obedience in our lives, what does it say about our remaining?

Overflowing Joy. How can we not get excited when we have an intimate love relationship with the Creator? Right after the last two verses of loving and obeying, Jesus gave another aspect of remaining: "I have told you this so that my joy may be in you and that your joy may be complete" (John 15:11). Joy indicates that we've reached a significant level of satisfaction in our walk with Jesus. Even when life seems to fall apart, we have no other place we'd rather be. We've discovered that following Jesus far exceeds all other options.

If we examine the joy in our lives, what does it say about our remaining?

Security in Christ. Now comes a marvelous promise, one that connects with the possibility of choosing to stop following Jesus: "Remain in me, and I will remain in you" (John 15:4). Jesus gets very clear and convincing with saying that if we choose to remain, then he will remain in us. As long as we remain in a faith relationship with Jesus, we have security.

I have no doubts that Mom continued both in faith and productivity. Randall saw no evidence of either in his dad. Jesus established both as essential targets for his followers.

If we examine the level of security we experience in our lives, what does it say about our remaining?

Complacent Faith and Bailing Out

Over my years in ministry, I couldn't begin to count the number of people who started to follow Jesus, then bailed out somewhere along the way. Some chose to leave for a variety of reasons; others allowed the relationship to die by neglect. Without questioning the genuineness of their faith, they began. But they didn't finish. For some, I saw the end of their lives, but I couldn't see any evidence of remaining in Christ. As a consequence of leaving their faith, according to Jesus, they don't receive eternal life: "If anyone does not remain in me, he is like a branch that is thrown away and withers; such branches are picked up, thrown into the fire and burned" (John 15:6). A very heavy result.

Remaining involves more than continuing to affirm Jesus. Remaining encompasses fruitfulness, effective prayer, obedience, a love affair with Jesus, joy, and security. The essential target of remaining includes what we've called the productive life. What consequences accompany a lack of productivity? In a parallel passage Jesus said: "The ax is already at the root of the trees, and every tree that does not produce good fruit will be cut down and thrown into the fire" (Matt. 3:10).

Followers of Jesus stick with him and continue to aim for impact all through their lives. Even to their last day. Like Mom. We may leave Jesus, and Jesus will wait for our return, like the prodigal son. But failing to remain gives us no security.

Understanding Radical Discipleship

I love the novels of Andrew Greeley. A Roman Catholic priest and sociologist, Greeley suggests that God pursues us, and that we can best see the depth of God's love in the passion found between a man and a woman.

That beautifully expresses the importance of radical discipleship. God doesn't want a one-night fling with a groupie, but a permanent marriage with a follower. When I gave my vows to Sheila on February 10, 1979, I first promised to become one with her, and we continue to discover how to do intimacy better. Second, I vowed that oneness would continue "until parted by death." Third, I vowed to cherish her, part of which includes helping her reach her personal best.

INTIMACY

We find connection at the very heart of our relationship with God. Remember, Jesus used the term *remain* twelve times in those seventeen verses. The New King James Version, the New American Standard Bible, and New Revised Standard Version all translate that as *abide,* which implies a settled, living relationship. In John 17:3, he taught the essence of the union: "Now this is eternal life: that they may *know* you, the only true God, and Jesus Christ, whom you have sent." The Bible also uses that term *know* for sexual intercourse between a husband and wife.

Once more, Jesus modeled remaining with his relationship with the Father: "As the Father has loved me, so I have loved you; abide in my love. If you keep my commandments, you will abide in my love, just as I have kept my Father's commandments and abide in his love" (John 15:9–10 NRSV). He wants us to copy what he and the Father have: intimate love.

Jesus amplified that two chapters later in John 17:20–23 (NRSV).

I ask not only on behalf of these, but also on behalf of
those who will believe in me through their word, that they
may all be one. As you, Father, are in me and I am in you,
may they also be in us, so that the world may believe that
you have sent me. The glory that you have given me
I have given them, so that they may be one, as we are one,
I in them and you in me, that they may become completely
one, so that the world may know that you have sent me and
have loved them even as you have loved me.

God desires a tremendous oneness with his people, an essential target
of remaining.

PERMANENCE

I didn't make a five-year commitment to Sheila with an option
to renew. I pledged the rest of my life to her. We've had some struggles,
and even separated once about twelve years ago, to give each other
some space to allow healing to begin. But even then, we had the goal
of making the marriage work, and we continued with a marriage counselor the entire period.

The radical nature of following Jesus includes continuing, we
saw that in the twelve uses of the word *remain* in our John passage.
Didn't Jesus remain with the Father, from the beginning all the way
through? Too often, people begin to follow Jesus and bail out. Anyone
can begin a relationship, completing it shows our commitment.

God desires that his people have a permanent relationship with
him, an essential target of remaining.

CONTRIBUTION

In the first wedding ceremony I performed, I began to ponder
what *cherish* means. At least part of the meaning includes valuing them

as a unique person, and helping them to fulfill their created intent. Ephesians 5 makes that clear.

> Husbands, love your wives, just as Christ loved the church and gave himself up for her to make her holy, cleansing her by the washing with water through the word, and to present her to himself as a radiant church, without stain or wrinkle or any other blemish, but holy and blameless. (vv. 25–27)

Husbands cherish their wives as they help them develop their abilities and to reach their goals. Jesus modeled that with the Father, "If you obey my commands, you will remain in my love, just as I have obeyed my Father's commands and remain in his love" (John 15:10). On another occasion he said: "I have brought you glory on earth by completing the work you gave me to do" (John 17:4). Throughout our John passage, Jesus talked about the importance of bearing fruit.

As followers of Jesus, we need to follow Jesus' example of contributing to reaching the Father's goals for the world. We arrange our lives, manage our resources, and give our time to bear fruit for God. Just like Jesus.

A Radical Following

I grew up in church, but left God for about four years of searching and sinning. At twenty-three, I came back to God. Out of that love, I began going down to the Tijuana Christian Mission, an orphanage and church in Tijuana, Mexico. About once a month, a semi-regular group of us would head south to do construction, clean things up, paint, and play with the kids.

I learned firsthand about the old chicken and the egg controversy: which came first? These trips began out of a love for God; we went down to serve him and people. We honestly expected nothing out of it. But we all felt so good serving them, and so much closer to God, that I soon called this "the most selfish thing I do." From this, I discovered that causes and effects can become circular: the first cause brings an effect, but that effect influences and amplifies the original cause, which increases the next result, and the circle continues.

I think that principle applies the six dimensions of remaining in the earlier section, "The Impossible Demand: Continue in Productivity." When we choose to remain in Christ, we'll see these six increase in our lives. But when we nurture them, we also become more imbedded in Christ. The circle continues.

FRUITFULNESS

In our John 15:1–17 passage, Jesus used some form of *fruit* nine times. For us followers of Jesus, we need to intentionally aim for this to deepen our intimacy with Jesus. Fruit represents production. An apple tree produces apples. A car manufacturing plant produces cars. And followers of Jesus produce followers of Jesus.

Truly, I don't want to lay a huge guilt trip on everyone, "You have to bring five people to Christ each year or you'll burn in hell." We've had enough of that. But if Jesus gave fruitfulness as an essential target, do we aim for that? Do we deliberately and intentionally seek to impact people who don't yet know Jesus? Do we deliberately and intentionally seek to challenge and help other followers to follow more intently? Do we do this even when it comes with significant personal cost? Yes, some have the gift of sharing their faith, but Jesus wants all of us involved in the process in some way.

I've discovered that living for impact addicts me. When I write something, and a person mentions how they specifically used it, I get excited and want to write more. When I speak, and a person says, "I always wondered what that passage meant, now I can live it more effectively," I get excited and want to speak more. When I share Christ in premarital counseling and the couple accepts Christ, I get excited and want to share more.

Do these things happen every day? Not to me, nor to most of us. But I want them to happen more frequently, because when they do, I get so much closer to Jesus.

EFFECTIVE PRAYER

Why don't we have more effective prayer? First, we don't spend enough time connecting with God. Surveys consistently show that most Christians feel guilty about how much time they spend in prayer. Count me in that group. I typically pray some each day, and try to nurture an awareness of God's presence every moment, but I don't give God the blocks of time that I give to other priorities in my life.

I heard once that heaven is filled with the unrequested answers to prayer. I suspect that's true. "You want something but don't get it. You kill and covet, but you cannot have what you want. You quarrel and fight. You do not have, because you do not ask God" (James 4:2). What more might we receive from God if we merely asked him for it?

But effective prayer has another condition, that we ask for God's will to be done, not our own. This last verse slides into the next: "When you ask, you do not receive, because you ask with wrong motives, that you may spend what you get on your pleasures" (James 4:3). I hate that verse. It reminds me of George Bernard Shaw's line, "Most people do not pray; they only beg."

When followers of Jesus commit themselves to more time in prayer, they can get addicted to the intimacy they develop with God.

A LOVE AFFAIR WITH JESUS

Most of us struggle with the tension between rules and relationship. We know that behavior impacts closeness, and the pages of the Bible contain a lot of rules. I found four sources that each say they've found 6,468 commands. I'll trust them in lieu of counting myself. And we've seen some people with such a nebulous relationship with God that it never changes their behavior.

But a genuine focus on love can bridge those two extremes with reality. Jesus connected love and obedience in our passage. Legalism supposes that love results from doing the right thing first. Love supposes that doing the right thing results from love. Jesus supported the latter in John 14:15: "If you love me, you will obey what I command."

Followers of Jesus obey out of love, to demonstrate their love, to do the loving thing. The more love we imbed within ourselves, the more depth we develop.

OBEDIENCE

Here comes the flip side of our previous dimension of remaining. We begin with love and then obey, but our very obedience demonstrates and increases our love. This verse may sound contradictory to the last section, but think of it as circular. Like the Tijuana orphanage experience.

Jesus linked love and obedience. Obedience lets us remain in Jesus' love. Or, we start with loving God, so we obey. But if we don't continue to obey, we don't continue to remain. Why? We don't continue in love: "He who does not love me will not obey my teaching."

Obedience is an essential target, but only obedience prompted by love counts at all. Our motives come in here. If we obey out of a legalistic duty, out of a desire to win God's grace, then our obedience doesn't benefit us a bit. But it we obey out of love, a desire to please the God who has done so much for us, then it brings the tremendous benefit of intimacy.

OVERFLOWING JOY

We choose our emotions. If we like the situation we find ourselves in, we choose happiness. If we interpret the situation as a loss, we choose sadness. If we interpret our life situation as something far greater than we deserve, something that exceeds our imagination, then we choose joy.

Specifically, what can cause us to respond with joy? Look at what Jesus said: "I have told you this so that my joy may be in you and that your joy may be complete" (John 15:11). What did he tell us that can bring us joy? In verse 10 he just affirmed that if we obey, we will remain in a love affair with him. That's good news. In verse 7 he promised effective prayer to those who remain. More good news. In verse 5 he promised a productive life to his followers. And the good news just continues.

So, as we regularly interpret our situations in light of what God is doing for us and in us, we nurture joy. In turn, that joy causes even more connection with Jesus, and the beat goes on.

SECURITY IN CHRIST

Although Mom did have a solid relationship with Christ, and remained in him, she did struggle in one area. Security. We talked about heaven one day, probably twenty years before her death. "I just hope I'm good enough to get there." I imagine memories of her earlier days brought some doubt.

We then talked about security, how our obedience flows from our faith, how it doesn't justify us before God. We talked about the solid promise in John 15:4: "Remain in me, and I will remain in you." It must have helped; those concerns never seemed to bother her again. But she did represent the questions of many. They reason, "If I can leave Christ, then how can I know if I'm really saved?"

The answer seems clear. If we remain in Christ, and we know how to determine that, then we have a solid security. We can rely on Jesus' promise. All followers of Jesus can continually remind themselves of their security. That security will then enhance their intimacy.

The Payoff

Many of us yield to the tendency to rely upon our initial profession of faith. However, Jesus blasts us out of the complacency that says beginning is finishing. We must remain in Christ to receive all the benefits Jesus gave. But when we do, our lives can impact the world. We see our prayers change ourselves and others. We find great motivation to obey. We enjoy intimacy with God. Joy floods our lives. And, we have the assurance of life in heaven, with the Father, Son, and Spirit.

Let's aim at remaining in Jesus.

Disciples Must Continue in Jesus' Teachings: We Abide in His Word, Not Ours

Brad and Scott began teaching at Grace Christian High School at the same time; Brad taught Bible and Scott taught English. As the only two new male teachers at the Colorado school, they hung around some at break times. Even so, they didn't quite click. Scott favored a more relaxed approach to life; Brad had a tightly coiled spring within. Scott had a winning way with the students; Brad focused on knowing, following, and enforcing the rules.

Those differences contributed to their confrontation. When covering literature and writing, Scott wove in biblical principles. "What spiritual themes can you find in 'A River Runs Through It?'" or "How did Maclean's father, the Presbyterian pastor, connect fly fishing and faith?"

That practical approach intrigued the students and some asked if they could have a Bible discussion once a week at lunch. The lively talks helped the group grow to about twenty, and Scott loved the interest the students had in God. They already had one Bible class, so giving up lunch for more Bible expressed their hunger.

After a month or so, Brad ran into Scott in the break room with no one else present. "Scott, you're stepping on my toes. I don't like it, and I want you to stop. This week."

"Hey man, what are you talking about? What do you mean about 'your toes'?"

"That Bible group that meets each week. You probably just aren't aware of professional respect. I teach Bible, so leave the Bible material to me. That's my responsibility. You handle the English; I'll handle the Bible."

"Brad, this is a Christian school. We're all Christians, and they want us to integrate faith into all we do. That's all. I'm sorry you feel like this, but the students want it, it helps them, and I plan on continuing."

Brad took the issue to the administration, but they liked the idea of students spending more time dealing with the Bible and hearing more voices. But Scott and Brad's minimal closeness dissipated. Brad pretty much hung by himself.

Then one Monday, a substitute taught his Bible classes—and Tuesday, along with the rest of the week. Scott wondered about it, so he asked James, the principal, if Brad was sick. James asked Scott not to tell the students, but Brad's wife, Ginny, had come to him and revealed that Brad had become sexually involved with a friend of theirs from church and had moved out with her. James had been talking to Brad for the last week but finally had to let him go. Brad saw nothing wrong with it.

He said Ginny didn't meet his sexual needs, so he had the right to get his needs met outside marriage. When James mentioned the scriptural teaching on adultery and marriage, Brad merely replied, "My God wouldn't want me to live my life like it's been. I gave Ginny the option of staying together. She just didn't want to share."

At the core of the issue, Brad didn't respect God's Word. For many of us, in cases perhaps less extreme than this, we think our ability to determine right and wrong exceeds God's. George Barna, in his 2003 book, *Think Like Jesus*, revealed that only 14 percent of born-again adults rely on the Bible as their authoritative moral compass.

The Impossible Demand

This demand may not fully qualify as impossible, but it does meet the standards for rare. Jesus gave another essential target: "If you hold to my teaching, you are really my disciples" (John 8:31). That word *hold* is the same word we covered in the last chapter, to continue or to abide. The New Living Translation says it well: "You are truly my disciples if you keep obeying my teachings."

Jesus wants his followers to use the Bible as their source of determining right and wrong in how they act. And, he wants them to not just follow those teachings some of the time, but all of the time.

Why did I say we rarely meet this demand? Barna gave the foundation for what many of us do. We make the decisions for our lives. We choose among the options. We determine our values that drive our actions. We think we know best. We often know what God says about an issue, yet we do what we desire.

I certainly put myself in that group. After four years of wandering, I recommitted my life to God at the age of twenty-three. I stopped searching, but I didn't stop sinning. That was back in the early '70s, with the sexual revolution in full swing. I did accept God's value of keeping intercourse within marriage, but I went right up to the edge too many times. Loose sexual living filled much of my life.

Did I know God considered this wrong? Kind of. I read the verses about purity, like: "I made a covenant with my eyes not to look lustfully at a girl" (Job 31:1), even though I did that. I knew the verse: "Flee from sexual immorality" (1 Cor. 6:18), and realized it had a broader scope than just avoiding genital intercourse.

But I rationalized. "God, I don't find any specific prohibition of oral sex." "God, I won't go over the line into intercourse. I have limits." But to get to the bottom line, I didn't keep obeying Jesus' commands. I didn't act like a follower of Jesus should. I thought I knew better.

Looking back, that disobedience opened the door to tremendous long-term damage to my behavior and my character. Weakness in those two areas contributed to my later vulnerability to online pornography. That contributed to significantly damaging my wife and our marriage. Why? In the very beginning, I didn't trust that Jesus knew best.

Jesus made it very clear that following his teachings demonstrates we truly follow him. The implication: If we don't continue to obey, we don't follow him. Remember, Jesus gave this as an essential target, not a legalistic requirement. Keep that in mind. But let's also not diminish the strength of his statement.

Why did he speak so strongly? Four principles underlie this trait of his followers.

AUTHORITY

I love Cold Stone Creamery. You choose a flavor of premium ice cream, then a variety of mix-ins: berries, fruit, candy bars, etc. While you watch, they put the ice cream on a frozen marble slab and cut in your chosen ingredients. It yields a totally custom made ice cream, made to your specifications and taste.

Don't we often do the same with determining our values? Many sources encourage us to accept a certain value. Our governments deal in values, as does the media, our families, peers, and the culture. Our own backgrounds, preferences, and reasoning adds more. Then we choose which we'll mix in to establish our ethical standards. As time goes on, we change the mix. Perhaps a family member comes home and says, "I'm gay," so we wrestle with the issue of homosexual behavior and become more broad-minded. Perhaps we get laid off at work, and we modify how we view helping the poor.

But we remain as the authority, we choose. This contradicts Jesus' essential target that we follow his words, not our own. But why do his words possess the authority that ours do not?

First, he's God and we're not. John identifies Jesus as the Word in these terms: "In the beginning was the Word, and the Word was with God, and *the Word was God*. He was with God in the beginning. *Through him all things were made*; without him nothing was made that has been made" (John 1:1–3).

Because of those two stressed items, Jesus begins with more authority than we could ever possess. But in a verse we examined earlier, Jesus gained more authority over us by his sacrificial death on the cross: "You are not your own; you were bought at a price. Therefore honor God with your body" (1 Cor. 6:19–20).

Jesus has the power to establish values, flowing from his identity and his sacrifice for us.

ACTION

As a verb, "follow" requires some kind of action. The one followed certainly has the right to set the terms of following. So when we choose to follow Jesus, we simultaneously choose to follow the conditions he imposes. Otherwise, how can we call ourselves followers if we don't follow?

APPLICABLE

Following Jesus has relevance for our two deepest spiritual needs. In John 6, huge crowds came to Jesus, and he wanted to test their willingness to follow. So in verse 26, he began to challenge them with some difficult dimensions of following him. Jesus got his expected result in verse 66: "From this time many of his disciples turned back and no longer followed him."

Even though he seemed to encourage this, he appeared a bit discouraged in verse 67: "'You do not want to leave too, do you?' Jesus asked the Twelve."

At times, Peter could rise to surprising heights of insight. He did here: "Simon Peter answered him, 'Lord, to whom shall we go? You have the words of eternal life. We believe and know that you are the Holy One of God'" (vv. 68–69).

Following Jesus' words leads to eternal life. As followers we can rely on the fact that following will lead us to heaven forever. Not bad, but following Jesus' words gives another result.

In my early twenties I started fooling around with woodworking. I made coffee tables out of large wooden wire spools by burning them with a propane torch, wire brushing the soft wood out to reveal the burned grain, and then putting on a clear finish. For another project, I made a box to carry my eight-track tapes. If you don't know what they are, don't even ask, you're in the wrong generation. I cut the wood to size, glued and screwed it together, and stained it.

When I started to put the finish on, Dad made a suggestion on how to get the best result. Dad had worked as a painter for several decades, and he knew his stuff. But in the arrogance of my twenties, I thought I knew better. So, I did it my way. Then, I redid it . . . his way. The lesson? I wasted a good amount of time not listening to the expert.

We can do the same in our spiritual lives. Who best knows how to follow God?

Psalm 119 has 176 verses, the longest chapter in the Bible. It focuses on the glory, benefits, and joy of knowing and following God's words, which give us guidance for the spiritual life. Verses 129–130 summarize it: "Your statutes are wonderful; therefore I obey them. The unfolding of your words gives light; it gives understanding to the simple." Because God's words give understanding and direction, followers obey them. God best knows how we should follow him.

AMPLE

Not only do God's words give us guidance in following him, they also have all the wisdom we need. Paul gave that promise to Timothy.

> But as for you, continue in what you have learned
> and have become convinced of, because you know those
> from whom you learned it, and how from infancy you have
> known the holy Scriptures, which are able to make you wise
> for salvation through faith in Christ Jesus. All Scripture is
> God-breathed and is useful for teaching, rebuking, correct-
> ing and training in righteousness, so that the man of God
> may be thoroughly equipped for every good work.
> (2 Tim. 3:14–17)

That can give us a lot of security, knowing that we can find all we need in the words of God.

Following Jesus requires that we build our value system around him. When his values conflict with our desires, followers of Jesus follow Jesus. Perfectly? No, but we aim for that as an essential target. We move beyond our emphasis on self to an emphasis on him.

Complacent Faith and Relativism

Two factors combine to build complacency when we develop our values. Many of us tend to take the path of least resistance. We'd rather relax than get stretched, so we choose values that accommodate us. Second, we'd rather get our way than yield to another. We want to run our lives, so we resist anyone who tells us what to do. Even Jesus.

As a consequence, we resist following his words fully. We know that obedience will stretch us. We know that obedience will oppose what we desire. So we obey when it doesn't cost us too much. We obey when it matches what we desire. Josh McDowell refers to a survey that says 75 percent of evangelical Christians don't accept the concept of absolute truth. Most followers of Jesus don't believe that what he says is always correct.

We call that relativism. *Merriam-Webster's Collegiate Dictionary* defines relativism as "a view that ethical truths depend upon the individual or groups holding them." Relativism suggests that absolute truth doesn't exist, nothing is always right or wrong; morality depends upon the situation. Individuals or groups choose their morality.

That philosophy didn't arise in the last few decades; Israel experienced it as well. The kings represented both spiritual and political leadership; they kept the people on track with God. But when no spiritual leadership existed, a vacuum of morality developed. "In those days Israel had no king; everyone did as he saw fit" (Judg. 17:6).

Relativism. Each person determines right and wrong. No one has the authority to require morality of others. That directly contradicts Jesus' claims that disciples follow his words. All of them. All of the time.

This issue becomes a critical tipping point in our following. Does Jesus have the wisdom and authority to give absolute commands? If we resist him here, we don't fully follow. Again, let's not get sidetracked by imperfect obedience, imperfect people obey imperfectly. But Jesus gives us an essential target, so we need to acknowledge that although we miss the target at times, it *is* the target. And not accepting the target impacts us and the kingdom negatively.

Personal confusion results from not accepting Jesus' words as the source of morality. I remember a new convert at a church I pastored in Fallbrook. A thoughtful guy, Dave and I once discussed sources of right and wrong. All of a sudden he grinned and said, "You know, until now, I always got my morality from TV. I figured that *they* wouldn't allow anything wrong on TV." That didn't work back in the early '80s, so don't try this at home today!

In my college years of wandering, I battled in trying to figure out the source of sexual morality. The hippie movement and sexual revolution drove the youth culture, but I also knew the Bible taught different values. Which should I follow? Or, should I craft my own? We still see this today. Following the example of a former president, many teens don't consider oral sex as sex. Various segments of our culture offer different standards. Just read the news about gay marriage, civil unions, embryonic stem cell research, and abortion.

Our society has lost our sense of shared morality. Up until about forty years ago, society accepted the Judeo-Christian ethic as the foundation for morality. Not all followed it, but most recognized it and many respected it. But we've now returned to those "thrilling days of yesteryear," when "everyone did as he saw fit."

Personal complacency also accompanies a lack of following Jesus' words. When I got caught up in the inappropriate internet viewing, I didn't rigorously seek out what Jesus might say about it. Why? I feared I would lose my wiggle room. I didn't want high standards that stretched me. I wanted standards that allowed me to meet my desires.

As a result, I spent nearly a year caught up in that sin. And because of that year, I now need a constant vigilance to avoid slipping back in. I didn't seek to follow Jesus' words, and it brought a huge negative impact. Did Jesus forgive me? Absolutely. Do I still face the consequences of my choices? Absolutely. But I must acknowledge that all of these problems merely came from not letting Jesus' words provide an absolute standard that I would consistently follow.

Church division also comes along when a group of followers don't follow Jesus' words consistently. A Christian from outside Valley Church approached one of the associate pastors with some troubling news. He had some business dealings with one of the members where the member bragged about having had sex with one of the young girls in the youth program. When the leadership team rightly began to investigate, some members of the church went ballistic.

"We don't want to be part of any church that intrudes into the private lives of the members. We just want to love and accept everyone. Let that stuff stay between them and God."

Did Jesus tell the church to discipline members in serious unrepentant sin? Yes, in Matthew 18:15–17:

> If your brother sins against you, go and show him
> his fault, just between the two of you. If he listens to you,
> you have won your brother over. But if he will not listen,
> take one or two others along, so that "every matter may be
> established by the testimony of two or three witnesses." If
> he refuses to listen to them, tell it to the church; and if he
> refuses to listen even to the church, treat him as you would a
> pagan or a tax collector. (See also Gal. 6:1; 1 Cor. 5:1–5)

As a result of conflicting values, about 30 percent of the members left the church. Short term, it hurt the ministry of Valley Church. Long term, it allowed the church to double in the next year. Why did the church grow? They finally had a clear consensus on the role that Jesus' words would play in the church. They decided to continue in Jesus' teachings, not their own or those of the culture.

Whenever followers of Jesus don't follow his words, we deny the essentiality of the target.

Understanding Radical Discipleship

In the previous section we explored some of the reasons that following all of Jesus' words gives us an essential target. But on an even deeper level, we do that because Jesus modeled it for us. We follow his words, because he followed the Father's words.

A GODLY SOURCE

Just a few days ago, I had an interesting discussion with two Mormon missionaries. We talked about consistency between different claims to authority. Particularity, the New Testament must not contradict the Old Testament. It can add complementary material, but not contradictory. Similarly, the Book of Mormon must not contradict the Bible, not if they claim to have the same source.

Jesus realized that need for consistency of revelation, and linked his words directly to the Father. "These words you hear are not my own; they belong to the Father who sent me" (John 14:24). Did Jesus give a different message at times from the Old Covenant? Yes, but it built on what had come before, and complemented it.

We accept Jesus' words as an essential target because they came from the Father.

A GODLY FOLLOWING

But Jesus didn't want us to just accept his words; he commanded that we continue in obeying them. Again, he patterned this. "I have obeyed my Father's commands and remain in his love" (John 15:10).

Intellectual assent without obedience means very little to God. Knowing his words means very little, unless we put them into practice. Satan knows the Word of God far better than any of us. He's had more time at it. Ezekiel apparently faced some discouragement when his hearers loved what he said but never changed, and God encouraged him.

> As for you, son of man, your countrymen are talking together about you by the walls and at the doors of the houses, saying to each other, "Come and hear the message that has come from the LORD." My people come to you, as they usually do, and sit before you to listen to your words, but they do not put them into practice. With their mouths

they express devotion, but their hearts are greedy for unjust gain. Indeed, to them you are nothing more than one who sings love songs with a beautiful voice and plays an instrument well, for they hear your words but do not put them into practice. When all this comes true—and it surely will—then they will know that a prophet has been among them. (Ezek. 33:30–33)

We obey Jesus' words as an essential target because he did the same with the Father's words.

A Godly Cost

Radical discipleship requires a willingness to pay the price that comes from following. God's agenda may interfere with our plans, our ease, our agenda, our health, our finances, and our comfort. God wants to disrupt our lives in order to bring grace to the world. Disciples follow the pattern that Jesus gave, a desire to serve God knowing that a price will come along. On the night before his death, Jesus needed some time with the Father and support from his followers.

Then Jesus went with his disciples to a place called Gethsemane, and he said to them, "Sit here while I go over there and pray." He took Peter and the two sons of Zebedee along with him, and he began to be sorrowful and troubled. Then he said to them, "My soul is overwhelmed with sorrow to the point of death. Stay here and keep watch with me." Going a little farther, he fell with his face to the ground and prayed, "My Father, if it is possible, may this cup be taken from me. Yet not as I will, but as you will." (Matt. 26:36–39)

Jesus would soon take on all our sins (1 Pet. 2:24), become sin (2 Cor. 5:21), and face excruciating pain. Did Jesus look forward to that with great anticipation? Not at all, he wanted to avoid that price. If he could. But if he couldn't, he would accept it.

We pay the price of obeying Jesus' words as an essential target because he did the same with the Father's words.

Radical discipleship makes sense, and Jesus gave us the model.

A Radical Following

We can summarize how to continue in Jesus' words in five steps. They are easier to understand than to apply, but that's the Christian life.

Accept It

The first step must come with accepting Jesus' words as authoritative, consistent with and having the same authority as the words of the Father. Rather than buying into the relativism that permeates our culture and encourages us to choose our values, followers of Jesus need to yield to the absolute truth that Jesus had the authority to give commands to his followers.

Learn It

Even though knowledge alone won't please God, we have to know Jesus' words before we can follow them. I love how the early church did that. As a predominantly Jewish group in the beginning, they knew the Old Testament Scriptures. But they thrilled to listen to the apostles teach how the prophecies applied to Jesus, and how to follow him more closely. "They devoted themselves to the apostles' teaching" (Acts 2:42).

We have tremendous resources and tools today to learn God's Word, take full advantage of the privilege of imbedding it in your mind.

Follow It

We've already covered this one in depth. "Do not merely listen to the word, and so deceive yourselves. Do what it says" (James 1:22).

Teach It

This gets a little more involved, since part of obeying Jesus' words involves telling others about them.

> Then Jesus came to them and said, "All authority in heaven and on earth has been given to me. Therefore go and make disciples of all nations, baptizing them in the name of the Father and of the Son and of the Holy Spirit, and teaching them to obey everything I have commanded you. And surely I am with you always, to the very end of the age." (Matt. 28:18–20)

We typically focus on the going and making disciples, the baptizing, and even Jesus' continual presence. But we can't skip the last part of making disciples: teaching them to obey everything Jesus taught. Followers teach the words. Followers teach the need to obey.

Of course, we do that in a multitude of methods. Some preach, some teach Sunday school, some lead home groups, some tell their friends and family members. But followers pass the words on from one spiritual generation to another.

Protect It

This may fit into the previous category of teaching, but its importance requires the emphasis of standing alone. Think back to why we often resist fully following Jesus' words: They can force us to change in areas we'd prefer not to. G. K. Chesterton said, "Christianity has not been tried and found wanting; it has been found difficult and not tried."

Because of the radical demands of Jesus, many try to soften them. We minimize them, explain them away, and try to escape their challenge. That occurred in the first-century church as well:

> For the time will come when men will not put up with sound doctrine. Instead, to suit their own desires, they will gather around them a great number of teachers to say what their itching ears want to hear. They will turn their ears away from the truth and turn aside to myths.
> (2 Tim. 4:3–4)

How should followers of Jesus react to attempts to change or soften Jesus' words?

> But even if we or an angel from heaven should preach a gospel other than the one we preached to you, let him be eternally condemned! As we have already said, so now I say again: If anybody is preaching to you a gospel other than what you accepted, let him be eternally condemned!
> (Gal. 1:8–9)

We need to avoid getting harsh, judgmental, and legalistic over minor issues. But on core gospel teachings, we need to take a stand. So, evaluate what people teach. Determine if it represents a matter of opinion or an essential core issue. And teach the full truth of Jesus' words, even in the face of opposition, ridicule, and disdain.

The Payoff

We've seen that following Jesus and his words will push us way out of our comfort zone. Why should we do that? Out of utter self-ishness. I say that in jest, but only in part. We may pay a high price; his words may challenge and stretch us. Following provides far more benefits than costs.

Eternal Life

Following the words of Jesus as an essential target gives us the assurance of eternal life with God and Jesus. "Watch your life and doctrine closely. Persevere in them, because if you do, you will save both yourself and your hearers" (1 Tim. 4:16).

Not a bad result of continuing in Jesus' words.

Clear Values

We can avoid the moral morass of competing value sources like we saw in the Judges passage about everyone doing what is right in their own eyes. When we face a decision, we determine what principle or value from Jesus applies to it. We can recognize teachings that can lead to problems if followed. And we know that we don't have to rely on our own faulty and incomplete opinions, because when we follow Jesus' words, we know they have absolute authority.

Guidance

I have screwed up so many times over the years. I've impulsively jumped into decisions that I didn't take time to research. I've allowed relationships to move into areas of problem and sin. I've rationalized against following Jesus' words, thinking I knew better, and paid the price.

And as I look back at those, and compare them to the life advice I see in God's Word, I could have avoided nearly all of the pain and problems. If only I had looked first at what God said, and then done it.

The unknown author of Psalm 119 knew that. "I will never forget your precepts, for by them you have preserved my life" (v. 93).

I've made those mistakes, and will again. But I've chosen the essential target of continuing in Jesus' words. They'll preserve my life.

Disciples Must Give Up Family: We Adopt a New Family

Several generations ago, members of my dad's family played a key role in the Mormon church, also known as The Church of Jesus Christ of Latter-Day Saints (LDS). My great-great-grandfather, Colonel Jesse Carter Little, served as president of the LDS church for the eastern United States. At a time when war with Mexico seemed imminent and the Mormon church had no funds, he convinced President James K. Polk to authorize the Mormon Battalion, a group of young Mormons who enlisted in the army and journeyed to California in 1846. The government paid their salaries directly to the church, and that money proved crucial to their migration west. This is the Place Heritage Park, outside Salt Lake City, depicts him on the monument, astride a horse.

Both Little and another great-great-grandfather, Thomas Jefferson Thurston, participated in the first migration to the Salt Lake valley. Thurston later pioneered a mountain valley east of Ogden, along the Weber River. He carved a wagon road alongside the river that allowed the towns of Milton and Morgan to develop.

Those early winters provided a challenge. Temperatures could hit twenty degrees below zero, and snow accumulated so much that wagons couldn't be used, just sleighs that would glide over the surface. Thurston's dedication to the Mormon church led him to became a bishop, where he supervised churches in the area.

But it also caused a rift in the family. The best information from family members who still live in Utah, and from searching the LDS records, indicates that not a single child of his chose to join the LDS church. What led to that?

The pioneers had few resources in those early years, and the next waves of migrants often needed assistance. Many left the East pushing handcarts that contained all their belonging and supplies for the trip. Church leaders frequently called on members to give sacrificially, far beyond the required tithe. Consequently, his children went without shoes in the harsh Utah mountain winters. Food fell into short supply.

That next generation decided that a church that caused a father to deprive his children so much didn't deserve their allegiance. That seems to make sense, doesn't it? A good church shouldn't damage the members. Did Thurston faithfully serve God, or did he fail him along with failing his children?

The Impossible Demand

Jesus seems to support Thurston. "If anyone comes to me and does not *hate his father and mother, his wife and children, his brothers and sisters*— yes, even his own life—he cannot be my disciple" (Luke 14:26). If loving acts benefit the person you love, then we could logically conclude that Thurston didn't seem to love his children, but hated them instead. So, he followed Jesus' demand, right?

Jesus' statement seems ever more radical when we explore the context. In the overall passage of verses 25–33, large crowds began to follow Jesus. His response? To thin them out by giving some of the impossible demands we've explored. He said that followers must carry their cross (v. 27), that they must give up all they have (v. 33). But he began with a requirement for following that must have struck the hardest at the family-oriented Jewish audience.

Hate your family, or you cannot follow me. The stark contrast to much of God's previous requirements seems to reveal an utter lack of consistency.

LOVE OUR FAMILIES

Creation testifies about the importance of family. What did the Father do shortly after creating the world and Adam? He crafted a woman and developed the marriage relationship for them. The blueprint he gave back then echoes in most wedding ceremonies even today: "For this reason a man will leave his father and mother and be united to his wife, and they will become one flesh" (Gen. 2:24).

He then completed the family by adding children. Genesis 4:1 gives an intriguing twist, one that I hadn't noticed before: "Adam lay with his wife Eve, and she became pregnant and gave birth to Cain. She said, '*With the help of the LORD* I have brought forth a man.'" I thought just Adam and Eve participated in that process! But God played a vital role in extending the concept of family from a husband and wife to include children. And Eve reminded herself of that every time she called her firstborn by his name.

When God offered a covenant relationship to the descendants of Abraham, he laid out the guidelines for people to follow. The first four of what we call the Ten Commandments dealt with connecting to God; the next six focused on dealing with other people. How did he begin that last group? "Honor your father and your mother, so that you may live long in the land the LORD your God is giving you" (Exod. 20:12). At the top of the list for how to treat people we find the command to honor the family. Notice the promise of long life, a result that obedience to no other injunction has.

When some first-century Jewish leaders developed a tradition that allowed them to not honor or take care of their parents, Jesus chastised them by saying: "Thus you nullify the word of God by your tradition that you have handed down" (Mark 7:13). Jesus affirmed the requirement to take care of family.

Taking it a step further, Jesus required that all of his followers love all people: "A new command I give you: Love one another. As I have loved you, so you must love one another. By this all men will know that you are my disciples, if you love one another" (John 13:34–35). Since family fit into the category of people, he commanded that we love our families.

That contrast seems logically inconsistent, but we can't ignore it.

HATE OUR FAMILIES?

Clearly, Jesus said we cannot follow him unless we hate our families. *Strong's Exhaustive Concordance* translates *hate* as "to hate, to pursue with hatred, to detest." Pretty strong. But we easily realize that Jesus used hyperbole, an intentional overstatement to emphasize a point. The logical inconsistency makes that clear; Jesus wouldn't contradict himself so badly.

Vine's Expository Dictionary helps explain that, defining hate as "a relative preference for one thing over another." Later in Luke, Jesus uses *hate* like this: "No servant can serve two masters. Either he will hate the one and love the other, or he will be devoted to the one and despise the other. You cannot serve both God and Money" (Luke 16:13).

So when Jesus tells us we must hate our families, he meant that we must love him supremely, or we cannot follow him. In comparison to the great passion we have for him, love for others will seem like hatred. In a parallel passage, Jesus used Vine's definition:

Do not suppose that I have come to bring peace to the earth. I did not come to bring peace, but a sword. For I have come to turn "a man against his father, a daughter against her mother, a daughter-in-law against her mother-in-law—a man's enemies will be the members of his own household." Anyone who loves his father or mother more than me is not worthy of me; anyone who loves his son or daughter more than me is not worthy of me. (Matt. 10:34–37)

He obviously proclaimed the primacy of our love and loyalty to God as having more importance than our love and loyalty to our blood family. Do we literally hate our family? No. But we dare not allow them to become more important to us than God.

What we've just done is logical, clear, and true. It also rips the heart out of why Jesus chose to use the term *hate*. We've taken a radical statement by Jesus and made it fairly innocuous. When we do this, we miss the danger to radical discipleship that Jesus intended to warn us about. Families can encourage our complacency and keep us from extreme following.

Complacent Faith and Family Ties

In the week that I wrote this chapter, I took my grandson Joshua to view *Star Wars 3: Revenge of the Sith*. The gifted young Jedi knight Anakin Skywalker had a vivid dream in which his bride, Padme, died in childbirth. His dreams often foretold the future, and he couldn't imagine living without his wife. Then the Supreme Chancellor Palpatine baited his trap in telling about his own mentor.

"He had such a knowledge of the dark side that he could even keep the ones he cared about from dying."

That idea entranced Anakin, and Palpatine let it brew for a while. Later, he closed the trap, "Only through me can you achieve a power greater than any Jedi. Learn to know the dark side of the Force, Anakin, and you will be able to save your wife from certain death."

Anakin makes that choice to save his wife, abandons the Jedi, and becomes Darth Vader.

Why did Anakin do that? He valued family above all else. Ironically, Padme still died while giving birth to twins, Luke and Leia Skywalker. He sold his soul to save his wife and lost her along with it.

Jesus knew that families can encourage spiritual complacency. Because of their great importance, we can allow them to rival our love for God. Friends, coworkers, and neighbors come and go. Blood family tends to stay. The very importance God placed within the human family helps them continue. At their best, our families typically know us the most and still love and support us.

But at their worst, they abuse one another physically, verbally, or sexually, and they remain together. I once read a cartoon in which a banner announcing a conference hung across the front of a huge auditorium. It read: "National Conference of Adult Children of Normal Families." Six people sat in the seats. Despite decades in pastoral ministry, I still find it hard to believe why some families put up with one another. We don't easily let go of the bonds that hold our families together.

Families can give us a comfort zone, an acceptance that doesn't stretch us and in some cases can hurt us. Our connection to them can keep us from following Jesus fully.

In his book *Follow Me*, Greg Sidders tells this story about Kenny. During a college conference, he sensed God calling him to become a missionary to France, where less than one percent of the people call themselves Christians. Then Kenny met just the right woman. After dating for some time, he asked her to marry him, and she agreed. Not long after, though, she told him she would not become a missionary to France.

Kenny battled within—whom did he love the most? The Jesus who called him to France, or his fiancée? But Kenny had already decided to truly follow Jesus, and though difficult, the choice was clear. Later, he met a young woman who willingly went to France with him, and they had a solid ministry together there. Kenny continued to have a dynamic walk with God, in large part because he loved Jesus above all else. Even family.

Jesus frequently found prospective followers who hesitated because of family ties, and Luke clumps three occasions together. One man proclaimed he'd follow Jesus wherever he went. Jesus replied, "Foxes have dens to live in, and birds have nests, but I, the Son of Man, have no home of my own, not even a place to lay my head" (Luke 9:58 NLT). In other words, "Will you follow me if you have to become homeless and sleep under the stars with a rock for a pillow?" Following might include leaving behind the comforts of home.

Jesus next asked another to follow, and he hesitated, saying he had to bury his father first. Jesus bluntly responded, "Let those who are spiritually dead care for their own dead. Your duty is to go and preach the coming of the Kingdom of God" (Luke 9:60 NLT). Commentators surmise that his father hadn't died yet, and that as the oldest son he bore the responsibility for making the final arrangements when the time came. But Jesus made it clear that followers follow *now*, and do their ministry *now*. Following means we obey at the time of the command, even if it means not carrying out family responsibilities. Realize, however, this refers to following a clear command of Jesus, not ignoring valid family needs in order to chase your own style of spirituality.

With the third prospective follower, Jesus seemed to become even more hard core on family values. The man readily agreed to follow, but just wanted to say good-bye first, so they wouldn't think he'd gone missing. That doesn't seem like such an unreasonable request. Except to Jesus: "Anyone who puts a hand to the plow and then looks back is not fit for the Kingdom of God" (Luke 9:62 NLT). Why did Jesus come down so hard on him? He'd made a commitment to the mission; he'd already placed his hand on the plow and then left. Perhaps he had some second thoughts, and found it hard to leave the comfort of his family. But he backtracked from a commitment he made.

Again, God created our families as the foundation for relationships. But we can give too much importance to them when they interfere with what God calls us to do.

Understanding Radical Discipleship

I don't think we've yet plumbed the depths of what Jesus wanted to convey here. We've done the necessary foundation work, but an essential element remains. One time Jesus talked about loving family more than we do him, which expresses the basic meaning. But another time he used the term *hate*. I suspect he used it to let us know the radical break with our normal lives that he wants us to make.

But when Jesus demands that we put our families in second place, what comes in first place? Obviously, he does. We touched on this topic in the chapter on taking up our cross. We can't value our families more than we do him. When we begin a relationship with Jesus, we embark on a new relationship with God, one that turns our family relationships upside down. That new relationship brings in a new dimension. When we give up the priority of our blood family, we simultaneously adopt a new family. A new family based on our new Father. This forms the heart of why Jesus used such radical terminology.

Primary Fatherhood

Jesus told us about this new relationship with God: "But to all who believed him and accepted him, he gave the right to become children of God. They are reborn! This is not a physical birth resulting from human passion or plan—this rebirth comes from God" (John 1:12–13 NLT).

Ron barely knew his birth parents; he had a few memories mixed in with some facts that others told him about them. Gene and Ginny had met in the church youth group. Chance put them together as partners in a game at a picnic, and they each felt attracted. Gene and Ginny dated through high school and married after two years of college. Two years later, Ron joined the family. When Ron was three, a drunk driver ran into his parents at an intersection, and both died instantly. Ron was at home with a babysitter.

His parents had made prior arrangements with some good friends from church, Bob and Sue, to raise Ron if anything happened to them. So Ron joined the Markoff family and instantly gained two brothers and a sister. If you ask him now about his parents, he mentions Bob and Sue. Although Ron received his genes from Gene and Ginny, he thought of Bob and Sue as his parents.

Our spiritual lives parallel that. We get our genes from our blood parents, along with some raising. But our permanent raising comes with God as our Father.

Many Americans believe that all can legitimately claim to be children of God. In one sense that's true: all human life came from God. But not all have the relationship with God as Father. That only comes when we accept Jesus as our Savior and Lord. Jesus taught: "Don't address anyone here on earth as 'Father,' for only God in heaven is your spiritual Father" (Matt. 23:9 NLT). Does that mean we can't call earthly fathers "Father"? No more than we need to literally hate our blood parents. But we must continually keep our priorities in mind.

We have a new Father. One in Heaven. One who's saved us. One who gives us a new family.

PRIMARY FAMILY

When we come to Christ, we enter a new family because we share a common father. A family united across all racial, economic, and skill backgrounds. A family not from genetics but from grace. A family not by inherited blood but by blood shed on a cross. A family not from our parents' choice but from our choice of a parent. A family not together for just a short time but forever.

If the two ever come into conflict, our spiritual family must take precedence over our blood family. Why? Because our spiritual Father takes precedence over our earthly father.

I haven't always done that well. Many years ago while interviewing at a church for the position of associate pastor, they asked me not to drink alcohol if they hired me. A reasonable request. Not necessarily a biblical command, but I agreed. They hired me, and I didn't want anything to hurt the ministry.

About a year later, Dad and I sat talking. He'd come down with emphysema, and had just a few months to live. I cherished every chance I had to talk and spend time with him, knowing the opportunities wouldn't last long. He had so many stories, so much knowledge, and I wanted to absorb it all like a sponge while I still could. As we sat in the living room, he said, "Tim, why don't you get us a couple of beers?"

The alcohol in the beer seemed to help Dad breathe. Honest! I walked into the kitchen, grabbed a can from the refrigerator, walked back and handed it to Dad.

"Where's yours?"

"Well, the church asked me not to drink, so I'm on the wagon."

"Gosh, I think they just meant when you're outside, when people can see you. I don't think they'd care now."

I quickly ran it through my mind. Dad hadn't come to Christ, and I desperately wanted to see that. I also didn't want him to think I'd become legalistic and judgmental, that might hurt the first goal. Dad's argument made sense, it wouldn't hurt my witness, but I'd given my word. My quick judgment: I'd rather enhance the connection with Dad, so I went back into the kitchen, grabbed another, and popped the top.

Yes, we did have a good conversation. No, he didn't accept Christ then. He may have later; we had deeper conversations after that. I just don't know for sure. Did having a beer help or hurt? I know it didn't hurt our conversation, and it may have helped. Dad had a strong aversion to legalism, because of his family's religious background that I shared earlier in this chapter.

I still feel conflicted about the choice I made that day. I don't want to fully equate a promise to a church with following God, but at one level I chose to please Dad over keeping my word. If I had to make the same choice today, I'd probably do the same. But I'd still feel bad about it.

Jesus radically turns our world upside down. Our blood family, the one God gave to raise, love, support, and encourage us, cannot remain as primary. God's family, the church, takes over that role.

A Radical Following

I find it very difficult to give specific ways that we hate our blood family and love our spiritual one. Each of us faces tremendously different families, situations, local churches, and ministries. But we can explore two basic principles that can guide us in restructuring our family connections. Please work with God to discover your individual path.

LOVE YOUR BLOOD FAMILY

Loving Jesus more than our blood family doesn't mean we don't love them. It doesn't mean we don't serve them. It doesn't mean we don't meet their needs. It doesn't mean that my great-great-grandfather Thurston properly followed Jesus' command.

God gave the family as a source of support: Jesus' demand complements that rather than contradicting it. In writing to a group of Christians, the apostle Paul said, "But if a widow has children or grandchildren, these should learn first of all to put their religion into practice by caring for their own family and so repaying their parents and grandparents, for this is pleasing to God" (I Tim. 5:4).

Paul affirmed that following Jesus doesn't mean neglecting blood family. Rather, meeting their needs pleases God. We don't abandon them. Just a few verses later, Paul demonstrated this as an essential target for followers of Jesus: "If anyone does not provide for his relatives, and especially for his immediate family, he has denied the faith and is worse than an unbeliever" (I Tim. 5:8). We could paraphrase Paul as: "If you don't meet the needs of your blood family you cannot follow Jesus."

Not supporting them denies the faith we proclaim. Better that we never claim to follow Jesus than to make the claim and not help our family. That help certainly involves material help when needed. But it also includes our love and presence.

We met Wayne and Cassandra at a church function, hit it off well, and then stopped off at a local restaurant for some pie and coffee. I'd just taken my first bite of boysenberry pie when Sheila asked if they had children. The wrong question. A tear slipped down Cassandra's cheek.

"Just one. Lori's twenty-one and lives in San Diego."

"Does she go to college there?"

That brought out a heartbreaking story. Wayne and Cassandra had always taken their faith seriously and were consistently involved in churches and ministries who did the same. Lori had that same fire, and soon joined a group of Christians when she began studying at San Diego State University. Unfortunately, the leader's passion exceeded his wisdom. In a study one week, they came across our theme verse that we must hate our family to follow Jesus.

"Lori, you want to follow Jesus, don't you? Then you know what to do. You must cut off all contact with your parents. Your love for them keeps you from fully loving Jesus."

She told this to her parents, and that she loved Jesus the most. She moved, changed her cell phone number, and left no way for them to contact her short of hiring a detective. Wayne and Cassandra hadn't heard from Lori for over a year. Nothing at Christmas, Mother's or Father's Day, or birthdays. Their heartbreak and confusion ruined the pie for all of us.

But I want to strongly emphasize: Jesus didn't intend this. Unless we face extreme circumstances, we don't abandon our blood families when we follow Jesus. We don't stop loving them. We just love Jesus more. Christianity doesn't require supreme allegiance to the institution of a church, but to God. It allows us to love our family in the context of Christianity.

LOVE OUR SPIRITUAL FAMILY MORE

All who call on God as Father through Jesus Christ make up our spiritual family. That includes the church universal: all those who follow Christ. That includes the local assembly of followers to whom we all must commit ourselves. And as the primary trait within that family, Jesus commanded us to love one another. "A new command I give you: Love one another. As I have loved you, so you must love one another. By this all men will know that you are my disciples, if you love one another" (John 13:34–35).

Years ago, Francis Schaeffer concluded in his book *The Mark of a Christian* that the world has the right to call us hypocrites if they cannot observe love between us. The last sentence of Jesus made that clear. But let's go a step deeper to the standard of how we should love. The second sentence gives the guideline that we must love one another as Jesus loved us. Doesn't that stretch us beyond our comfort zone? Doesn't that sound like an impossible demand? Love at times, yes. Love in some ways, yes. But like Jesus? We recoil at the impossibility of it.

We find how Jesus loved that in the first verse of that chapter. "It was just before the Passover Feast. Jesus knew that the time had come for him to leave this world and go to the Father. Having loved his own who were in the world, *he now showed them the full extent of his love*" (John 13:1).

Humility overwhelms me when I read what Jesus next did. Can I do this? Absolutely. Do I often do it? Not really. Jesus, the Son of God, Creator of the universe, took off his outer clothing, wrapped a towel around his waist, poured water into a basin, and began to wash the dirty, stinky feet of his followers. Since Jesus did all things well, he must have gone between the toes to clean out the toe jam. He then dried those twenty-four feet with the towel in his lap. Two of those feet belonged to Judas, who would soon send him to the cross. Two belonged to Peter, who would soon use curses to deny that he even knew Jesus.

Jesus took on a task usually left to the lowest servant. An act of love to people who didn't deserve it. Then he nailed us. You and me. Right here were we are.

> When he had finished washing their feet, he put on his clothes and returned to his place. "Do you understand what I have done for you?" he asked them. "You call me 'Teacher' and 'Lord,' and rightly so, for that is what I am. Now that I, your Lord and Teacher, have washed your feet, you also should wash one another's feet. I have set you an example that *you should do as I have done for you.* I tell you the truth, no servant is greater than his master, nor is a messenger greater than the one who sent him. Now that you know these things, *you will be blessed if you do them.*"
> (John 13:12–17)

Do we want Jesus to bless us? Then we serve our spiritual family. Humbly. At a college mountain conference years ago, we had a foot-washing service. Washing filthy feet humbled us, and it moved me like few events ever have. Must we wash each other's feet? I don't think so.

Foot washing fit into a pedestrian culture where people wore sandals; it had a practical role then but it doesn't today.

But Jesus, our Teacher and Lord, gave us an example of humble service that his followers must emulate An essential target. Exactly how we all serve with humility will vary. But we radically follow Jesus when we look for opportunities to meet the needs of others. That demonstrates the genuineness of our following.

Two chapters after this, Jesus taught the depth of our service. "My command is this: Love each other as I have loved you. Greater love has no one than this, that he lay down his life for his friends. You are my friends if you do what I command" (John 15:12–14). We can't blow this off as hypothetical; the very next day Jesus laid down his life for us, his friends. The apostles understood this literally. All except John died as martyrs for their faith.

We follow Jesus when we love and serve others as he did. And how does the greatest degree of love express itself? With a willingness to give our lives, and the stuff of our lives, for others. Or, we choose to decrease our lifestyle and comforts to impact others. That may involve our very life. It may involve our stuff. But we use what we have to benefit the people we love. Just like the early church.

> All the believers were one in heart and mind. No one claimed that any of his possessions was his own, but *they shared everything they had.* With great power the apostles continued to testify to the resurrection of the Lord Jesus, and much grace was upon them all. *There were no needy persons among them.* For from time to time those who owned lands or houses sold them, brought the money from the sales and put it at the apostles' feet, and it was distributed to anyone as he had need. Joseph, a Levite from Cyprus, whom the apostles called Barnabas (which means Son of Encouragement), sold

a field he owned and brought the money and put it at the apostles' feet. (Acts 4:32–37)

These early followers showed a willingness to go all the way with their following. Can we do less if we choose to follow Jesus? That's what it means to love one another like Jesus did.

The Payoff

Let's go back to Luke. Chapter 9 describes the excuses that some potential followers used. Chapter 14 describes the radical demands Jesus gave for all followers. Luke 18 tells the story of the rich young ruler who wanted to follow Jesus. He claimed to have kept all the commandments from his youth. Without arguing, Jesus merely told him to sell all he had, and to give the money away, and then he could follow. The young man made a choice: his stuff over eternal life. Jesus then talked about how difficult it can be for the wealthy to put God before stuff.

Apparently, Peter started putting all of this together. How excuses don't work. How we must hate our families, take up our cross, and give up all of our stuff. How material goods can interfere with following. And perhaps with a sense that the apostles really did want to follow, he proclaimed: "We have left all we had to follow you!" (Luke 18:28). I imagine Peter put a little stress on *we*.

What payoff did Jesus give for their sacrificial following? "I tell you the truth, no one who has left home or wife or brothers or parents or children for the sake of the kingdom of God will fail to *receive many times as much in this age* and, in the age to come, eternal life" (Luke 18:29–30).

When we love Jesus more than our family, he gives us a new family. Instantly. One that lasts forever. And he gives us eternal life. A nice deal, isn't it?

Disciples Must Give Up Stuff: We Relinquish Ownership

I'll never claim to have more holiness than the next guy. I fully know my faults, some of which you would never guess. And don't hold your breath waiting for me to reveal those I already haven't. But I don't particularly struggle with greed or with an overwhelming desire to become wealthy. I learned the promise in Sunday school that if I give first place in my life to God, then he'll ensure that my needs get met. I learned the verses that tell us to serve God now and he'll reward us in heaven. I've tried to live by these.

I tend to choose jobs for ministry impact, not for the money. The professions I've chosen—pastor, Christian school teacher, and Christian author—don't have reputations for high pay. We don't have a lot in savings, except some from my mom's inheritance.

We've always had our physical needs met. The few extra pounds I still pack demonstrate that. We have a nice home, although not huge or custom. We have three vehicles, not brand new, but they all look nice and run strong. Sheila and I try to live by I Timothy 6:8: "But if we have food and clothing, we will be content with that."

On the whole, I can say with some fair honesty, that I feel content financially. We're not wealthy, but we are comfortable. Compared to most of the world, we live quite well.

I do have a couple of things that I care about deeply. My classic 1978 Honda Gold Wing motorcycle fits into that category. I've ridden bikes for thirty-six years now, and have toured all but eleven states. I've taken at least seven major cross-country rides, and once cruised all day at 90 to 100 mph. That happened decades ago, and since the statute of limitations has run out, I can share that.

I rode my first bike, a 1970 Honda 350 Scrambler, to Canada as a college graduation present to myself. That was a big mistake with such a small bike. I next had a legendary 1973 750 Honda Four and took it on several trips, including a three-month journey that explored thirty states.

We also have a 1995 Mustang convertible, deep blue with a white top. It's carried us over the continental divide in Colorado numerous times, with snow on the surrounding countryside, the top down, and the heater running full blast. I can't even imagine not having a convertible.

In no way can I make the argument that these represent needs. I acknowledge them as wants, as desires, as fun toys. And I can't help but think of the bumper sticker: "He who dies with the most toys wins." These two toys make me a winner.

But if an important ministry opportunity came up, would I willingly sell the bike? If our life situation changed and we needed a more "traditional" vehicle for ministry, would I willingly give up the convertible? Forgive me, but these sound like small areas, don't they? And perhaps they are. But they cause me to struggle with the next essential target Jesus gave.

The Impossible Demand

In our last chapter, we examined how Jesus said we must hate our family to follow him. He ended that passage like this: "In the same way, any of you who does not *give up everything he has* cannot be my disciple" (Luke 14:33).

Expressed in both example and command, that demand runs through the New Testament. Jesus had run into Simon Peter and his brother Andrew, along with their fishing partners, John and James, several times before. They had talked about the kingdom of God, but decision time had now arrived. After a large catch of fish, Jesus told them that from now on they would catch men. Their response? "So they pulled their boats up on shore, *left everything* and followed him" (Luke 5:11).

Not much later, Jesus approached a tax man named Levi, whom we know as Matthew. Jesus simply said, "Follow me." Levi's response? "Levi got up, *left everything* and followed him" (Luke 5:28).

Paul had it all. Position, prestige, and power. Then he met a person who demanded that he give all that up. His response? "But whatever was to my profit I now consider loss for the sake of Christ. What is more, I consider everything a loss compared to the surpassing greatness of knowing Christ Jesus my Lord, for whose sake *I have lost all things.* I consider them rubbish, that I may gain Christ" (Phil. 3:7–8).

To Paul, following Jesus had enough value that he would gladly give up everything, just to know Jesus. But not all people did that.

Another prospective follower, a very wealthy one, asked Jesus about inheriting eternal life, and claimed to have followed the Ten Commandments. Jesus' demand? "You still lack one thing. *Sell everything you have and give to the poor,* and you will have treasure in heaven. Then come, follow me" (Luke 18:22). The man's response? He loved his wealth too much to do that, and walked away.

We all face that dilemma. Jesus said we cannot follow him unless we give up everything. Some follow, some don't. But exactly what did Jesus mean by give up everything?

Did he command that we fully and permanently give away everything we have, and forever live as homeless people who have to beg for food? We fear Jesus meant exactly that.

The phrase "give up" means to set apart or to separate, and we only find it six times in the New Testament. It can include to renounce or forsake, and Luke 14:33 may fit into this category. But every other use refers to a temporary separation. Paul demonstrated that when he left his fellow followers of Jesus at Ephesus: "But as he left, he promised, 'I will come back if it is God's will'" (Acts 18:21). When Paul left, he held out the possibility of returning.

So, from the meaning of the phrase, to give up everything doesn't require that we give everything away forever and ever in every instance. Other Scriptures support that. 1 Timothy 6:17–19 tells wealthy believers how to live faithfully.

> Command those who are rich in this present world not
> to be arrogant nor to put their hope in wealth, which is so
> uncertain, but to put their hope in God, who richly provides
> us with everything for our enjoyment. Command them to
> do good, to be rich in good deeds, and to be generous and
> willing to share. In this way they will lay up treasure for
> themselves as a firm foundation for the coming age, so that
> they may take hold of the life that is truly life.

Paul didn't command them to sell all they had, like Jesus did to the wealthy young man. They could even enjoy their stuff! Did you notice the phrase "God . . . richly provides us with everything for our enjoyment." Great news! I can keep and enjoy my Gold Wing and Mustang. God is good!

But let's not try to rob Jesus' demand from its radical meaning. And it is radical.

WE RENOUNCE OWNERSHIP

At a bare minimum, following Jesus means that we renounce our ownership of our stuff. Like my Gold Wing. Like my Mustang. Like my house. Like my life. In effect, we sign over the pink slip. Obviously, we don't do that physically. I doubt the state of California would allow that, how could they collect the license fees from God? But God owns our stuff, and allows us to use it. Temporarily.

David knew that: "The earth is the LORD's, and everything in it, the world, and all who live in it; for he founded it upon the seas and established it upon the waters" (Ps. 24:1–2). Because God created the universe, he owns it. He lets us use our stuff, but we need to remember who really owns it.

I battle that. I work for my stuff. I take care of it. I purchase it. I pay to keep it up. Now, I do have an interest in my stuff, but I don't own it. Not if David had it right. Not if Jesus said what he did.

Several years ago when my mom had to stop driving, I picked up her car, a Ford Escort. Slow but economical, it became my transportation between home and the church I pastored ninety miles away. After I resigned, it became an extra car. We knew it belonged to God, so we sometimes loaned out "God's car" to friends in need. A buddy from a home Bible study needed short-term wheels, so I let him use it. He liked it and asked to buy it.

We agreed on a price, he made a small down payment, then promptly quit paying. He didn't change the registration with the state, so we remained liable. Soon after, he quit returning my calls. He did respond to an e-mail, saying he'd take care of the registration; he never did. Months later I received notice of a parking violation and other problems. I contacted our church, but he had quit attending. Short of tracking him down and taking him to court, Mom's car and the money have disappeared. That ticks me off. We had counted on that money and didn't have a lot to spare. Justice plays a role in my anger.

But I try to remind myself, God owns that car. He didn't steal it from me, but from God.

Renouncing ownership means we keep a loose grip on our stuff; we try to not get too attached. And, we remember it all belongs to

God, and he can call in the loan at any time he desires. This radical principle can change how we accumulate and use our stuff, can't it? Yes, we can have stuff. Yes, we can enjoy it. But whenever God wants it, he has the right to take it.

However, this can lead to a problem. I can easily say, "God, all my stuff belongs to you, just let me know when you want it for something else." I mean it, but I don't always hear those gentle whispers from God. Too often we act like the pastor who took the Sunday offering and said, "God, this offering is yours. All of it. Now, I'm going to give it to you by throwing it all up in the air. You take what you want, and I'll take anything you let fall to the ground."

If our stuff belongs to God, we need to take it to a deeper level than merely affirming that God owns it. This becomes a more radical threat to our complacency.

WE INVEST IT FOR THE KINGDOM

We give up everything as intended for our needs, use, and pleasure, and factor God into the equation. We switch from an ownership role to a stewardship role. Jack had started a computer programming company that focused on small businesses and churches. He found a niche and the company grew nicely. Within a few years, it caught the attention of a larger programming firm who wanted to expand into that area. They contacted him, began negotiating, and made an offer he couldn't refuse. They gave a generous purchase price, and wanted him to continue to run the company at a very good salary. But within several months, his frustration had grown.

"You know, their offer gave my family great financial freedom. I still have to work, but I have a big enough nest egg now that we don't have to worry about money anymore. I can give more to the church's mission projects, and I like that. But they want to take the company in a direction I just don't like."

"I thought they liked the way you set the company up."

"I thought so, too. We gave the churches a nice discount, they paid not much more than our cost, the companies paid our bills, and it all worked out fine. I made a good living, the churches benefited, and the companies got great service at a reasonable expense. But the new owners want us to eliminate working with churches; the small profit with them doesn't justify their investment."

"Can they do that?"

"Sure, they own the company! I have to run it the way they tell me."

"Couldn't you just quit, and start another business doing the same thing?"

"No, I had to sign a non-compete clause. I can't start another company or work in that field for anyone but them for three years. I don't really know anything else."

That hauntingly represents our lives in Christ. *"You are not your own;* you were bought at a price. Therefore honor God with your body" (I Cor. 6:19–20). God owns us and our stuff. The owner calls the shots. Jack had to run the company to benefit the owner. And followers of Jesus use our stuff to benefit the owner. God.

Not just when God makes a specific command. But consistently, we use our stuff to carry out the desires we already know the owner has. And the owner will check on us. Jack learned that. As the new owners checked the books, they discovered that the profit margin on the churches didn't match that on other businesses. Jack had to please the owners.

And God audits how we use his stuff as well. Jesus told a story to make that point. "There was a rich man whose manager was accused of wasting his possessions. So he called him in and asked him, 'What is this I hear about you? Give an account of your management, because you cannot be manager any longer'" (Luke 16:1–2).

So what will our owner look for when he audits us? Have we used worldly wealth to advance the kingdom? Greg Sidders said,

"What we hoard; we squander. What we spend on God; we invest."
Jesus hinted at that just a few verses later: "I tell you, use worldly
wealth to gain friends for yourselves, so that when it is gone, you will
be welcomed into eternal dwellings" (Luke 16:9). Or, God expects us
to use his stuff for his purposes for our eventual benefit.

This forces us to a quantum leap regarding stuff. We can't justify acknowledging that God owns our stuff, on keeping a loose grip
on it, and turning it over to him if he ever asks. We need to deliberately use our stuff to benefit him. Intentionally. Strategically. Worldly
wealth must impact eternity.

Jesus made that clear: "Sell your possessions and give to the
poor. Provide purses for yourselves that will not wear out, *a treasure in
heaven* that will not be exhausted, where no thief comes near and no
moth destroys" (Luke 12:33).

Jesus gave us this essential target of giving up our stuff because
he knows that when we do, we get a phenomenal return on our investment. Yes, this will disrupt our lives, and we'll explore some specifics
of that a little later. But Jesus turns our approach to stuff upside down.
We can't satisfy ourselves with tithing 10 percent of our income to
our church, to supporting some other good ministries, and then do
whatever we desire with the rest. It all belongs to God. If we desire to
use much of our stuff primarily for our own desires, God is not safe
for us.

Complacent Faith and Stuff

Our attitude toward wealth and stuff can bring complacency to
our spiritual walk. For many of us, when we get baptized, we hold our
wallet above the water. We serve God with some of our substance, but
rarely with all of it. Me too, remember my Gold Wing and Mustang?

Bible students love to count how many times God refers to an
issue to determine its importance. But since God inspired all Scripture,

he just has to mention something one time to make it important. But repetition does imbed itself on the mind. God views faith as significant; he mentions it almost 500 times. He views prayer as significant; he mentions it over 500 times. Where does money fit? According to Crown Ministries, over 2,350 times. Jesus spoke more about money than judgment.

Jesus gave us a stark choice. "No one can serve two masters. Either he will hate the one and love the other, or he will be devoted to the one and despise the other. *You cannot serve both God and Money*" (Matt. 6:24).

We must choose—which has our primary allegiance? God? Or comfort, meeting our needs and enjoying our stuff as we desire. Jesus said we cannot blend them.

But why do we struggle with this choice? God created us as physical beings with physical needs. We must eat, drink, and sleep. Our physical needs don't surprise God, at least, not according to Jesus: "So do not worry, saying, 'What shall we eat?' or 'What shall we drink?' or 'What shall we wear?' For the pagans run after all these things, and *your heavenly Father knows that you need them*" (Matt. 6:31–32).

As a person who deeply loves food, I appreciate this. God created us with these needs, and he imbedded pleasure in getting them. Don't we all love to sit down to a good meal? Think of your favorite food, and your mouth begins to salivate. And after a long hard day, my body yearns for the comfort of a bed, just to sink into its welcoming softness.

Second, we know these needs get met from our activity. Paul taught that we shouldn't feed people who won't work for their food (2 Thess. 3:6–12).

The problem comes when we overemphasize our responsibility for meeting these needs. Notice Jesus' description of this tendency: "the pagans run after all these things." Having needs doesn't present a problem; focusing on them does. So, how do we strike a balance?

Needs only become a problem when we run after them more than we run after God.

We tend to rely upon having stuff, and savings, and wealth, to insure that we don't miss out on our needs. That can threaten the primary love we have for God. This happened to Demas. While imprisoned in Rome in AD 60, Paul wrote Colossians and Philemon. In both letters he identified Demas as a key part of his ministry team, grouping him with Mark and Luke. Nice company. Paul then left prison and went on his fourth missionary journey, before Nero put him back in prison. By AD 66, as he once more wrote from prison, Paul's evaluation of Demas had changed: "Please come as soon as you can. Demas has deserted me because he loves the things of this life" (2 Tim. 4:9–10 NLT).

An effective ministry ended because a love for stuff eroded his love for God. Stuff led to spiritual complacency. When we don't give up our stuff, we run the same risk.

Understanding Radical Discipleship

Doug and Carrie Vom Steeg had a comfortable and productive life, and they loved Jesus deeply. Doug had taught fourteen years at a public high school and had worked with the youth at their church for eight years. Carrie had stayed at home with Micah since his birth. She loved their spacious house that allowed for entertaining and for her to lead a writers' critique group.

Then God became unsafe to them.

Doug had a concern for the large numbers of high school young people that left their faith in Jesus when they left high school. Some returned, some didn't, and many experienced spiritual difficulties. They faced a sometimes hostile world, typically with a university lifestyle in which they had no training on how to cope.

While sitting on a bluff overlooking the Pacific Ocean, Doug realized that a year off between high school and college could have a productive impact on young lives. Doug could teach them a Christian worldview, the essentials of faith and how to express them to others, show them how to work as a team, and expose them to other cultures. The goal: that one year would change their lives, by giving them a foundation to last.

Doug and Carrie prayed about it and began Ventana Ministries, the Spanish word for "window," representing the window of time of which they hope to take advantage of. You can learn more at www.ventanaministries.org. The method: to take a group of high school graduates to a variety of locations: camps in the U.S. for training, sites in Mexico for ministry. They began to pack. Doug left his teaching position. They sold most of their possessions and sold their house, and paid off their bills. Carrie announced their garage sale in a newsletter:

> We are trying to live out the verses in the Bible that touch on the subject of our material possessions, but it's not easy! Doug has always been better at letting things go, but lately I've been wrestling with what to get rid of and what to keep. Almost 11 years of marriage and 2,500 square feet later . . . yes, we have a lot of stuff. So unless it's an heirloom or an incredibly functional item we could use in the future, it's for sale!

In talking about it later, she said, "It sounds insignificant in the big picture (and maybe to most men who don't care about material possessions as much), but selling our house was probably the hardest part for me. Selling about half of what we owned was hard, too, but I loved our house."

What a tremendous step of giving up stuff to serve Jesus. Once more, Jesus patterned this for us. But more than material stuff, he left behind equality with God.

> Do nothing out of selfish ambition or vain conceit,
> but in humility consider others better than yourselves. Each
> of you should look not only to your own interests, but also
> to the interests of others. Your attitude should be the same
> as that of Christ Jesus: Who, being in very nature God, did
> not consider equality with God something to be grasped,
> but *made himself nothing*, taking the very nature of a servant,
> being made in human likeness. And being found in appear-
> ance as a man, he humbled himself and became obedient to
> death—even death on a cross! (Phil. 2:3–8)

Jesus left behind far more than we ever will. Far more than Doug
and Carrie left behind. For disciples of Jesus, just following his example
should be enough to motivate us. But some of us need to know why.

BREAK THE BACK OF SELF-INTEREST

Our primary resistance to God comes from our desire to look
after ourselves. Didn't Paul refer to that in the first two sentences of
the above passage? We struggle with ambition and conceit. We focus
on our interests, not those of others. So as we loosen our grip on stuff,
we can tighten our grip on God.

Paul affirmed "But godliness with contentment is great gain. For
we brought nothing into the world, and we can take nothing out of it"
(I Tim. 6:6–7). We choose godliness and loosen our grip on stuff, or
we hang onto our stuff and lose godliness. This essential target plays
a primary role in crafting the direction of our lives.

CHANGE THE WORLD

Dare I say Paul made a mistake in the above passage? Correctly,
we can't take any stuff with us. We entered with nothing, we leave
with nothing. But we can send spiritual stuff ahead. Doug and Carrie
gave up their stuff to change the world. One thought that came to

Doug on that bluff dealt with the personal significance he had. Was he maximizing his impact on others? Could he become more effective? And, what price would he and Carrie have to pay?

As we give up our stuff and invest it for God, we help change the lives of people.

I'm a Christian today because people sacrificially gave of their time and money to start Parkcrest Christian Church in Long Beach, California. Some taught me in Sunday school. Some worked as youth sponsors. Some gave financially to support the work of the church. Each of us has spiritual forebears, some of which we never know on earth, that contributed and made an impact on our lives by how they relinquished their stuff for Jesus.

A Radical Following

Most spiritual changes don't completely occur all at once, and giving up our stuff fits into that category. The grammar for "give up" in Luke 14:33 is the present tense, which has the idea of continuing, of a process. We give up all we can think of today, we give it up again tomorrow. And if tomorrow brings a new awareness of the stuff we can use for Jesus, then we give up more the next day. We talked about this earlier, how we take up our cross daily, to remind ourselves of what we most want to do.

Remember the use of the phrase where Paul says good-bye, hoping to return? Doug and Carrie have done the same. He took a leave of absence from his job. They sold their house and they kept some of the family heirlooms. They would give all of those up, if they need to. Now, let's get practical.

CHOOSE GODLINESS

At times, we must choose between stuff and God. Let's make a decision now that God comes first. If we wait until the decision gets critical, we can easily feel stressed, unless we establish a core value that God counts more than stuff. We previously examined Matthew 6:31–32, then Jesus added: "But *seek first his kingdom and his righteousness, and all these things will be given to you as well*" (v. 33).

We need both God and stuff, but we can strive for the latter and lose the former, or we can strive for the former and gain the latter.

CHOOSE CONTENTMENT

We can only choose contentment when we distinguish between needs and wants. Needs deal with the basic necessities of life. Wants exceed that. Wants aren't bad, they just don't qualify as necessities. I need food; I want a New York steak. I can live without the latter, but not the former. Contentment can keep us from dissatisfaction with what we have, when we realize we have what we need. G. K. Chesterton said: "There are two ways to get enough: One is to accumulate more and more. The other is to desire less." But we must learn contentment, not many of us have that as a natural gift.

> I have learned to be content whatever the circum-
> stances. I know what it is to be in need, and I know what it
> is to have plenty. I have learned the secret of being content in
> any and every situation, whether well fed or hungry, whether
> living in plenty or in want. I can do everything through him
> who gives me strength. (Phil. 4:11–13)

Paul had to learn that! And the last verse promises that God will give us the strength to choose contentment. I wonder how many resources we could free for the kingdom if we chose contentment when our needs get met, rather than pursuing our wants so passionately.

CHOOSE MINISTRY

We can also use our stuff to impact people. We can use it to support others in their ministry, like Joanna:

After this, Jesus traveled about from one town and vil-
lage to another, proclaiming the good news of the kingdom
of God. The Twelve were with him, and also some women
who had been cured of evil spirits and diseases: Mary
(called Magdalene) from whom seven demons had come out;
Joanna the wife of Cuza, the manager of Herod's household;
Susanna; and many others. *These women were helping to support
them out of their own means.* (Luke 8:1–3)

We can use it to help the poor. Do not be afraid, little
flock, for your Father has been pleased to give you the kingdom. Sell your possessions and give to the poor. Provide
purses for yourselves that will not wear out, a treasure in
heaven that will not be exhausted, where no thief comes near
and no moth destroys. (Luke 12:32–33)

We can use it to connect with people who don't yet know
Christ. "I tell you, use worldly wealth to gain friends for yourselves, so
that when it is gone, you will be welcomed into eternal dwellings"
(Luke 16:9).

Pat Boone had a connection with Pepperdine University when
I attended there. Some criticized him for living in a nice house in
Beverly Hills. They reasoned that Pat could have sold the house,
bought a smaller one in a regular neighborhood, and used the money
for ministry. But because of the house, Pat had a ministry to the
entertainment industry that most people couldn't begin to have. He
baptized quite a few in the pool that some criticized.

Pat used his possessions for ministry, and a lot of people will
welcome him in heaven. Maybe we can spring some cash loose to have
our neighbors over for a barbeque. We can even call it ministry! If a
neighbor loses his job, buy a few bags of groceries for him. Hire him
to mow your lawn.

Let's follow Jesus' example of giving stuff up for God, that's an essential target.

The Payoff

Assuming we follow Jesus radically and give up our stuff, what impact does that have? Obviously, as we've discussed, more people get to know Jesus, more go to heaven, and we know more people there. Obviously, we conquer our self-interest and become more outwardly focused. But a passage we used gives a tremendous promise in the next verse, one we didn't read before.

Remember Luke 12:32–33, and then read verse 34. "For where your treasure is, there your heart will be also." Doesn't that seem backward? We typically think that we invest in what we value. But Jesus says that if we invest in God, we build a deeper intimacy with him. That intrigues me. As I tithe, I get closer to God. As I support other ministries, I get closer to God. As I help others with my stuff, I get closer to God.

That all seems backwards. I thought I would lose if I gave up my stuff to God. Instead, I gain intimacy with God, something far more important than stuff. That intimacy lasts forever. Not a bad essential target.

Acting Like Jesus

In "Acting Like Jesus," Jesus and his apostles
describe following in imperative terms: what disciples *always* do.
These essential targets look at critical behaviors
that express how we value Jesus.

Acting Like Jesus

Disciples Must Pursue Purity: We Change Our Values

Over 210 million people in 185 countries have attended crusades led by Billy Graham. The Billy Graham Evangelistic Association magazine *Decision* has a circulation exceeding one million. Several of his twenty-four books have made best-seller lists. He founded the magazine *Christianity Today*, which has become the standard bearer for American evangelicalism. Worldwide Pictures, part of the ministry, has produced fifty-eight films, resulting in over two million decisions for Christ. Graham's ministry even allowed a junior high student a brief escape from legalism.

Peter Chattaway, in *CT Direct* of August 2005, told how Denny Wayman became a decision counselor for a Billy Graham film in 1965. One of his reasons? He could step inside a movie theatre. "Free Methodists, at that point in our denomination, were not allowed to go to movies."

We followers of Jesus often get ensnared in a confusing host of rules that we just cannot find in Scripture. When I was in my late teens, I read the Bible passages about not causing others to stumble in their walk with Jesus, and resolved that I shouldn't drink alcoholic beverages. Every Christian needs to apply biblical principles, but we can't force our applications on others. I made that mistake, and looked down on Christians who had a drink on occasion, thinking my personal rule should apply to all others. Funny, though, that God never saw fit to make the same prohibition; he seemed content to tell us to avoid getting drunk.

Why do we think we know better than God? Many people over the years have considered Christianity, only to reject the host of rules that seemed to go along with it. We tend to make following Jesus more difficult than it should be.

Like the rich young man who couldn't give up his wealth to follow Jesus, many others see those demands and decide, "I didn't sign up for this," and they leave. People see these absolutes, know they can't live up to them, and don't bother trying.

And in this mess of rules, Jesus raises the bar.

The Impossible Demand

First-century Judaism had a group called the Pharisees, who meticulously followed every rule and made up thousands in addition to those in Scripture. Yet their strict rule keeping didn't qualify as success to Jesus: "For I tell you that unless your righteousness surpasses that of the Pharisees and the teachers of the law, you will certainly not enter the kingdom of heaven" (Matt. 5:20).

Later in the same chapter he continued: "Be perfect, therefore, as your heavenly Father is perfect" (Matt. 5:48). If you catch me on a good day, I may claim to be OK. But perfect? Never. Paul gives that as a goal of his ministry: "We proclaim him, admonishing and teaching everyone with all wisdom, so that we may *present everyone perfect in Christ.*

To this end I labor, struggling with all his energy, which so powerfully works in me" (Col. 1:28–29). If Paul tried to present me as perfect, his labor would have been wasted.

These high standards get worse, according to the apostle John: "No one who is born of God will continue to sin, because God's seed remains in him; he cannot go on sinning, because he has been born of God" (1 John 3:9). Do you continue to sin like I do? It sounds like we haven't been born again, doesn't it?

Doesn't the spiritual superiority of "holy" people grate on us? We know they fake it. But Peter the apostle requires our holiness: "But just as he who called you is holy, so be holy in all you do; for it is written: 'Be holy, because I am holy'" (1 Pet. 1:15–16).

Let's pull this together. God requires high righteousness, perfection, that we not sin, and our holiness. We can do that, right? And what does God have in store for us to accomplish tomorrow? Fly to the sun? Both seem equally impossible. And that impossibility feeds spiritual mediocrity.

Complacent Faith and Purity

Typically, we respond to these impossible demands in two ways, and both keep us from blasting out of complacency and mediocrity. They keep us from stretching ourselves beyond what we thought we could do.

LEGALISM

Sometimes we accept these as just more rules to follow, and we give it our best shot. We may feel overwhelmed, but we slog on through. After all, we've committed our lives to serving God, and we'll do what we must. I got caught up in that. In our church youth groups, we heard a lot about rules. I tried to follow them, I really did, but my inability increased my guilt. We could go to movies, but we still had a lot of rules.

Our group joined hundreds of high school young people at a midwinter conference, and at the invitation time I went down to rededicate my life to Christ. I knew I didn't do the Christian life well enough. My youth pastor said, "I'm not sure why Tim is up here, he's a good Christian, but let's pray for him." I didn't dare share that I felt like a fraud. Just one year later, my faith tumbled down, in part from an inability to follow all the rules.

Remember those Pharisees who strictly followed the rules? Jesus said they didn't make it either, as did Paul. "For no one can ever be made right in God's sight by doing what his law commands. For the more we know God's law, the clearer it becomes that we aren't obeying it" (Rom. 3:30 NLT).

Apart from our inability to please God by following the rules, we get no pleasure from such a life. The church in Galatia became enmeshed in rules and Paul saw the result: "Where is that joyful spirit we felt together then?" (Gal. 4:15 NLT).

In the end, legalism fails us. We always fail to follow all the rules perfectly. We get stuck in spiritual quicksand.

LIBERTY

We could view these demands for perfection and rightly realize that we can't do them. So, we give up. We accept them as vague goals that have few consequences if we don't do them. After all, why would God require the impossible of us? Therefore, we have the liberty to do whatever we desire, including sin. Some followers in Rome thought through this dilemma with care. We can't avoid imperfection, and so God provided grace and forgiveness. If we can receive forgiveness for all of our sins, then the sting of sin disappears. And, the more we sin, the more forgiveness we get, and the more that grace flows.

But as people sinned more and more, God's wonderful
kindness became more abundant. So just as sin ruled over
all people and brought them to death, now God's wonderful
kindness rules instead, giving us right standing with God
and resulting in eternal life through Jesus Christ our Lord.
Well then, should we keep on sinning so that God can show
us more and more kindness and forgiveness?
(Rom. 5:20–21; 6:1 NLT)

On its face, it makes some sense. But Paul disagreed: "Of course
not! Since we have died to sin, how can we continue to live in it?"
(Rom. 6:2 NLT). When we come to Christ, we decide to leave sin, and
this approach denies the essence of following Jesus. It ignores all the
commands for purity that Jesus and the apostles gave.

In the end, liberty fails us. It allows us to slip back into the same
sin that following Christ takes us away from. Once more, we don't
progress in delving deeper into the transformed life.

Understanding Radical Discipleship

Fortunately, we have a third option for dealing with these
demands for perfection. This option takes the grains of truth from
each and integrates them into a comprehensive system. Legalism correctly says that God cares about what we do and our character. Liberty
correctly says that God realizes we cannot live without sin and provides forgiveness. But let's first define some of these key terms. These
represent different dimensions of the purity God demands of us, and
they don't mean what we typically think they mean.

HOLY

Holy means "separated, or set apart," not sinless perfection. We
must be holy, but we cannot be sinless: "If we claim to be without

sin, we deceive ourselves and the truth is not in us" (I John 1:8). We choose holiness when we determine that we won't live to please ourselves but to please God.

PERFECT

Perfect means "complete, finished, or mature." Ironically, perfect doesn't mean sinless perfection either! It means we reach the goal God has given for us. Perfect means we've gotten on the track, like Paul, and that we pursue it:

> Not that I have already obtained all this, or have already been made perfect, but I press on to take hold of that for which Christ Jesus took hold of me. Brothers, I do not consider myself yet to have taken hold of it. But one thing I do: Forgetting what is behind and straining toward what is ahead, *I press on* toward the goal to win the prize for which God has called me heavenward in Christ Jesus. (Phil. 3:12–14)

We choose perfection when we pursue his design for our lives.

PURE

Several Greek words get translated into pure, but the basic concept means that we have no values that fight against what God desires for us. Yes, temptations will clearly contradict God's best, but we realize they fight against our deepest desires. Jesus taught the importance of purity: "Blessed are the pure in heart, for they will see God" (Matt. 5:8). Or, to see God we need a heart that purely yearns for him.

We choose purity when we choose values that complement God and that don't fight against him.

RIGHTEOUS

Righteous refers to a life in a right relationship with God, in a condition acceptable to him. It involves integrity, virtue, and a purity of life. We can't be righteous on our own: "There is no one righteous, not even one" (Rom. 3:10). We can't be righteous by following the rules: "Therefore no one will be declared righteous in his sight by observing the law; rather, through the law we become conscious of sin" (Rom. 3:20).

We can only be righteous through faith in Jesus: "But now a righteousness from God, apart from law, has been made known, to which the Law and the Prophets testify. This righteousness from God comes through faith in Jesus Christ to all who believe" (Rom. 3:21–22).

We become righteous when we accept Jesus as our Lord and Savior.

Now, with these definitions in mind, what did Jesus and the apostles intend when they demanded our holiness, perfection, purity, and righteousness?

EXPRESS FAITH THROUGH LOVE

This typifies our concept of an essential target. With all our strength, we pursue purity through reliance upon the power of God which comes to us through our faith in Jesus. Galatians 5:6 tells us: "For in Christ Jesus neither circumcision nor uncircumcision has any value. The only thing that counts is faith expressing itself through love."

Our behavior means absolutely nothing, unless it flows from loving God. But if we have faith, we must lovingly express it in what we do. Jesus calls this essential. We won't express it without failing sometimes, but we must always strive for it. And when we fail, we acknowledge it and get back on track.

We may act in just the same way, but our motives change. Rather than acting out of legalism (the vain effort to please God by what we do), rather than acting out of liberty (the vain effort to minimize the wrongness of sin), we yearn to act lovingly to God. And that motive makes all the difference.

I've had a beard since my college days; it's become part of my core identity. When I met Sheila, my beard covered most of my face; so that's all she knew. After a few years of marriage, I wondered how my face had changed underneath the obscuring whiskers, so I shaved it all off. Sheila complimented the new look, but graciously mentioned she liked the old look best. She never nagged, she never insisted that I grow it back or face dire consequences.

But before long, the beard came back. Out of obligation? No, out of love. I wanted to please my wife. We express our love for God in a similar fashion.

Obviously, we must begin with faith, believing in Jesus. That faith brings righteousness to our lives: "However, to the man who does not work but trusts God who justifies the wicked, his faith is credited as righteousness" (Rom. 4:5). Again, we see that actions not based on faith mean nothing. Doing good will never make us righteous, because we always have some sin within us. And like the worm that ruins the apples, a little sin keeps us from that right relationship with Jesus.

But we don't stop there! "Offer yourselves to God, as those who have been brought from death to life; and *offer the parts of your body to him as instruments of righteousness*" (Rom. 6:13). Once we come to Christ, we give our lives to him as righteous tools for him to use however he desires.

And because God is holy, we strive for holiness: We set our lives apart for him and we strive to decrease the sin in our lives. Because God is perfect, we strive for perfection: We work on becoming all he desires for us. Because God is pure, we strive for purity: We eliminate values and behaviors that contradict his desires. Because God is righteous, we strive for righteousness: We continually evaluate our walk with God to discover anything that keeps us from fully following.

Yes, this essential target seems close to impossible, but God doesn't require sinless perfection. When we come to Christ, we embark on a lifelong process of transformation. God doesn't expect sinless perfection but progression toward sinlessness. Jesus himself helps us. "For by that one offering he perfected forever all those whom he is making holy" (Heb. 10:14 NLT).

By his sacrifice, Jesus made us perfect. Past tense. He did everything necessary for us to become mature and complete spiritually. At the same time, he is making us holy. Present tense. A process that continues. We become more set apart from sin and for holiness all the time.

When I returned to Christ after my years of college searching, I knew of one primary area that God desperately wanted to change in me, and my desperation matched his. After we made some progress, God pointed out another area. I thought that would finish the process, that I'd be fairly complete spiritually. In the decades since, God continues to show me new areas in which to change. Areas that I felt pride in before I feel shame in now. As we continue to follow Jesus, God gives us a greater sensitivity about what holiness entails for us.

The question for each of us: Do we embrace the process of this essential target?

A Radical Following

The New Testament links a number of acts to pursuing purity, as we incorporate these, we'll see holiness grow in our lives.

PRAY

Prayer intimately connects us with God; it renews our commitment, it lets us listen to him, and it allows us to share our heart with him. Paul knew the link between effective prayer and holiness: "I want men everywhere to lift up holy hands in prayer, without anger or disputing" (I Tim. 2:8).

We choose purity when we pray.

KNOW THE WORD

We really can't follow Jesus unless we know what he told us to do. Once we come to Christ, we continue the process by yearning to learn: "You must crave pure spiritual milk so that you can grow into the fullness of your salvation. Cry out for this nourishment as a baby cries for milk" (I Pet. 2:2 NLT).

When Sheila and I began dating, we'd stay up for hours talking, wanting to learn more about each other. I wanted to discover if she had the qualities that would lead to a permanent relationship, and how to please her.

Followers of Jesus have such a great opportunity to learn, especially knowing where it leads us: "All Scripture is God-breathed and is useful for teaching, rebuking, correcting and *training in righteousness*, so that the man of God may be *thoroughly equipped* for every good work" (2 Tim. 3:16–17). Knowing the Word allows us to grow into righteousness, we have a clear target.

We choose purity when we know the Word.

OBEY THE WORD

But we cannot stop with knowing Jesus' words; we need to do them: "You have purified yourselves by obeying the truth" (I Pet. 1:22). Every time I choose to resist viewing online porn, I feel closer to God. Every time I forgive someone who has wronged me, I feel closer to God. That makes sense, doesn't it?

Several specific behaviors fit in here. We need to watch our words (James 3:2); to live in sexual purity (Heb. 13:4); to help the needy (James 1:27); and to continue in holiness (Rev. 22:11).

We choose purity when we obey the Word.

Flee Evil

Learning the Word lets us know what to avoid. We simultaneously do what Jesus told us to do, and we move away from wrong. That will eliminate values in our lives that increase impurity. *"Flee the evil desires of youth, and pursue righteousness, faith, love and peace, along with those who call on the Lord out of a pure heart"* (2 Tim. 2:22).

Following Jesus means we choose to follow his path of righteousness, which eliminates the option of liberty, doesn't it?

We choose purity when we flee evil.

Confess Sins

Jesus gives us great grace on this one. Because pursuing purity is a process, we'll never fully arrive while alive on earth. But when we sin, if we acknowledge that to God, we can get back on the purity track. "If we confess our sins, he is faithful and just and *will forgive us our sins and purify us from all unrighteousness"* (1 John 1:9).

I have to confess: I battle this. For years, I hated to acknowledge that I had done wrong. I couldn't easily do that to either God or other people, and that damaged a lot of relationships. But in my middle years, I began to learn the freedom that comes from agreeing with God and the truth.

We choose purity when we confess our sins.

Accept Discipline

I've battled this one also, for the same reason I just mentioned. God uses the consequences of our sins to discipline us, to get our attention when we've slipped off track. It can range from a gentle whisper to a devastated life. Typically, how soon we listen determines how minor the damage is. "Our fathers disciplined us for a little while as they thought best; but God disciplines us for our good, that we may share in his holiness" (Heb. 12:10).

Last week, while eating dinner at an oceanfront Mexican restaurant, Sheila asked about the porn viewing. After we talked about it, she said, "I've asked God to whack you hard with a two-by-four if you slip back into that." Honestly, I asked her to continue, because God's discipline lets us share in his holiness.

We choose purity when we accept discipline.

As we incorporate all of these more intentionally in our lives, we'll follow Jesus more radically, and we'll see our lives transformed.

The Payoff

A life that grows in purity will enable us to see God, and to live forever with him. "Make every effort to live in peace with all men and to *be holy; without holiness no one will see the Lord*" (Heb. 12:14). As we pursue holiness, we can count on seeing God, and that he'll be smiling on us.

We'll also change our mindset about life; we won't get caught up in all the problems, negativity, and difficulties. I really like this promise that Paul gives: "*To the pure, all things are pure,* but to those who are corrupted and do not believe, nothing is pure. In fact, both their minds and consciences are corrupted" (Titus 1:15). Have you seen how some people only focus on the bad things in life? Yes, bad experiences exist. But when we pursue purity, God opens up a new dimension to us, we no longer have to feel overwhelmed by evil.

And to highlight all of this, when we embark on the pursuit of holiness, we take control of our lives. As we cooperate with God in wanting righteousness, we can stand against temptation. We can flee evil. We can share in the very holiness of God. "Each of you should learn to *control his own body* in a way that is holy and honorable. . . . For God did not call us to be impure, but to live a holy life" (1 Thess. 4:4, 7).

We don't feel like paper boats that get blown all over the lake, we become an ocean liner that charts the course under the direction of our Captain. Purity: A great essential target.

Disciples Must Rejoice: We Transcend Adversity

By 1994, my wife Sheila and I had built a solid foundation of not treating each other well. We didn't listen enough, and we reacted to surface messages instead of trying to discover the meaning and pain underneath. We each brought in a number of personal issues and never really worked to resolve them. I didn't marry until the age of thirty-one, and struggled with incorporating her into my life and leaving behind my independence. For Sheila, the combination of an alcoholic father and an unfaithful first husband brought trust issues to the forefront of her mind. My independence amplified that.

Then, during a sabbatical from pastoring, we reached a crisis point. Neither of us could take it any longer. We saw a Christian marriage counselor twice a week. We explored why we acted like we did, and how we could better act. But we couldn't change enough to stop wounding each other deeply. Old habits die slowly; we kept picking at one another, reopening old wounds and opening new ones.

Then I suggested we try a separation. Sheila feared I did so as the first step toward divorce, but I wanted it so we could avoid one. We needed some distance, a chance to let wounds heal, a chance to redis-cover our love and how we could treat each other better. We continued counseling, and I rented a room from friends. I thought two or three months would do it. Optimistic me.

When two or three months didn't accomplish the task, I rented a small house. We continued counseling. I prayed and hoped for rec-onciliation. A friend commented that I seemed to handle it all well; I just smiled. I felt like the proverbial duck that appeared calm on the surface but desperately paddled underneath. But I did have some peace. I clung to God. I shared the situation with a few close friends. I did all the things I had to do; I kept life going on.

But in truth, I felt devastated. I had little hope for either my mar-riage or my ministry. Counseling made little progress in resolving our issues; I saw no improvement in our attitudes or actions. My sabbatical would soon expire and I would need a job, but I knew divorced pastors don't have a high desirability quotient in the evangelical community. The two major passions in my life, short only of my love for God, seemed about to end. The impending destruction of my dreams led me into a deep depression. Except for God, I had little reason to go on.

A person telling me that I must rejoice in all things would have risked serious bodily injury.

The Impossible Demand

But Jesus and the apostles had already told me that. I just chose to ignore it, and paid a much higher price in discouragement during those days than I needed to. Jesus began the parade of this impos-sible demand in the evening before his crucifixion. He told them he would soon go to the Father, but would return. In response to their bewilderment he said, "So you have pain now; but I will see you again, and your hearts will rejoice, and *no one will take your joy from you*" (John 16:22 NRSV).

Focus on the statement that once Jesus returned, no one could take a way the joy of his followers. Question: Did I feel joy in those months of separation, with my marriage and ministry on the rocks? Not much. If I had read this verse then, I would have felt like an even greater failure. Something had surely taken my joy from me. So, did Jesus fail me, or did I fail Jesus?

Then the apostle Paul twisted the knife that Jesus had driven into my guts. "Rejoice in the Lord always. I will say it again: Rejoice!" (Phil. 4:4). Another twist came, *"Be joyful always;* pray continually; *give thanks in all circumstances,* for this is God's will for you in Christ Jesus" (I Thess. 5:16–18).

Get this. God wants me to be joyful when facing the end of my marriage and ministry? He wants me to thank him for these? He hates divorce but wants me to rejoice when facing it. He called me to the ministry but wants me to thank him when its end appears imminent.

That sounds like a totally impossible demand, to respond to every situation with rejoicing. I can understand feeling joy when things go well. But Jesus and the apostles talked about a joy that never disappears, that we can always experience. Now, it gets worse.

They specifically linked rejoicing with suffering and difficulties. "Consider it *pure joy,* my brothers, *whenever you face trials* of many kinds" (James I:2). That also applies to torture and death, according to Paul, "But even if I am being poured out like a drink offering on the sacrifice and service coming from your faith, I am glad and rejoice with all of you. So you too should be glad and rejoice with me" (Phil. 2:17–18).

OK, Paul, rejoice in your death if you choose to, but why ask me to rejoice with such masochism? Once more, it hits deeper.

The theme of joy permeates Philippians; we can find some form of it eleven times in the brief four chapters. Think of that context as you read this verse: "For it has been granted to you on behalf of Christ not only to believe on him, but also to suffer for him" (Phil. I:29).

Most of us resist suffering, but Paul tells us it's a privilege. So we should rejoice because God grants suffering as a benefit? This sounds like madness.

Our human nature resists suffering; it infringes on our plans, our contentment, our pleasure, even our enjoyment of life. Typically, adversity impacts us negatively. We become depressed, discouraged, and often we quit in the face of what seems to be impossible difficulties. Much like I responded during my marital uncertainty. I didn't see that as part of God's plan or will; they didn't match my desires for my marriage or my ministry. I didn't quit, but I did experience the depression and discouragement.

Reacting to pain and problems with joy doesn't match our nature, does it? And that doesn't just apply to us. A biblical character named Heman (no, not He Man) had the same experience.

May my prayer come before you; turn your ear to my cry. For my soul is full of trouble and my life draws near the grave. I am counted among those who go down to the pit; I am like a man without strength. I am set apart with the dead, like the slain who lie in the grave, whom you remember no more, who are cut off from your care. You have put me in the lowest pit, in the darkest depths. Your wrath lies heavily upon me; you have overwhelmed me with all your waves. You have taken from me my closest friends and have made me repulsive to them. I am confined and cannot escape; my eyes are dim with grief. I call to you, O LORD, every day; I spread out my hands to you. Do you show your wonders to the dead? Do those who are dead rise up and praise you? Is your love declared in the grave, your faithfulness in Destruction? Are your wonders known in the place of darkness, or your righteous deeds in the land of oblivion? But I cry to you for help, O LORD; in the morning my prayer comes before you. Why, O LORD, do you reject me and hide your face from me? From my youth I have been afflicted and close to death; I have suffered your terrors and am in despair. Your wrath has swept over me; your terrors have destroyed me. All day long they surround me like a flood; they have completely engulfed me. You have taken my companions and loved ones from me; the darkness is my closest friend. (Ps. 88:2–18)

In the entire psalm, we don't see a glimpse of joy. Not a hint of seeing good coming from the pain. But we see oceans of despair flooding over Heman. We see him questioning God's love and presence. We see him thinking his life has essentially ended. He merely continues breathing until he stops.

I relate to Heman. Although I yearn for it, I don't easily relate to rejoicing in trials. Once again, Jesus holds out an impossible standard. But once again, he does so to blast us out of complacency and into a more full experience of life.

Despondency and Joy

We like happiness. We pursue it. That value permeates our national psyche, even finding its way into the Declaration of Independence. When good things happen to us, we feel happy. When they don't happen, we feel unhappy. The stock market rises with good news and sinks with the bad. We resent anything that interferes with our happiness. We link our emotional response with how nice things go for us.

So when serious difficulties come, we easily get caught up in the "slough of despondency" and can't find our way out of it. But God holds out an option, one that David revealed. In Psalm 31, David faced a conspiracy that caused even his friends to abandon him. David reacted as many of us would:

> Be merciful to me, O LORD, for I am in distress; my eyes grow weak with sorrow, my soul and my body with grief. My life is consumed by anguish and my years by groaning; my strength fails because of my affliction, and my bones grow weak. Because of all my enemies, I am the utter contempt of my neighbors; I am a dread to my friends—those who see me on the street flee from me. I am forgotten by them as though I were dead; I have become like broken pottery. For I hear the slander of many; there is terror on every side; they conspire against me and plot to take my life. (Ps. 31:9–13)

We don't see a lot of joy here. David didn't seem to be a happy camper, at least not at this point. But in the next two verses, he showed a deeper level of dealing with difficulties. "But I trust in you, O LORD; I say, 'You are my God.' My times are in your hands" (Ps. 31:14–15).

Here we see David begin to escape the trap of despondency. Now, read the last verse as he ended the chapter: "Be strong and take heart, all you who hope in the LORD" (Ps. 31:24). David realized that the problems don't show the entire picture. Sometimes we only see the problems and, therefore, see no solution. David revealed that by encouraging us to take heart by hoping in God. How could he do that?

Earlier, he linked joy and affliction: "I will be glad and rejoice in your love, for you saw my affliction and knew the anguish of my soul" (Ps. 31:7).

David didn't care much for the situation, but he trusted in God during it. Specifically, he relied upon God's love, that God continued his involvement in David's life, and that God knew what David experienced.

That, I can relate to. During our separation, I did rely on God's love. I knew he both cared for me and knew the pain I felt. I did draw strength from his presence. However, I missed the joy part of the equation. The depression overwhelmed me, and I didn't escape it. But, I could have.

Why did I miss it? Because I committed the all-too-human mistake of confusing joy with happiness. We rejoice when we get what we desire. Give me one of the new retro Mustang GT convertibles, and you'll hear rejoicing from California to Maine.

This reduces rejoicing to circumstances. But focusing on circumstances will keep us locked into despondency and will kill joy. When we focus on the immediate, the short term, the present, true joy escapes us. We get stuck in place—a place we don't like.

Understanding Radical Discipleship

Joy is the result when we focus on the big picture, on the long term. We cannot avoid discouragement when we suffer, but we can develop joy. This joy doesn't ignore the reality of pain and suffering. Rather, joy acknowledges the reality of both the pain and a greater reality. Jesus experienced that in the Garden of Gethsemane just before his execution. After the Last Supper, he led the apostles to the garden and then enlisted some extra prayer support for the ordeal soon to come.

> He took Peter and the two sons of Zebedee along with him, and he began to be sorrowful and troubled. Then he said to them, "My soul is overwhelmed with sorrow to the point of death. Stay here and keep watch with me." Going a little farther, he fell with his face to the ground and prayed, "My Father, if it is possible, may this cup be taken from me. Yet not as I will, but as you will." (Matt. 26:37–39)

Jesus well knew what it meant to face the physical agony of the crucifixion, along with the even greater torment of becoming sin for us. He heard their approaching hoof beats and didn't want to face them alone. If possible, he wanted out. He would accept the Father's will, but he knew the pain it would bring.

Another component amazes me. "Let us fix our eyes on Jesus, the author and perfecter of our faith, who for *the joy set before* him endured the cross, scorning its shame, and sat down at the right hand of the throne of God" (Heb. 12:2).

Despite dealing with difficulties that I could never imagine, Jesus connected joy with the cross. Did his divinity allow him to do that, a quality I don't have? Not at all. The New Living Translation makes it clear that I have access to what allowed Jesus to experience joy. "He was willing to die a shameful death on the cross because of the *joy he knew would be his afterward*" (Heb. 12:2).

Jesus chose a long-term view. He didn't allow himself to obsess over the horrors soon to come. He accepted them as reality, but as just a *part* of reality. He didn't get caught in the momentary morass of misery but looked ahead. That allows us to link joy and suffering without falling into masochism. Unlike my experience, we can have joy in suffering by looking beyond the suffering. We don't ignore either the short- or long-term realities. I could have used that long-term view back then; it would have helped me realize that the present doesn't amount to the total of my life. God had more in store for me. I could trust in his love and involvement without knowing the specifics of what he would later bring.

Genuine joy can only truly express itself in suffering; otherwise we tend to feel happiness based solely on what's happening. The presence of suffering teaches us that our joy transcends the trials. In the thirty-six primary verses I researched on joy for this chapter, twenty-three involved suffering. I don't claim to be a rocket scientist, but even I can see that link. Those verses seemed to group together to give four principles on how choosing joy in suffering will take us to a deeper level of following Christ.

CHOOSING JOY BALANCES SUFFERING

Let's face the truth: Suffering makes up a huge part of life. We all encounter difficulties and trials because we live in a fallen, decayed world. Some attempt a rose-colored glasses approach that denies suffering; others proclaim that problems come to us because we have weak faith. These approaches deny both reality and Scripture.

Try to tell people that Jesus promised we won't have difficulties: "In this world you will have trouble" (John 16:33). Try to tell Stephen, the first martyr, that we won't have difficulties: "And as they stoned him, Stephen prayed, 'Lord Jesus, receive my spirit.' And he fell to his knees, shouting, 'Lord, don't charge them with this sin!' And with that, he died" (Acts 7:59–60 NLT). Try to tell James, the apostle and brother of John, that we won't have difficulties: "[Herod] had James, the brother of John, put to death with the sword" (Acts 12:2).

Read both sides in the Hall of Faith from Hebrews 11. Yes, let's read about those victorious lives:

> Who shut the mouths of lions, quenched the fury of the flames, and escaped the edge of the sword; whose weakness was turned to strength; and who became powerful in battle and routed foreign armies. Women received back their dead, raised to life again. (Heb. 11:33–35)

But let's not neglect the other side:

> Others were tortured and refused to be released, so that they might gain a better resurrection. Some faced jeers and flogging, while still others were chained and put in prison. They were stoned; they were sawed in two; they were

put to death by the sword. They went about in sheepskins and goatskins, destitute, persecuted and mistreated—the world was not worthy of them. They wandered in deserts and mountains, and in caves and holes in the ground. (Heb. 11:35–38)

Yes, reality includes suffering, but choosing joy provides a balance. When we act as Jesus did, we can get beyond the immediate and add the long term. Yes, we suffer. But the suffering doesn't tell all of the story.

CHOOSING JOY IMPACTS PERSONAL DEVELOPMENT

I found sixteen passages that link our approach to suffering with deepening our spiritual connection with God. Most of us desire more spiritual character; choosing joy in our troubles will enhance that.

First, we'll have more of *God's peace*.

Rejoice in the Lord always. I will say it again: Rejoice! Let your gentleness be evident to all. The Lord is near. Do not be anxious about anything, but in everything, by prayer and petition, with thanksgiving, present your requests to God. And the peace of God, which transcends all understanding, will guard your hearts and your minds in Christ Jesus. (Phil. 4:4–7)

We gain peace when we choose joy in troubles because we increase our reliance on God. We don't feel like it all rests on our actions. Yes, I relied on God during that separation, but I didn't take it far enough to rejoice and experience the best of God's peace.

Second, persecution demonstrates that we *make a spiritual impact*. Satan seems to operate on the principle of letting sleeping dogs lie. In other words, if we don't cause trouble for him, he won't cause trouble for us. Some suffering comes because we stir things up, according to

Jesus: "Blessed are you when people insult you, persecute you and falsely say all kinds of evil against you because of me. Rejoice and be glad, because great is your reward in heaven, for in the same way they persecuted the prophets who were before you" (Matt. 5:11–12).

Why rejoice? Because the trials put us in good company: the prophets and Jesus himself.

Third, problems *build perseverance*. "Not only so, but we also rejoice in our sufferings, because we know that suffering produces perseverance" (Rom. 5:3).

Trials force us to revaluate, to examine unproductive methods, to think about our values, and to learn how to better face the realities of life.

Once we survive a trial, we learn that God can get us through it. The first time a girlfriend broke up with me in high school, I felt devastated. I'd always ended relationships before. Somewhat surprisingly, I survived. Then I experienced getting dumped again. This time, I could handle it better, based on my experience and what I had learned from the first dump. It didn't feel good, but I realized that life didn't have to end. Does this sound minor? Think back to your high school days. Few tragedies can match the emotional upheaval that brings.

Fourth, we rejoice because suffering prepares us for a future glory. "Therefore we do not lose heart. Though outwardly we are wasting away, yet inwardly we are being renewed day by day. For our light and momentary troubles are achieving for us an eternal glory that far outweighs them all" (2 Cor. 4:16–17).

We can rejoice in troubles because we experience an ongoing spiritual renewal. We know the future holds something far better. Some of our suffering comes from making an impact for God, and we've well earned that. Pain benefits us because it helps us look to the future glory and not get caught up in the immediate.

Fifth, we can rejoice because suffering *increases our reliance on God's strength*. A phrase I heard years ago intrigued me: "If you want to see

God act, attempt something he desires that is so impossible that you're doomed to fail." Only when we attempt the impossible do we make room for God to act.

Rejoicing in suffering fits that category. We face difficulties that we know we cannot handle, and that we've failed in before. Naturally, we respond with discouragement. But spiritually we can respond with joy because it forces us to rely on a power outside ourselves, a power greater than ourselves.

Paul dealt with that. He had some physical difficulty, and asked God to remove the source of torment. God said no, but notice why.

> But he said to me, "My grace is sufficient for you, for my power is made perfect in weakness." Therefore I will boast all the more gladly about my weaknesses, so that Christ's power may rest on me. That is why, for Christ's sake, I delight in weaknesses, in insults, in hardships, in persecutions, in difficulties. For when I am weak, then I am strong. (2 Cor. 12:9–10)

During separation from my wife, I relied much more on God's strength, because I just didn't have enough of my own. I missed the logical next step of rejoicing, but at least I made the start of reliance. Rejoicing in suffering, however, does more than merely impact us.

Choosing Joy Allows Continuing Ministry Impact

Ministry will always cost us. It costs our time, our talents, and our resources. It brings frustration when others want to do it differently, or when they don't do their part. We then face two primary responses. Many of us get discouraged, or even quit. One praise team member at a previous church quit "because it wasn't fun anymore." It took more work than he anticipated and the leader didn't cater to him, so he bailed out. That pattern has followed him into other ministries and other churches, but he isn't alone.

Others respond with a joy stronger than their discouragement. That alone allows them to continue to make an impact for the kingdom. Paul regularly experienced a variety of suffering when he ministered. He had opposition from civil leaders, other religious leaders, ministry team members, and the churches. But he kept his focus on the privilege of touching people for Jesus: "Now I rejoice in what was suffered for you, and I fill up in my flesh what is still lacking in regard to Christ's afflictions, for the sake of his body, which is the church" (Col. 1:24).

Paul didn't deny the reality of suffering, but he remembered why he willingly suffered: to benefit them spiritually, moving them closer to God. The joy he received from doing that far exceeded the suffering, and he continued ministry without losing heart. Combining all of these leads inescapably to the step in understanding why radical discipleship requires joy.

CHOOSING JOY INCREASES INTIMACY WITH GOD

Twenty-one verses explored this concept. Bitterness from things not going as we desire poisons our intimacy with God. We question his love for us, we doubt that he works in our lives, and we slowly drift away from intimacy. Or, we can choose joy in our suffering, see God's long-term working, and draw closer to him.

Despite encouraging early progress, Paul and Silas faced significant troubles in the city of Philippi. Unhappy residents dragged them before the magistrates and accused them of breaking the law. Guards stripped and beat them severely, threw them into the inner cells of the prison, and fastened their feet in the stocks. That qualifies as trouble, doesn't it? Even in the worst difficulties of my life, I've never encountered that level of trouble.

I could easily understand Paul and Silas becoming a trifle discouraged. "God, we came here to serve you. We even brought some people to faith. We cast out an evil spirit. And how do you respond?

Not a single 'Attaboy.' Instead, we get falsely accused, blood flows from our wounds, our muscles are cramping because of these stocks, and what do you do? Nothing."

But they didn't respond like that. As radical disciples, Paul and Silas did something different. "About midnight Paul and Silas were praying and singing hymns to God, and the other prisoners were listening to them" (Acts 16:25).

Rather than allowing bitterness and a "poor me" attitude to poison their spirits, they intentionally chose to praise God and rejoice. Perhaps they rejoiced because the persecution proved they had made an impact on people. Perhaps they rejoiced because they felt the peace of God that comes from choosing joy. Perhaps they rejoiced because they'd experienced this before, and had seen God work. Perhaps they rejoiced because they looked to the future glory God had for them. Perhaps they rejoiced because they experienced an extra measure of God's strength.

They reacted in a totally non-typical manner. No wonder the other prisoners listened! They'd never seen anyone react like this. Paul and Silas used the trouble to get closer to God. Later, the head jailer and his family accepted Christ. They saw an attractive intimacy with a God that allowed his followers to make behavioral choices that transcended troubles. Radical.

A Radical Following

How can we deliberately choose joy when we face the trials of life? How can we develop joy as an essential target that blasts us out of how we typically react to trouble with depression?

ENHANCE OUR INTIMACY WITH GOD

A close connection to God provides the source of joy. Perhaps that gave David the foundation for how he didn't allow the troubles we mentioned earlier to overwhelm him: "You have made known to me the path of life; you will fill me with joy in your presence, with eternal pleasures at your right hand" (Ps. 16:11).

He knew that the presence of God far outweighed the impact of any difficulty. When we begin to walk with Christ, the Holy Spirit comes to live in our being. He then brings the very character of God and imbeds that into our life. That brings joy: "But the fruit of the Spirit is . . . joy" (Gal. 5:22).

Without the strength that intimacy with God provides, we're simply unable to consistently choose joy when troubles overwhelm us. Continually nurturing our closeness with God gives the foundation for the ability to choose joy.

CHANGE OUR PERSPECTIVE

But we also need to develop the habit of looking beyond the moment. Several years ago I picked up a book by Dean Koontz, a well-known mystery author. I'd never seen such twists and turns woven into a story. Anticipation and fear built within me, so I cheated. I read the last chapter. Did it ruin some of the reading? Yes, a bit. But it also eliminated the fear of wondering how the story would turn out. I could read the rest without uncertainty.

Doing the same spiritually allows us to choose joy. We can't always know the details of how difficulties will turn out, but we do know the overall result. God wins, along with those on his team. Just read Revelation 20–22. Despite the confusion of interpreting much of the book, we can all understand the conclusion.

We move our vision beyond the immediate to consider the overall situation. Proverbs 14:12 says: "There is a way that seems right to a man, but in the end it leads to death." Similarly, some situations seem like nothing but trouble, but in the end we can find benefits. I learned that in our marital struggles.

They forced me to look at some issues in my life that desperately needed examination. Particularly, I had to address how my independence impacted my marriage and how it wounded Sheila. She genuinely felt excluded from key parts of my life, and that didn't enhance our oneness. Now, looking back, I can truly rejoice because those struggles forced us to make some changes that have improved our marriage significantly. I would have done much better during that time if I had adopted more of a long-term perspective.

Choose Joy—Always

I agree, this sounds much too simplistic. And, it may be. But simple doesn't mean easy. When we face difficulties, we choose our response. We can choose to embrace joy. Many emotions call to us: anger, despondency, depression, confusion, frustration, and more all battle for our attention. We will feel many of these, almost simultaneously.

But Jesus and Paul tell us to go deeper, to not allow those understandable emotions to take preeminence. They tell us to avoid the trap of just looking at the surface. We can redefine the situation to look for what God may do in it. We can look beyond the pain. We can delve deeper into our walk with Jesus. And with that, we can choose to blend joy into the mix. We can choose to let joy become the dominant element. The others will remain, and many times they should. When we experience loss, we should feel grief as a normal, healthy response. But we can avoid allowing it to dominate our lives.

We'll need to continually remind ourselves to rejoice, since it goes against our grain. But God does give us that option. We can do it.

The Payoff

Choosing joy in the midst of pain and loss and trouble allows us to transcend the situation. Our lives become more than just the current struggle; we realize that life offers so much more. During the separation between Sheila and me, sometimes only God's involvement kept me going. Only the desire for reconciliation moved me beyond despair. But I didn't choose joy very often then, and I paid the price.

Don't make the mistake I made. Live radically. Live rejoicing—always.

Disciples Always Check Things Out: We Test Everything

Just last week I received another petition that brought the total close to fifty. Pretty much the same message each time, always telling me how urgently I needed to respond to the Federal Communications Commission (FCC). They began as mailed petitions, but they've followed technology and have become e-mail messages.

They warn that the late atheist, Madalyn Murray O'Hair, petitioned the FCC to ban all religious broadcasting on radio and television. The message even came with an official FCC petition number, RM-2493. Now, I can easily understand why some would get upset. It violates the Constitution in several ways and would be a major attack on the expression of faith.

Many have taken a stand, requiring the FCC to respond to millions of concerned Americans. In just the first five years, these patriots spent over $1 million in postage. An issue well worthy of opposition.

Except, it isn't true. Petition RM-2493 did exist, back in 1975. But it didn't seek to ban religious broadcasting; Madalyn Murray O'Hair had nothing to do with it; and the FCC promptly denied the petition that same year. In the thirty years since, Christians have tilted at windmills. We've spent millions of dollars, taken years of time, and filled the in-boxes of our friends.

Why? Because we don't critically evaluate. We don't check things out. We accept assertions much too easily. And so we often look foolish. When I heard the rumor back in 1980, I called the FCC directly and learned the truth. With each new e-mail message I receive about this, I hit "Reply All" and tell them the whole story. I've only received one response.

Now, do you believe me? My story sounds plausible, doesn't it? You've probably heard the rumors, but this may be the first time you've heard the other side. Which do you believe? I hope you don't blindly believe me any more than so many have blindly believed the rumor. So, check it out. Here's an official FCC Web site about it at www.fcc. gov/mb/enf/forms/rm-2493.html. Or, if you think I faked the page (some could do this, although I confess I don't have the tech savvy), do a search for FCC 2493.

In fact, please *do* your own search and convince yourselves of the truth. More importantly, convince yourselves of the need to always check things out. Disciples should test everything.

The Impossible Demand

God wants us to do that. Through the apostle Paul he says: "*Test everything.* Hold on to the good. Avoid every kind of evil" (1 Thess. 5:21–22). Doesn't that sum up the Christian life? Grab onto the good. Stay away from the evil. But how can we do that? We first have to discern between the two. We have to judge. We have to check things out.

That theme permeates the Bible. The words *judge, test, truth, prove,* or *discern* occur in various forms over 540 times. When God established a covenant with the Jewish people, he wanted them to think critically. If someone began teaching about different gods, or different ways of following God, he gave the solution: "Then you must *inquire, probe and investigate it thoroughly*. And if it is true and it has been *proved* that this detestable thing has been done among you, you must certainly put to the sword all who live in that town" (Deut. 13:14–15). They had to investigate and prove it.

Don't just accept what anyone says. Thoroughly check it out. Thoroughly. Prove assertions. Probe. Investigate. Read this list of specific judgments that followers of Jesus should make.

Test Jesus' Claims

When a new follower of Jesus invited a friend to join him, the friend responded with skepticism. Phillip simply told him, "Come and see" (John 1:46). Or, check it out. See for yourself. When Jesus began disrupting the religious way of life, the authorities asked about his authority. Rather than ignoring the question, he answered that his resurrection would demonstrate that (John 2:18–21). He wanted them to check out his truth claims.

Jesus continued to use his resurrection to establish the truth of his teaching. "After his suffering, he showed himself to these men and *gave many convincing proofs* that he was alive. He appeared to them over a period of forty days and spoke about the kingdom of God" (Acts 1:3). Rather than condemning people who asked questions, Jesus seemed to invite them. When Thomas wouldn't blindly accept the evidence that others gave about the resurrection, Jesus told Thomas to put his finger in the wounds for proof (John 20:24–29).

Test Doctrine and Teaching

When Paul went to the city of Berea and began to teach that Jesus fulfilled the Old Testament prophecies about the Messiah, the people didn't blindly accept what he said. Instead they "examined the Scriptures every day to see if what Paul said was true" (Acts 17:11).

Any statement by anyone should face the test of consistency with Scripture.

Church Leaders Test Church Leaders

Sometimes leaders feel they don't have to account to others for what they teach, since God called them to leadership and followers must respect that, echoing David: "But the LORD forbid that I should lay a hand on the LORD's anointed" (I Sam. 26:11). However, God tells leaders they need to regularly test the accuracy of the teaching of other leaders. "Two or three prophets should speak, and *the others should weigh carefully what is said*" (I Cor. 14:29).

Test Church Workers

Even before followers become leaders, we need to check them out before giving them the privilege of serving: "*They must first be tested*; and then if there is nothing against them, let them serve as deacons" (I Tim. 3:10). Willingness and a warm body don't make up all the qualifications to serve Christ's church.

Test Ourselves

Participating in the Lord's Supper provides a great opportunity to examine our own lives.

> *A man ought to examine himself* before he eats of the bread and drinks of the cup. For anyone who eats and drinks without recognizing the body of the Lord eats and drinks judgment on himself. That is why many among you are weak and sick, and a number of you have fallen asleep. *But if we judged ourselves, we would not come under judgment.*"
> (I Cor. 11:28–31)

Self-examination should play a regular role in our lives.

TEST THE WHOLE STORY

Like our opening example, we can easily make a decision before we gain all the facts. Wise followers hear it all before they begin evaluating. "The first to present his case seems right, till another comes forward and questions him" (Prov. 18:17).

TEST THE ACTIONS OF OTHER CHRISTIANS

We may get into the touchiest area here, but God clearly tells us to judge the behavior of other Christians.

> But now I am writing you that you must not associate with anyone who calls himself a brother but is sexually immoral or greedy, an idolater or a slanderer, a drunkard or a swindler. With such a man do not even eat. What business is it of mine to judge those outside the church? *Are you not to judge those inside*? God will judge those outside. "Expel the wicked man from among you." (I Cor. 5:11–13)

TEST LEGAL CASES

Rather than have followers going to the courts to resolve legal disputes between them, God tells the church to make those decisions. "If any of you has a dispute with another, dare he take it before the ungodly for judgment instead of before the saints? Do you not know that the saints will judge the world? And if you are to judge the world, are you not competent to judge trivial cases?" (I Cor. 6:1–2).

TEST ANGELS

The next verse says that we can legitimately judge legal cases because in the future we'll judge angels. *"Do you not know that we will judge angels?* How much more the things of this life!" (I Cor. 6:3). What does that mean? I don't have a clue! But it does affirm that followers of Jesus have a role in judgment. The next amplifies that.

Test the Twelve Tribes of Israel

Again, I don't know clearly what it means, but it does intrigue me: "Jesus said to them, 'I tell you the truth, at the renewal of all things, when the Son of Man sits on his glorious throne, you who have followed me will also sit on twelve thrones, *judging the twelve tribes of Israel*'" (Matt. 19:28).

That list forces me to change how I think about judging and testing. God does want us to judge. But, that doesn't seem impossible. Distasteful and daunting, but not necessarily impossible. Not yet.

Complacent Faith and Sloppy Thinking

Our typical resistance to judging and thinking critically cannot please God. Sloppy thinking, not discovering the full situation, not dealing with facts, and not seeking the full truth dishonors the God of truth. God commands that we test all things. Why do we resist? A number of possible reasons combine for that result.

Jesus Said to Not Judge

Last year I taught about the life of Christ to a group of eleventh graders, and they surprised me a bit. As we read over the Sermon on the Mount, we came to Matthew 7:1: "Do not judge, or you too will be judged." They all agreed wholeheartedly that Christians should *never* judge. That led to a spirited discussion where we incorporated some of the passages I previously mentioned. Some reluctantly saw the need to judge at times; others never did. But all began by resisting it.

That ethos of not judging permeates Christianity. In part from Jesus' statement here, in part from a counterreaction to decades of

Christians acting very judgmental, and in part from accepting the value of tolerance from our culture.

CULTURAL TOLERANCE

With the growing influence of postmodernism, relativism has moved from the culture into much of the church. Based on the view that "ethical truths depend on the individuals and groups holding them" (*Webster's Dictionary*), relativism eliminates the ability of one individual to tell another that an act is wrong. Why? No one can tell me what's right for me. That's why my students resisted judging: it requires some sort of absolute truth that applies to all people, regardless of their acceptance of it.

With relativism, we hesitate to make moral judgments on others.

LIMITED TIME

On a purely practical level, we find it difficult to check *all* things out. I can't count all the e-mail petitions I receive that call me to take some kind of action to protect Christian liberties. For the majority, I just delete them. Otherwise, I would do nothing but become "Rumor Control Central." That leads to much of the impossibility of this demand: we don't have the time to check everything out.

CONTENTMENT

Sometimes we resist examining issues because we feel very comfortable with where we are. "My mind is made up; don't confuse me with the facts." We find a good position and don't want to modify it. Change takes us beyond our comfort zone, so we avoid anything that might threaten it.

LAZY THINKING

Socrates first said, "The unexamined life is not worth living." Even in the golden age of thinking, not all thought well. Rather than submit to the rigors of probing, exploring, researching, and actually thinking, we find it easier to just accept what others tell us. We find sources that appear credible and accept their statements as truth. As perhaps some of you did with my statements about the petition.

And we fall prey to the problem we mentioned earlier: "The first to present his case seems right, till another comes forward and questions him" (Prov. 18:17). Unfortunately we don't wait for the second person. We don't become the second person.

So, we resist judging. We resist checking things out. We find it easier and safer to stick with the status quo. But what's the problem with this? We never grow in our faith, our intellect, or our emotional maturity. We stagnate. We accept stuff as it is. We don't believe "the good is the enemy of the best." Good is good enough.

God wants to blast us out of mediocre lives. So, he requires that we test everything to determine the best. Only as we become willing to do that can we move from the good to something better. Yes, we resist that demand, but God gives it so we can embark on that process of finding the best.

Understanding Radical Discipleship

Lies, partial truths, and imperfections fill our world. Ignorance causes some of that. Information has exploded over the past several decades; no one can keep up with all the new material. Perhaps no one taught us some important truths. Perhaps we haven't wanted to pursue them. But many flaws come intentionally. People lie to advance their interests, and we don't challenge what they say. People shade the truth to benefit themselves, and we don't take the time to learn the full story. People take shortcuts to increase their profits, and we don't ask for documentation.

The radical step of questioning everything moves us closer to full truth. If we accept all that we encounter, then we buy into the imperfection and partial truths that surround us. Let's examine why we must test everything.

GOD'S CHARACTER

Truth expresses the character of all three persons of the godhead. David described the Father like that: "Into your hands I commit my spirit; redeem me, O LORD, *the God of truth*" (Ps. 31:5). Jesus gave that same trait to himself: "*I am* the way and *the truth* and the life. No one comes to the Father except through me" (John 14:6). Jesus included the Spirit in that truthful threesome: "But when he, *the Spirit of truth,* comes, he will guide you into all truth" (John 16:13).

God wants us to yearn for the full truth, because that expresses his own character. We cannot get closer to God without a passion to get closer to truth.

SPIRITUAL GROWTH

We cannot grow in spiritual maturity without increasing our connection to accurate truth. As we've already discussed, complacency keeps us from fully knowing God. Since none of us totally knows truth, we continually need to seek it. "Instead, *speaking the truth* in love, we will in all things *grow up into him* who is the Head, that is, Christ" (Eph. 4:15). We can't speak the truth in love unless we have an intimate relationship with it.

INTELLECTUAL RIGOR

Let's not confuse intellectual rigor with intelligence. Some geniuses never really think; they merely parrot back what others tell them. But a good number of people with average minds have chosen to train themselves to think critically, to examine claims, and to not accept all they hear. But we cannot develop to our intellectual potential unless we investigate claims.

Our minds play a central role in our spiritual transformation. I love the process that Paul describes.

> Therefore, I urge you, brothers, in view of God's mercy, to offer your bodies as living sacrifices, holy and pleasing to God—this is your spiritual act of worship. Do not conform any longer to the pattern of this world, but *be transformed by the renewing of your mind.* Then you will be able to test and approve what God's will is—his good, pleasing and perfect will. (Rom. 12:1–2)

God wants us to give our lives to him so we can be transformed into the likeness of Christ. What kick-starts that process? Renewing our mind. Making sure that we only put true material into it. Removing any material that isn't true or good. We test everything, so we can cling to the good and avoid the evil. Christianity pushes our envelope in a number of arenas. Developing intellectual rigor is one.

A Radical Following

Getting practical here means getting into trouble. We make our own lives more difficult and we risk stepping on the toes of others. But following Jesus compels us.

CLARIFY A STANDARD OF TRUTH

Before we can check things out, we need a standard to measure them against. Fishermen have a well-deserved reputation for exaggeration, and while browsing through a sporting goods store I came across "The Fisherman's Scale." Guaranteed to make you look better, the ruler marked off "inch" increments about every half inch, easily turning a decent twelve-inch rainbow trout into a prize twenty-four incher. It did the same for the weight.

Did I buy one so I could brag to my fishing friends about the huge trout I began to catch? No, but it really did tempt me. I could honestly say, "I measured that one at twenty-six inches."

Our culture presents us with numerous standards to determine right or wrong. Some promote feelings: "Listen to your mother's heart." But as I write this chapter, the news tells of a mother who stripped her three children, ages one, two, and six years, and dropped their bodies into the frigid October waters of San Francisco Bay. Three days later, they have only recovered one dead body. But she listened to her "mother's heart." Can we call relying on our emotions good?

Others tell us to follow society. Our society allows fetuses, at eight months of development, to be ripped apart while still in the womb. Can anyone argue that Nazi Germany met the standard of good? After World War II, the Nuremberg War Trials convicted and executed many who merely followed the orders given them by their societal or military leaders. That judgment required a higher standard of good than what the society provides.

Still others encourage us to "look out for Number One"—ourselves. To act in our own best interests, as we determine them. The year 2005 saw the arrest of Dennis Rader, also known as BTK, for bind, torture, and kill. Over a thirty-year period, he stalked and murdered at least ten people, terrorizing Wichita, Kansas, and living up to his acronym. He followed his desires. An extreme example? Perhaps. But how many marriages end because one partner placed their desires above the best for the family?

An age of relativism provides no consistent standard to determine good and bad. If no absolute moral truth exists, who can tell me what to do? Taken to its logical extension, relativism yields nothing but moral anarchy. Anyone can do what they can get away with.

Unless we have a source with sufficient authority to apply to all people at all times. That will give us a ruler that can measure all trout accurately, by the same standard. Only the author of life has the authority to do that. His words give that: "Sanctify them by the truth; your word is truth" (John 17:17). An awesome claim. If the author of life gives the words of truth, then we can consistently rely on them. Standards based on the character of God won't change, like the shifting standards of society: "I the LORD do not change" (Mal. 3:6).

If his words don't express truth, or if they change like the culture, then his claim is a lie and has no more validity than another standard a person chooses.

So, followers of Jesus can use the words of God to determine right and wrong, good and bad. But do all of God's words carry equal weight as we test all things? In *Essays on New Testament Christianity*, Dr. Scott Bartchy, Director of the Center for the Study of Religion at UCLA, divides all passages into three groups. *Normative* texts declare a standard that applies to all, and transcends culture and individual preferences. For example, Jesus told his followers to remember him in the Lord's Supper (Luke 22:17–20). *Descriptive* texts tell us what happened, without making it a command. The early church practiced it weekly in the worship service (Acts 20:7), but we don't find a command that all should do it like that. And in I Corinthians 11:18–34, Paul gave a *problematic* passage, where he addressed specific problems in how the church did Communion, and gave specific solutions to resolve them. So, we give the most weight to the normative passages, less to descriptive ones, and we follow the problematic ones when we have a similar problem. But even the normative passages can give us some difficulties.

When they give a *general principle*, such as don't commit adultery, then we all follow that standard. But we also need to apply that, which can require that we make individual interpretations. For instance, to decrease temptation, I've decided to not have meals alone with a woman. Does that flow from the general principle? For me, yes. And while I make this binding on me, I can't bind that on others, since I made an interpretative application. That application isn't inherent in the command. Others may do that and have no problems. That's fine (Rom. 14:23).

As followers of Jesus, we have a clear and absolute standard to test things: the normative Word of God. Next, we need to apply that.

TEST SOME TRUTH CLAIMS

Rich Klinsky and I grew up at the same church, and began riding motorcycles about the same time. Rich loves the appearance, mystique, and throaty roar of Harley Davidsons. I love the performance, reliability, and quietness of Honda Gold Wings. When he proclaims the superiority of Harleys, do I need to find chapter and verse to test his claim? Not at all. We want to focus on spiritual truth, not matters of motorcycle preference.

And even on spiritual matters, focus on the important ones. Don't stress over matters of opinion or personal applications. But test everything that people say is required to know and follow God. If someone says you must speak in tongues to follow Jesus, or that you cannot genuinely speak in tongues and follow him, then test it. Those qualify as essentials, so check them out according to God's Word.

MISCELLANEOUS TIPS

In our testing, let me give four quick tips. First, *go broad*. Or, get the whole picture, not just one side. Research the issues carefully. Keep Proverbs 18:17 in mind: "The first to present his case seems right, till another comes forward and questions him." In writing my second book, *A Passionate Pursuit of God*, I examined every verse in the Old and New Testaments that in any way applied to our relationship with God. Not all verses made their way into the final result, but they all contributed.

Do the same in testing truth. Listen to the best of all sides. Avoid using just one source. A few years ago I taught a class on Mormonism and advertised it in the newspaper. I received a phone call from a local

LDS bishop who feared I might just use "anti-Mormon" literature and represent his faith unfairly. We met for lunch and I gave him my notes. He read them and replied, "I have to admit, you're accurate." Why? Because I used direct quotes from their literature: the Book of Mormon, Doctrine and Covenants, and other official sources.

Second, *go deep*. Don't just look at the surface, but try to dig deeper. We typically err because we don't take the time this requires. Perhaps we don't want to experience the discomfort of exploring the assumptions that we and others have. Perhaps we fear rejection by others when we reject the current party line. Let's value the truth more than acceptance by others. Jesus said: "Stop judging by mere appearances, and make a right judgment" (John 7:24). Correct judgments come when we examine the history, motives, and background of an issue.

Third, *evaluate your sources*. Never blindly accept what anyone says or writes. We can learn which sources prove themselves trustworthy. You won't have to test them as much as those who often pass on ideas you've already tested as inaccurate. If a person speaks against their own interest, their credibility rises. If they speak in line with their own interests, exert more caution. Typically, trust *Consumers' Reports* more than your local car salesman. Can they validly claim some expertise in the subject? If so, give them a little more credibility.

Fourth, look for *faulty reasoning*. Discover the classic fallacies, and learn how to identify them. I teach the most common twelve in my university communication classes, but one Web site lists eighty. I encourage you to find some good Web sites or a good logic book and learn them. Now, let's apply all this.

NEVER JUDGE

Some things we should never judge. First, we *never judge unbelievers' actions*, at least not in this lifetime. In discussing discipline in the church, Paul says: "What business is it of mine to judge those outside the church?" (I Cor. 5:12). Why is this not our business? God cares most about their acceptance of his Son, not their unsaved behavior. "Whoever believes in him is not condemned, but whoever does not believe stands condemned already because he has not believed in the name of God's one and only Son" (John 3:18). We have no reason to change their behavior, only to encourage them to change their beliefs regarding Jesus.

Second, we *don't judge people's hearts*. Yes, we need to look below the surface, but only God and the individual know the inside. "For who among men knows the thoughts of a man except the man's spirit within him?" (I Cor. 2:11). We shouldn't judge what we cannot know.

Third, we *don't judge eternal destiny*. God has reserved that for Jesus, not us.

> When the Son of Man comes in his glory, and all the angels with him, he will sit on his throne in heavenly glory. All the nations will be gathered before him, and he will separate the people one from another as a shepherd separates the sheep from the goats. He will put the sheep on his right and the goats on his left. Then the King will say to those on his right, "Come, you who are blessed by my Father; take your inheritance, the kingdom prepared for you since the creation of the world." . . . Then he will say to those on his left, "Depart from me, you who are cursed, into the eternal fire prepared for the devil and his angels." . . . Then they will go away to eternal punishment, but the righteous to eternal life. (Matt. 25:31–34, 41, 46)

We can, and should, give the conditions for entering eternal life. We can validly say that if people don't know Jesus they face eternal fire. But let's not pronounce guilt and their destination. Let's leave that to Jesus, who sees the heart.

Fourth, we *don't judge hypocritically.* Hypocrisy has turned off more people to faith than just about anything else.

> Do not judge, or you too will be judged. For in the same way you judge others, you will be judged, and with the measure you use, it will be measured to you. Why do you look at the speck of sawdust in your brother's eye and pay no attention to the plank in your own eye? How can you say to your brother, "Let me take the speck out of your eye," when all the time there is a plank in your own eye? You hypocrite, first take the plank out of your own eye, and then you will see clearly to remove the speck from your brother's eye. (Matt. 7:1–5)

Jesus didn't condemn all judging, he merely condemned judging others when we first haven't judged ourselves for the same issues. Since how we judge determines the severity of how God judges us, then perhaps we need to err on the side of grace and understanding. That leads us to the next issue.

JUDGE OURSELVES

We must judge ourselves long before we dare to judge others. A number of passages tell us to evaluate our walk with Christ, including: "Examine yourselves to see whether you are in the faith; test yourselves" (2 Cor. 13:5).

We need to examine our priorities: do we truly put God in first place? We need to examine our behaviors: do they truly reflect our priorities? Do they best express the holiness of God? Do they best express genuine reverence for God? Do they best express our desire to minister for God? Can we move beyond some good things to better ones?

Earlier we mentioned Socrates' quote that the unexamined life is not worth living. As radical followers of Jesus, we need to continually test our attitudes and actions to determine if they represent God's best. Part of that involves carefully listening to criticism. Even our enemies can point out flaws that miss our gaze. Our spouses often see some aspects of ourselves better than we do. If you have exceptional courage, then ask a good friend to give you an honest appraisal of your strengths and weaknesses.

Only when we submit ourselves to rigorous self-examination by biblical standards can we think about the next step.

Judge Other Christians' Behavior

Christ placed his followers into one body, where each member impacts others and the whole, so what others do affects us. We don't generally think of toenails as critical parts of the body, but just a few days ago I stubbed my big toenail on a piece of wooden furniture. I've limped ever since. Wearing shoes hurts; going barefoot helps. But each step causes at least a twinge. Toenails matter.

I found seventeen New Testament passages about Christians dealing with the sinful behavior of other believers. So, how do we test others? First, we must focus on scriptural sins. Their hair length, style of clothing, or anything not clearly a sin according to God's Word doesn't enter the field of play.

Second, we act from love and a desire for reconciliation. We don't desire to seem better or more spiritual. "Dear brothers and sisters, if another Christian is overcome by some sin, you who are godly should gently and humbly help that person back onto the right path. And be careful not to fall into the same temptation yourself" (Gal. 6:1 NLT).

Paul addressed a serious problem in Corinth, and told the church how to handle it:

It is actually reported that there is sexual immorality among you, and of a kind that does not occur even among pagans: A man has his father's wife. And you are proud!

Shouldn't you rather have been filled with grief and have *put out of your fellowship the man who did this?* Even though I am not physically present, I am with you in spirit. And I have *already passed judgment* on the one who did this, just as if I were present. When you are assembled in the name of our Lord Jesus and I am with you in spirit, and the power of our Lord Jesus is present, hand this man over to Satan, so that the sinful nature may be destroyed and his spirit saved on the day of the Lord." (I Cor. 5:1–5)

Apparently, that hard act by the church had a good result. The man repented, and Paul provided the next step.

If anyone has caused grief, he has not so much grieved me as he has grieved all of you, to some extent—not to put it too severely. The punishment inflicted on him by the majority is sufficient for him. Now instead, you ought to *forgive and comfort him,* so that he will not be overwhelmed by excessive sorrow. I urge you, therefore, to *reaffirm your love for him.* (2 Cor. 2:5–8)

Many books explore church discipline and I don't want to repeat them. But I do desire to make clear that when God commands us to test everything, that includes the behavior of fellow followers of Jesus.

The Payoff

Very simply, only as we commit ourselves to testing everything can we move beyond good things and experience the best. God desires our perfection: "Be perfect, therefore, as your heavenly Father is perfect" (Matt. 5:48). Perfect doesn't mean sinless but complete, full, mature, reaching the goal. Or, we maximize our lives. We can never do that unless we're willing to check out everything that has a spiritual impact on our lives.

We hold everything against the standard of absolute truth of God's Word. We don't allow ourselves to become content with anything short of that. Radical? Absolutely. But possible. And good.

A Closing Thought

The preeminent problem for people of faith is that we've emasculated the radical demands of Jesus. The resulting small goals cause us to experience little transformation; we've become too much like the society around us. Therefore, we have no message for a world in desperate need of consistent truth coupled with hope that life can experience meaning. The world won't listen to the claims of Jesus because his followers won't listen.

My heart yearns to see individuals decide to follow Jesus. Followers who see Jesus not as safe, but as good. Followers who will accept these radical demands of Jesus as essential targets. Not just more legalistic rules, nor just something that we ignore.

These goals can blast us out of complacency; they can explode us out of lukewarmness, and they can help us achieve the radical life God designed us to experience. No, we will never fully follow them in this life. But that "failure" will eliminate our complacency, won't it? The very impossibility of fully reaching them keeps us from thinking we've arrived.

We can only do this with the indwelling Holy Spirit to motivate us, fill us, give us power, and transform us.

So, we face some choices. A choice to listen carefully to the Spirit. A choice to accept those impossible demands as something that Jesus *really* wants from you. A choice to embark on the process of radical transformation, one that utterly exhausts your ability and power. Or a choice for the complacent status quo.

If you accept the challenge of Jesus, then remember the wisdom of Mr. and Mrs. Beaver. "Safe? Don't you hear what Mrs. Beaver tells you? Who said anything about safe? 'Course he isn't safe. But he's good."

Follow these essential demands of Jesus. Move beyond your spiritual comfort zone. Realize Jesus loves you more than you can comprehend, and he'll walk with you each step of the way.